JAMES AXLER

DEATH LANDS®

Thunder Road

A GOLD EAGLE BOOK FROM
W RLDWIDE®

TORONTO • NEW YORK • LONDON
AMSTERDAM • PARIS • SYDNEY • HAMBURG
STOCKHOLM • ATHENS • TOKYO • MILAN
MADRID • WARSAW • BUDAPEST • AUCKLAND

First edition September 2008

ISBN-13: 978-0-373-62593-2
ISBN-10:   0-373-62593-6

THUNDER ROAD

He that has and a little tiny wit,
With hey, ho, the wind and the rain,
Must make content with his fortunes fit,
Though the rain it raineth every day.
                    —William Shakespeare
                    King Lear, III, ii, 76

THE DEATHLANDS SAGA

This world is their legacy, a world born in the violent nuclear spasm of 2001 that was the bitter outcome of a struggle for global dominance.

There is no real escape from this shockscape where life always hangs in the balance, vulnerable to newly demonic nature, barbarism, lawlessness.

But they are the warrior survivalists, and they endure—in the way of the lion, the hawk and the tiger, true to nature's heart despite its ruination.

Ryan Cawdor: The privileged son of an East Coast baron. Acquainted with betrayal from a tender age, he is a master of the hard realities.

Krysty Wroth: Harmony ville's own Titian-haired beauty, a woman with the strength of tempered steel. Her premonitions and Gaia powers have been fostered by her Mother Sonja.

J. B. Dix, the Armorer: Weapons master and Ryan's close ally, he, too, honed his skills traversing the Deathlands with the legendary Trader.

Doctor Theophilus Tanner: Torn from his family and a gentler life in 1896, Doc has been thrown into a future he couldn't have imagined.

Dr. Mildred Wyeth: Her father was killed by the Ku Klux Klan, but her fate is not much lighter. Restored from predark cryogenic suspension, she brings twentieth-century healing skills to a nightmare.

Jak Lauren: A true child of the wastelands, reared on adversity, loss and danger, the albino teenager is a fierce fighter and loyal friend.

Dean Cawdor: Ryan's young son by Sharona accepts the only world he knows, and yet he is the seedling bearing the promise of tomorrow.

In a world where all was lost, they are humanity's last hope....

Prologue

Thunder Rider rides again!

With a full-throttled roar from the throat of his magnificent iron steed, the masked avenger, the seeker of justice, the righter of wrongs, roared into the small town. Villainy trembled beneath his iron heel, and those with much to fear fled in abject terror at his approach.

There was much wrong with this town. For too long the forces of lawlessness had held sway over the land, allowing evil to flourish. He could see it in the faces of those he passed as they leveled their weapons, turning with the following wind of his trusty machine, their aim arcing to follow and intercept its trajectory. He narrowed his eyes against the slipstream of the wind, even though the thick Plexiglas goggles protected them. It was more an indication of his steely and grim determination as his face set into a mask of fury.

He threw the motorcycle into a skid, one hand diving to the battered leather holster—inherited from those who had rode this path before—and freeing the .44 Magnum gun he used for maximum effect. It wasn't just the damage inflicted by the bullets, it was the mighty roar of the weapon that struck fear into the hearts of those who

dared oppose him. With his free hand he gripped the specially modified steering, power-assisted to be as light as
the softest down to his touch. The bike responded to the
feather's breath of movement, the tonnage of screaming
hot metal beneath him scoring an arc of dirt that flew up
into a blinding shower, acting as a screen to the full angle
of his turn.

As the way in front of him cleared, he saw the first of
the coldhearted villains standing before him, defiant,
aiming a long-barreled rifle in his direction. Without
pause, without even the need to register and react, he
squeezed the trigger of the .44, the gun bucking and
rearing in his hand, the shock of recoil absorbed by the
whipcord tendons of his wrist.

The villain's sneer of menace turned into a gasp of dis-
belief as the slug from the mighty Magnum weapon
ripped into him, tearing a gaping maw in what had once
been his chest. Thunder Rider's lips parted in a tight smile
of satisfaction. One down, but many more to go. As the
rest of the villains scattered, he snapped off a few quick
shots. If one hit, then all well and good. Their real purpose
was to act as a deterrent, to drive the opposition back and
give him enough time to circle with greater care, rehol-
ster the gun and withdraw the MP-15 assault rifle from
the casing that kept it firmly strapped to the chassis of the
bike.

It was time to take out some trash….

Easing on the throttle, he headed for the center of the
town. From his recon, he knew that this was where the
young women were being held hostage. It was his task
to free them from their bondage. They were being kept

captive in a large building guarded by seven heavily armed men.

Although Thunder Rider had announced his arrival in no uncertain terms, he knew that the villains of this town had nothing as fast as his iron steed, nothing in their transport to match his speed and power. This, and the training he had put in to hone himself to the peak of fitness and to the mastery of his machine—until the point where he and the bike were almost as one—were more than enough to level the odds, no matter how outnumbered he may be.

The building where the women were being held was in his sights. Seven men approached him. They made it too easy. Clustered together, they presented an easy target. Without slowing, and without veering one degree from the course he had set himself, he raised the MP-15 and loosed the last of the grenades at the group of villains. Two of the men vanished as though they had never existed. One second they were there; the next they were a fine spray of blood, bone and flesh. The other five were wounded in differing degrees. Each fatally, the only difference being the amount of time it took them to die.

He slewed the bike to a stop and dismounted in one fluid movement. Erect, and with a swagger in his stride that bespoke a man not to be messed with, he racked the MP-15 and entered the building. A few craven souls cowered in front of him. He pulled the .44 from its holster and fired a few shots into the floor. They scattered.

"Ladies," he said, his stentorian tones resounding around the echoing and empty inside of the building, "you can come out now, you are free."

They emerged slowly, like small mammals blinking in the sunlight, staring at him with uncomprehending eyes.

"Your captivity is at an end. You may go where you wish, do as you wish. None shall hold you prisoner from this day forth, lest they fall beneath the wrath of Thunder Rider."

Crisply, he turned on his heel, after the briefest of bows, and strode out of the building into the wan sunlight. He mounted his iron steed, looking around at the peace that now reigned, and nodded to himself. It was good.

He kicked the massive engine into life and rode off into the distance, another wrong righted. Another step toward justice.

IT WAS A DAY like any other day. But not for long.

The ville of Casa Belle Taco was clustered around the remnants of a mall left from the days of predark. It was named after the gaudy house, which had been housed in the remnants of an old fast-food restaurant, and had grown over the years to cement its reputation as the finest gaudy in New Mex. Trade convoys and parties of marauding coldhearts would make special journeys to drink the psychotropic brew that was the house speciality, and to watch the sluts perform in shows with each other and selected members of the audience before offering services to the highest bidders. Not many men would bid for a gaudy slut, but these were no ordinary girls. It was said that they could do things that most men could only dream were possible.

Casa Belle Taco was a small ville. Rich in jack because of the gaudy house, those who lived there worked in some connection with the focal point of the ville. They either catered the gaudy, worked as staff or were sec. Even those who ran the local stores and ran sec on the perimeter were under the command of Mad Jack Flack, the baron of the ville—although baron was, in truth, a big title for a pesthole like Casa. Predark, he would have been the biggest pimp in the area, but no more.

The first indication of trouble had been the approach of the vehicle. Traffic in and out of the ville was no strange thing, but never before had the patrolling sec crews seen a single vehicle. Never before had they seen one that had eaten up the dirt and dust at such a pace.

"Sec force" was too dignified a name, in truth, for the two men in a wag, blasters idly at their sides, who watched the approach almost with disinterest.

Any danger from such a rapid approach was lost on them: the ville's reputation was such that no one wanted to upset the baron and get banned from the Casa.

The stranger burned rubber as he entered the ville. Astonished men with blasters at their sides were reduced to chilled corpses as the stranger pulled his blaster and fired indiscriminately. He was an expert rider on his machine, and it was almost impossible for the befuddled, bemused and still stoned men of the ville to get a bead on him. For the most part they ran for cover. Discretion was not so much the better part of valor as the chance to stay alive. All the same, many of them were chilled by stray slugs as he switched to a high-powered blaster. Then the first of the grens hit home, reducing much of the ville off the main drag to smoldering rubble, which meant most of the ville, as Casa Belle Taco was nothing more than a few buildings leading off the road to the gaudy house.

The sec force that manned the gaudy was a little more together than those who patrolled the outreaches. Even so, roused as some of them were in a stuporous sleep, they were still a ragged force as they rushed out to meet the oncoming danger.

Tactics and strategy weren't even words to them. They all arrived at the front of the building, following the sound of the vehicle, not even thinking of what an easy target they presented.

If they hadn't thought of this beforehand, they had less than no time to think of it when the stranger took advantage of their clustering to take them out with ease.

Baffled and scared, those still alive watched from hiding as the stranger dismounted and strode into the gaudy house. Inside, the gaudy sluts hid, also. Who knew what the triple-mad freak wanted from them.

The last thing they expected was his little speech, and for him to bow to them and leave them confused and staring with bemusement at the chaos around them.

Who the hell was this triple-stupe bastard? And what was the idea behind blasting their livelihood to shit and then telling them they were free? What use was that with no jack? Shit, they'd been happy with their lives until this asshole rode into town and screwed everything up. Now they had a gaudy house in a mess, and no sec to keep the customers in order.

Might as well have slit their throats and have done with it.

As one of them walked to the door and watched the

cloud of dust recede into the distance, she wasn't to know that they were just the first call of the day for the man who called himself Thunder Rider.

Chapter One

"Hot. Boring. Need action." Jak was sullen, hunched over at the front of the seat, holding the reins loosely in his grip while the emaciated horses tethered to the wag plodded on across the scrub and desert.

"My dear boy, I should have thought that we'd all had more than enough action to last us a lifetime," Doc replied laconically from the rear of the wag. He was lying propped against a rough hessian sack, once full and now alarmingly depleted. His shoulders slumped uncomfortably against the cans, self-heats and withered fresh produce that still lay within. His lips barely moved as he added, "Speaking for myself, I would welcome this respite from a life of constant peril. The merits of an adrenaline rush are, in my humble view, much overrated. Oh, for the balmy days when I could relax beneath the New England skies with a slim volume of poetry—"

"Not talk," Jak interrupted pithily. "Prefer you when crazy to this."

Doc gave a throaty chuckle. "Sometimes, lad, I think that I would agree with you."

Ryan was keeping watch out the back of the wag. It was hard enough to concentrate in the heat, without the added irritation of Jak and Doc. The flying bastard parasites who kept buzzing around him, diving to bite and take some more of his blood no matter how much he swatted at them, were irritation enough. The wasteland vistas out the back of the covered wag were endless: partly an illusion fostered by the heat haze and the stretches of scrub and desert dotted only with a few mutated cacti. They had been driving for days. It was as necessary to ration water to the horses as it was to ration the water for themselves. There was no other way they could make the distance. Paradoxically, in doing this, they had made their progress interminably slow. It was the lesser of the two, but still made days beneath the canvas cover of the bone-jarring wag hot, boring and seeming to stretch across time like the ooze from a stickie's pads.

There was a word for what the one-eyed man was feeling. Ennui. Ryan Cawdor wouldn't have recognized the word, but Krysty Wroth would have. She lay propped against him, idly stroking his leg, lost in her own thoughts. Sure, she could snap out of them in an instant, but right now there was no necessity, and so she let her mind wander back to the days of her upbringing in the ville of Harmony, where her education would have included some old texts that had used that very word. It was an idyllic time, rainbow-colored by learning, by youth and by the fact that it was a very long way away. There had been bad things, but her memory filtered them out to make room for only the good. And she was aware of this, using it as a place to escape when she had the chance. It helped her to relax. As she could feel the tension in Ryan's muscles and tendons beneath the rough material of his combat pants, she figured he could do with something to help him relax.

They had been heading in a southwesterly direction for—Ryan stopped to think—this was the fourth day. Fireblast, it seemed a lot longer. Four short days ago they had been riding sec for a ville baron who had hired them to help his men shift a herd of cattle across the plains. Doc had marveled at the job—"a return to the agrarian mores of yesteryear, my dear Ryan," whatever the hell that meant—and had seen it as a sign that the world was beginning to settle again.

Ryan hadn't seen it that way. To him, it had been a triple-stupe move. The cattle were the only asset the ville had; the baron was taking a hell of a chance using outsiders to augment his inept sec men; and there were coldhearts in every pass who could take the cattle and use them for ransom, for slaughter and for trade. But they were offered jack and, more importantly, this wag and some supplies. Coming as they were off yet another arduous trek, the latter was more than enough of an enticement.

The journey had been even shorter, swifter and bloodier than even he had expected. Two days out on their journey to the ville that had exchanged the cattle for goods, the route took them through a rocky mountain pass. To skirt around the pass in safety would have added a couple of days to the journey. Ryan had tried to argue for it, but had been shouted down by the baron's sec chief, already sore over the fact that outsiders had been brought in.

Six of Ryan's people against twice that number of

ville sec: in truth, the friends could have taken all of them out without even breaking a sweat, but that would have left them with the cattle and not enough personnel to go around. It wasn't worth it. The lesser of the options was to go with the majority, and just make sure that, if nothing else, their own backs were covered.

It was a wise move. Just as Ryan had feared, there was an ambush in that most obvious of places, and they rode straight into it. The fool sec chief was taken completely by surprise. Ryan and his people were ready.

The result was a bloody firefight in which the ville sec men were quickly disposed of, the friends pinned down in the pass and the cattle stampeded to a certain death— either under the hail of fire that crossed the narrow chasm, or by drought and starvation in the arid plains beyond. There were no winners here, only those who could survive.

It had been a bitter battle, in the end won only by the triple-stupe action of the ambush party, who had been torn between chasing the cattle and finishing off the people in cover. They chose the former, figuring that there were only a few left alive and they would be no threat.

There are bad calls, and there are those that go way beyond bad. This was one of them. Usually, it would have been a toss-up whether to waste the ammo by chasing the retreating coldhearts. This time, it was personal. Not a single one of the ambush party had survived.

Which left Ryan with this to consider: the sec men were chilled, the cattle were chilled, the ambushers were chilled. Apart from a charnel house full of corpses, both animal and man, there was nothing to back up their version of events. Should they go back? Should they go on to their destination and try to explain what had happened? Or should they just collect the wag of supplies that had accompanied them on the cattle drive and head off without looking back?

It was a no-brainer of a decision. Why risk being the messenger who got the shitty end of the stick? The whole operation had been a mess from start to end. Cut the losses and go.

The horses had been remarkably calm while chaos erupted around them. After their driver had been chilled, they had simply wandered into a shelter from the rain of fire. There they stood, ignoring the firestorm. Too stupe to notice, or just plain deaf? It was hard to tell, and in truth it didn't matter. All that mattered was that the wag was waiting for them when they got back to the pass.

Some of the water cans had been pierced by stray shots. Some of the cans and self-heats had been similarly hit. But, for the most part, the supplies were intact. Of course, there was nowhere near as much as they had been promised, but that was almost to be expected. All it did was reinforce their decision not to go back to the ville and the stupe double-crossing baron. Screw him.

So they had set off, not having any clear idea of where to go other than to avoid the ville from which they had come, and the one to which they had been headed. J.B. had used the minisextant that he found invaluable to determine their position, and the most expedient course had been to head toward the Grand Canyon and the nearest redoubt. It was territory that they knew, and although it harbored bad memories—which could have been said for most of the Deathlands—it was not a place where a welcome involving heavy firepower would await them if they returned.

Four days. The sky was clear of the taint of chem clouds, which meant that they could avoid the awful acid rains. But it meant that there was no cover for the oppressive heat of the sun. The canvas covering the wag was thick, but even that smelt at times as though it were beginning to smolder under the constant rays.

The seemingly endless boredom didn't help. A keening sound, underpinned by a dull roar that was all but masked in the air, broke the dead silence. It was a wag, or something like a wag…but unlike any Jak could ever recall hearing. Small, but powerful—he could tell by the note of the engine against the noise from the ground.

"Something out there." He spit over his shoulder. "Weird shit."

"What kind of weird shit?" Ryan said, his full attention now on his scanning of the landscape out the back of the covered wag. The hairs on the back of his neck began to prickle and rise.

Ryan's attitude communicated itself to the others without his having to say anything. They had been a unit for too long not to be able to read each other. Krysty, J.B. and Mildred shifted their positions and began to check their blasters, knowing they were primed and ready, but knowing the value of always making sure. Even Doc moved from his uncomfortable perch, the ancient but deadly LeMat coming easily to his hand.

"Still way off," Jak commented more than once.

Then, just as it seemed that the tension was to leave them, the sound became audible to their unattuned ears. It was like the angry hum of an insect, but growing louder with every second.

"There," Jak said simply, raising a hand to indicate direction. A cloud of dust and dirt rose toward the sky, a solitary blemish on the clear blue. It grew like a smokestack, spreading out to form a trail.

It was apparent that the vehicle was moving at a right angle to them. It was approaching, but not directly, which suggested that whoever was heading this way was not necessarily hostile.

The covered wag was an easy target, moving or still. That wasn't a consideration. What did concern Ryan—concerned all of them—was their own effectiveness in a moving as opposed to still vehicle. Particularly one that was little more than wood or canvas. As it moved, the wag gave them little in the way of options for firing. There was the uncovered front and rear, and little else. To fire from the front meant that whoever took the reins of the horses would be as impeded as the firer beside them. From the rear, there was a limited angle of vision. The only option would have been to strip off the canvas cover, which would merely leave the wag open and even more vulnerable than it was at best.

In truth, their best option was to stop the wag, unhitch the horses so that they could get clear—they had already demonstrated a propensity for avoiding crossfire—and use the wag for as best a cover as possible. They'd have to fire from under and around the structure to utilize the cover and also maximize the angle of fire.

In less time than it would have taken Ryan to explain the plan, the companions had complied. Each of them knew what was the best option, and they worked without words, knowing time was of the essence.

For the wag on the horizon was getting closer with every second.

As the horses wandered off, and they took up their positions, J.B. squinted through his spectacles at the approaching vehicle. It struck him that it was making one hell of a noise for something that seemed so small. It wasn't a tricked-out war wag; neither was it the kind of old predark truck that was still used for transporting goods within a short distance range.

"What is that thing?" Mildred asked to no one in particular. "I haven't seen anything go like that since NASCAR."

"What?" J.B. questioned absently.

Mildred gave a brief, bitter laugh. "Long time ago, John. Way, way before your time."

"Heads up, people. He's closing way too quick for my liking," Ryan stated.

ANOTHER SUCCESSFUL DAY for Thunder Rider. A one-man crusade against the forces of darkness was never going to be an easy task, but already he felt that he was making progress along his thunder road. More towns had been cleaned up: more scum had felt the scything sword of justice within the time between sunup and sundown.

Now to return to the secret base, where he could rest and recuperate in peace and security before venturing forth once more. Of course, he knew there would come a time when he would have to venture so far afield that it would be impossible for him to return home with the sun. Then, he would have to establish mobile bases that would serve as a secure haven while he rested. Perhaps in time he would be able to recruit others to his cause. There were good people out there, tired of being under the oppressive heel of the scum, who would join with him once they had a figurehead, once they knew they were not alone. He knew there were others from the communications that had been monitored at base since before he was fully trained. It was only a matter of finding them.

Though the dust streamed behind him, he had a clear view from all other angles. As darkness fell in such a barren environment, there was likely to be danger all around.

Like over to his right, and ahead of him. It was nothing more than a dot on the horizon to begin with, but as he approached, he could see that it was a horse-drawn wagon, with a small, hunched-over man driving it. It was covered, and he could not see within, but it was unlikely to be harboring danger. Those who would oppose him were not the sort to be driving a humble horse-drawn wagon, after all.

Nonetheless, he took one hand from the bar of the bike and flexed his fingers. He could find the .44 in a fraction of a second if necessary.

Perhaps it would be. He furrowed his brow as he watched the wagon pull to a halt. The small man leaped nimbly down and unhitched the horses, who wandered off. From each end of the wagon, men and women came forth. They were armed, he could see that, though not even his keen vision could make out their ordnance at such a distance. If he had worn the enhanced vision comp-visor that was a part of the bike's setup, then he would not have this trouble.

It was an oversight. He had been lax. That would not happen again.

Meanwhile, he fixed his eyes on the wagon in the distance. The people were adopting defensive postures. They were not looking for a fight, but rather they were responding to his approach. Oh, irony, they thought that he was one of the bad guys.

He determined to show them that all was well. Easing the throttle, he turned the bike toward them, slowing slightly. Raising one hand, palm up and out, he showed that he was unarmed. He could imagine the puzzlement on their faces as he approached them. What was this all about? Why was this powerful man not attacking them?

As he came within view, he could see them behind and around the wagon. Not enough to be able to identify them should they ever cross paths again, but enough to know that his gesture had achieved its intended effect. Their guns were not raised to him.

Perhaps they would recognize him. Surely the news of Thunder Rider had already spread far and wide. He could imagine the look of delight on their faces when they realized who he was; or, at least, that he was friend and not foe.

Perhaps in time they would join him.

He was past them in less than a moment. Righting his path, he opened up the throttle once more, the pulse engine responding to his deft touch. He returned both hands to the bars and sped on, once more, for home.

"HE'S COMING RIGHT FOR US," J.B. said incredulously. "Tell me I'm not imagining what I'm seeing."

"Oh no, freak boy's for real, John," Mildred whispered in tones that mixed awe with astonishment.

They could see that the vehicle was massively powerful. Wide and squat-bodied, it was obviously an engine-driven bike rather than a wag; yet its bulk suggested that it should be a trike, which would also account for its stability. Yet astonishingly, as it turned side-on to them, it became apparent that it was only dual-wheeled, the tires being of an immense width and thickness. And there was no trail of exhaust fumes to mingle with the dust in its wake. No smell of wag fuel that would have been so familiar and expected.

The most bizarre thing of all was the way in which the rider on the bike waved to them. There was no other word for it. He took one hand off the bike's steering and waved, as friendly as if he was an old friend greeting them after a long absence.

It was apparent that he was not going to attack them. As one, they lowered their blasters, watching in collective amazement as he turned away and roared off into the distance.

"Triple-good bike," Jak commented. "Weird bastard."

"Very succinctly put," Doc murmured.

"What was powering that thing?" Krysty asked.

Ryan looked at J.B., who returned his questioning gaze, then shrugged. "Don't know. But if he's that friendly to any old stranger who passes, then he's headed for a whole lot of trouble."

"Mebbe not," J.B. mused. "Anyone with wheels like that is going to have one bastard of an armory on board."

Mildred shook her head. "Yeah, well, there's too much weirdness there. Thank God he's headed in the opposite direction."

"Agree with that," Krysty added.

Chapter Two

When the sun went down, the companions pitched camp for the night. They had changed their direction, figuring that a ville lay on the line cut through the desert plain by the man on the bike. It was still in line with their original course, and a detour couldn't hurt if it gave them a chance to collect more supplies. Particularly water. They were on too tight a ration for the heat they had to endure during the day, and it was a primary concern.

Jak was on edge, senses straining for the return of the bike. What if the stranger hadn't attacked simply because he was on his own? What if he had been on a recce, and was now on his way back with other riders, heavily armed?

Ryan felt much the same, although without the heightened senses to give him warning. He did, however, have something that may have been even better than that: Krysty.

It was obvious from the way that she sat, staring into the fire, that something was bothering her. She was preoccupied. He could tell from the way that her flowing, prehensile hair had flattened itself, curled around her like a shield. Usually, the tresses were wild and free. The opposite could only mean one thing.

"Problem?" he asked her quietly. Jak was himself pre-occupied, Doc was sleeping and J.B. and Mildred were some distance off, grabbing themselves a little privacy. None of them had noticed Krysty's demeanor, and the one-eyed man was unwilling to draw their attention to it unless it became a necessity.

"Mebbe, lover," she replied in an equally soft tone. "Could be I was just spooked by that rider. Could be that there was just something that seemed odd about him."

"Man riding by on such a machine that doesn't try and blast the fuck out of you is weird enough these days," Ryan said with a small, tight grin.

Krysty gave a short bark of a laugh. "Yeah, true enough. But mebbe there's just this feeling that he wasn't as harmless as we thought. I can't say what. You know what this is like. It's like there was a scent of danger left, and I can't get the bastard out of my nose."

"Usually it's a good thing that it stays there," Ryan said, moving closer to her. "I trust that sense of yours. And this time it's backed up by Jak, and by something in my gut. Couldn't say what, just that I know the fucker's there."

Ryan left her to begin patrolling the camp's perime-ter. He looked at his wrist chron by the light of the fire before moving any farther: an hour remained until his watch was over and he could get some sleep. Time then to wake up Doc. Jak was also supposed to be getting some rest, but the albino couldn't sleep. Ryan knew him too well to counsel otherwise.

Moving away from the light and warmth of the fire, he shivered as the cold and dank of the darkness draped

itself over him. J.B. and Mildred were on the edge of
where the light petered out, and he skirted them, unwilling to disturb them. The Armorer and Mildred were on
last watch before sunup. They had plenty of time yet.

As THEY SET OFF next morning, the subject of the motorcycle rider wasn't mentioned. He was long gone, in the
opposite direction to that in which they now traveled, and
there was no sign of his return. The only way in which
he was relevant to their journey now was in the hope that
his path of the day before would lead them to a ville.

It was a hope that was realized within a few hours.
Before the sun had risen more than forty-five degrees in
the sky, they sighted a distant ville.

They could tell it was only a small ville by the fact that
there were only a few columns of smoke rising into the
sky.

"Oh, boy, do I have a bad feeling about this," Mildred
remarked heavily.

"Don't need a doomie sense for that," Krysty agreed.

It took an hour for the slow, horse-drawn wag to get
close enough to the ville to make out anything other than
the smoke. It was a journey that seemed as though it
would never end, the horses seeming to go slower with
every step. The lack of water was beginning to tell:
problem was, would there even be anything left in the
ville when they got there? Right now, they expected to
find nothing more than smoldering ruins.

A smell in the air wafted toward them on the light
desert breeze. It was, in part, horribly familiar—the smell
of burned, charred and roasting human flesh. There was

something else mixed in with it, a sweet smell with a bitter undertone. It was foreign to all but Mildred. She had no firsthand knowledge, but it reminded her of something she had read about when she was a child back in predark days.

Could it be napalm? Surely not. They had never come across much evidence of this surviving skydark, in all the time they had spent crossing the Deathlands. But if not that, then how had anyone come up with a hybrid that was so close?

Ryan stopped the wag. "We go on foot from here," he said shortly. "Triple red."

Jak tethered the horses to a fence post on the perimeter of one of the fields, and they began to move in on foot, along the trail that led to the center of the ville.

The smell hung over them like a pallid cloud, heavier than the smoke that rose to the skies, more oppressive. As oppressive as the quiet. The ville was only a small collection of residential dwellings. Some were cobbled together, and some were the remnants of predark adobe houses, patched badly over the years. Perhaps at some time this had been a small mall on the outskirts of a larger town. But it didn't matter right now. All that mattered was that they were drawing close to the center, and the quiet was replaced by the faint noises of people moving, people talking and people in pain, the small whimpers of those who had no fight left in them, and were hovering close to buying the farm.

The columns of smoke they had seen from a distance were now easily identifiable as coming from a small area in the center. The friends spotted scorch marks on some of the buildings, and debris that suggested some kind of explosion.

More than that, there was an orange tinge that spread over some of the walls and impregnated the dust on the sidewalks and roads that were, in themselves, little more than dirt tracks.

"What is that?" J.B. asked. His tone bespoke an almost professional curiosity. There was little about ordnance that he did not know, yet this was a new one.

"I fear, my dear John Barrymore, that it may be a portent of terrible things," Doc said with a quiet solemnity.

Ryan stayed them with a raised hand as they drew close to the center of the ville. "Keep it frosty, people. Anyone who can handle a blaster is going to be trigger happy and jumpy as jackshit after what must have happened here." He signaled for them to take whatever cover was possible as they approached.

So far, they had seen no one. That was strange. First thing anyone with any sense did when under attack was secure defensive positions. Ryan had expected to encounter at least one defensive sec patrol or lone blaster as they advanced. The fact that there had been none did nothing but fuel a dread of what may have happened here. Whatever had attacked this ville, its consequences had to have been severe.

But nothing could prepare them for what they saw as they entered the few streets that constituted the center of the ville.

The buildings were blackened, with orange streaks that ran across the blasted surfaces. Gaping holes pitted the frontages, with rubble strewed across the streets. Some of the buildings were little more than smoking piles of rubble, and in a few there were fires that still burned in small patches of red and orange flame.

Corpses littered the streets, bloated and gaseous in the heat. Some of them were burned and charred, which accounted for some of the smell. Others were beginning to stink of putrefaction, their sickly sweet odor adding to the olfactory overload. They were all male. And there were a lot of them. Ryan stopped counting at thirty, figuring that he now knew why there had been no sec or suspicious and paranoid ville dwellers to meet them. This was a small place. That many men had to have accounted for a good proportion of the ville's population.

The rest, he figured, if they were still alive, were in one of the burned-out shells, along with any other casualties. He could see from where he stood that this building, on the far side of the ville's central block, was full of people. Probably everyone left standing. Mostly women and children. They were clustered on the ground floor of what may have been the infirmary before whatever had happened here, but if nothing else had been converted to that purpose now.

"What happened here?" Mildred asked softly.

"Swift, sudden and brutal," Doc murmured, shaking his head sadly. "A veritable feast of carnage."

Ryan signaled to them to lower their weapons. Maybe not holster any blasters, in case someone over there got an itch to fire on them, but certainly at ease enough to avoid giving a hostile impression.

It looked like these people had seen enough of hostile to last them for some while.

Picking his way over the rubble, Ryan led the friends across the debris-strewed sidewalk and road. "Hey," he yelled, "what happened here?"

Some of the women and children looked up from their tasks, many with fear in their eyes.

All the while the friends had been moving closer to the building, its front an open wound. At least it allowed easy access, which was probably necessary. Women moved in and out, intent on their tasks: water, rags, something that looked like medical equipment, or could at least pass for it… Looking past them, Ryan could see where the soft cries of pain had originated from, and also why. The ground floor of the building was littered with makeshift cots and beds, crammed in no order except that which would make use of available floor space. Some of the things that lay on the beds bore little resemblance to anything human. He guessed that these were probably corpses, and that they were there only because there had been no time to clear them when they had given up their tenuous hold on life. Those that more closely resembled human beings were the ones who made the noises, the mewling, whimpering or weak-throated screams changing in proportion to how human the figures on the cots looked.

Some of them were women, most were men. Most were barely recognizable, at any rate, their hair burned off, skin either blackened or blistered a raw red. Some had wounds that were visibly weeping; bleeding that could not be completely stopped and that seeped through makeshift bandaging.

One of the women spoke as they approached.

"Mister, I don't know who you are, and I don't care. None of us do. If you want to chill us all, if you think there's anything worth taking here, then just do it. But if not, then just leave us in peace to try and deal with what's happened to our menfolk."

"Shit, if we coldhearts you be chilled for that," Jak said, echoing the thoughts that ran through them all. For the woman to speak that way to armed strangers, for the rest of the women and children to ignore them, bespoke of a tragedy that had driven them beyond the bounds of normal caution.

"We don't have an argument with you, and we don't want anything," Ryan said simply. "We're just passing through. Mebbe we can help a little." All thoughts of bartering for water and supplies left him at that moment. That could come later. Right now, it was time to perhaps earn that favor. And perhaps just time to act with a little civilization, a rare enough thing in the Deathlands.

Mildred and Krysty holstered their weapons and joined the women tending to the sick and dying. Each in her own way had skills that could help the ville women. Krysty's upbringing in Harmony had supplied her with an extensive knowledge of herbal medicines, and the natural healing properties that may exist in anything to hand. She had an expertise that was hard to come by.

Mildred's training as a doctor in conventional medicine in predark days was on shakier ground in this environment. She could administer and prescribe only those medicines that were available. In a ville like this, that wasn't exactly going to leave her with much in the way of options. It soon became clear that there was little medicine that she could use, but she had one invaluable skill: her diagnostic technique allowed her to prioritize the use of the medicines. As painful as it was to make some decisions, she assessed how bad each patient was, how much chance he or she had of pulling through, and how much of a waste or a benefit the administering of medicines would be. That enabled her to maximize the use of limited resources. Furthermore, she was able to work with Krysty in identifying the problems of each patient, so that the Titian-haired woman could also maximize her skills.

It was long, arduous and tiring work. They kept going for longer than they could keep track of time, and only realized the passing of the hours when lamps lit their path around the makeshift infirmary, rather than the sun.

While they worked, the others made themselves busy. The constant need for water had to be attended to. There was some rudimentary plumbing in the buildings, but all of this had been ruptured and rendered useless by what had gone on. Now, the water had to be carried in buckets, in anything that could be used as a container, from the more outlying buildings that were still serviced by the water system. A lot of the water was also going to waste, spilling out of ruptured and broken pipes, and it was vital to fix the ruptures and conserve as much as possible. J.B. and Jak set to this task with alacrity; Doc, being less practical in such matters, was only too glad to lend his strength to the constant relay of buckets and containers. He looked old and infirm, but as the women of the ville were soon to learn, that was deceptive. He may have been wrinkled and almost as whip-thin as Jak, but beneath his frock coat he was wiry, and the whipcord muscles that his occasional stoop served to disguise were soon brought into play. He felt, in some ways, useless. Mildred and Krysty had medicinal skills; J.B. and Jak were mechanically and practically minded; but Theophilus Tanner was, and would always be, an academic at heart. His skills lay in the mind, and were of little call in such a circumstance. He therefore determined to make himself of whatever use he could, working tirelessly.

Which left Ryan a little space to ease up on his part in the chain. Not from any desire to avoid work, but rather because he wanted to take the time to find out what had happened here. He had an uneasy feeling in his gut that it was connected with the stranger on the motorcycle who had passed them the day before. They had followed his trail, and the coincidence was too much. But how, exactly, did the two connect? Had one man been able to do this much damage? How?

It took him some time to gain the confidence of the woman who had initially spoken to him. She had shown them where they were to collect water, and formed part of the chain with them, if for no other reason than to keep an eye on them, lest they should prove to be an enemy. Not that there was much she would be able to do. Nonetheless, Ryan understood and appreciated her attitude.

For some time, her answers to his questions were noncommittal, which made progress seem next to impossible, particularly as his questions had been less than direct. He figured from her attitude that an outright demand to know what had happened would not achieve any result. So he had been cautious. But he was starting to run short on patience.

Eventually, he tired of it all and decided to go for broke.

"Fuck this not asking what we need to know," he said, taking her arm to stop her as they walked back from the water collection point. She looked down at his hand on her arm, then up into his eye, leveling her gaze with his. For a moment, he could see the fear in her eyes. Then it dissipated, replaced with acceptance.

"Okay, I figure by now that you don't mean us any harm, mister. So where do I begin?"

"I'm figuring that a man on a big motorcycle has something to do with it."

"You know him?" For a second, the alarm flared up once more in her eyes.

"Kind of," Ryan replied quickly, then told her of their brief encounter with the mystery rider the previous day.

When he finished, she laughed bitterly. "You got off lightly, mister. Shit, you don't know how lucky you are."

"Was he on his own, or were there others?"

She fixed him firmly with a stare. "You won't think it right, mister, but there was no one but him. No one. I tell you, there's no one left living here who's ever seen anything like it. Or would want to again."

Ryan whistled softly. "Coldheart bastard must have one hell of an armory on that bike. Tell me everything you can, from the beginning."

"You sayin' that you're gonna get him for us?" she asked with what was a palpably sardonic tone.

"No, I'm not saying that. I won't lie to you. But mebbe he's like a mad dog that needs chilling before it bites anyone else. We'll see. Tell me everything, first."

She nodded firmly. "Fair enough. But bear in mind that no matter how hard it is to believe, I ain't making any of it up. Or exaggerating, either."

And she began to tell him of the previous day.

"DAYS AROUND HERE GO much the same, no matter what. Guess they change with the seasons, mebbe even with the weather, but other than that there ain't much to disturb us. This ville's been here since skydark, and we ain't rich in jack, like some. Nor have we got much in the way of growing stuff. But we get by 'cause we can trade a little.

"And we don't get no trouble, either. A lot of these places, they got people buying the farm every day, people blasting each other for no reason. Now that's their business, if they want to chill each other for no reason, but we've always kinda stuck together here. When there ain't much to go around, you tend to look out for those next to you in case you need them to look out for you next.

"We were all going about our business like usual. The sun had just hit its peak, and it was no better or worse than any other day. Then we get word that this wag is coming to the ville. Really eating up the dirt, great clouds behind it. Faster than anything we'd ever seen come through here before. No one on the edges could explain what it was. Guess that's why we was all so curious. Nothing like something new to get you talking, right?" She gave a bitter cough of a laugh. "Shit, wish the coldheart bastard had just carried right on by.

"Anyway, it was obvious that the wag was comin' through here, and being as it was unlike anything we'd seen, mebbe we figured that it might have something on it for trade or jack. We get the same traders through here all the time, someone new, some fresh blood, would be more than welcome. Reason I tell you that is to explain why so many people were in the center of the ville when the wag came in… 'Cept it was no wag, but a bike. Weird-looking fucker—wheels big, like wag wheels, but it moved like a bike. Rider guided it in and pulled it up quick with a turn that he shouldn't have been able to do. Anyway, it was real impressive. Word had been spreading while it was approaching, so it was pretty full in the center, everyone crowding around to get a good look. There was stuff on the bike—lotta blasters, but also stuff that looked like packs, so mebbe he was some kinda solo trader. Dressed odd, threads like I ain't seen before, kinda shiny. Not hide or skin, but not wool or cottons, either. And he had these big, dark goggles on, like the kind you see sec men wearing on trade convoys, but more, y'know? There was something going on with them, but I don't know what. Only know that we had no idea what was about to happen.

"He takes off the goggles and looks around at everyone. No one says anything as there's this kinda weird feel about the whole thing. It's not like he's threatened us, so no one has gone for their blasters, but it's not like he's there to do us any favors. Y'know what it felt like? Felt like everyone breathed in and held it, waiting for him to speak. And then when he did, no one could understand what the fuck he was talking about."

Ryan stopped her with a gesture. "What do you mean? It was another language? What?"

The woman shook her head, then spit on the ground. "It was the same language we speak, boy, but not how we speak it. The words we could recognize, but not what they meant. Y'know when someone gets sick in the head?"

Ryan, thinking of Doc and starting to see what she meant, nodded.

"Yeah, well, it was kinda like that. The words made a kinda sense, but not what you could make out straight-away…I dunno, it was just…"

"Can you remember what he said?" Ryan asked.

She looked at him. He could see in her eyes that she would never forget. She began to intone, as though dragging them wholesale from memory.

"'Good people, I am Thunder Rider. I have come to deliver justice and peace. For too long there has been lawlessness in the land. There have been crimes committed against the good people of this and many other villes that have gone unpunished. The good and true cower in the shadow of evil. No longer shall the criminal go unpunished for his crimes. I have come to be your protector. You know who these wrongdoers are, and you stand in fear of them as they have greater strength, greater callousness, greater evil. You may fear no more, as I have a strength far greater than any they may possess. I carry with me the sword and shield of justice, and it is swift and sure. Vengeance will be yours, and I shall be the instrument. Turn your criminals over to me, and I shall deal with them, restoring peace and justice to your lands.'"

She stopped and fixed Ryan with a gaze that was defiant and bemused at the same time. "C'mon, One-eye, what kinda crazy stupe shit is that? What the fuck is a 'crime'?"

Ryan knew from old books about the concept of crime, which went hand-in-hand with the idea of law and order. But they lived in a world where such ideas had no place, which made the idea of the man on the bike triple screwed. Where had he gotten such ideas, and how did he think they applied to this world? But the one-eyed man said nothing of this. Instead he merely prompted, "What happened then?"

She shook her head. Now, she could not catch his eye, the memories too fresh and painful. In the past twenty-four hours there had been no time to think about it. Now she had to. Her voice cracked as she continued.

"No one did anything. What was there to do? We were all confused, didn't know what the hell he was talking about. Everyone was looking at everyone else, not knowing whether we should just blast the fucker and be sure. But there was something about him. He just didn't look like it'd be that easy to chill him, even though he was way, way outnumbered. Anyway, it must've been only a few moments before he spoke again. He said, 'So, you choose to ignore me. You choose the ways of lawlessness. I offer you protection, and you spurn me. Very well, those who side with the lawless shall pay as those they condone.' And then it started."

She stopped for a moment, gathering herself. Ryan waited, keeping down his impatience. He wanted to know every detail; she may not know herself what she was telling him, but he would be able to work it out. This was a chance to discover what weaponry Thunder Rider possessed, what kind of ordnance had wreaked such havoc.

"He must have known that his words would make

some of us fight. It was hard to understand most of what he said, but by the end it was pretty fucking well clear that he was gonna blast the shit out of us. He took a blaster out of a holster on his hip, a big long-barreled thing, and fired at the first man in his way. It was like the blood and shit that flew everywhere just shocked us more. Shoulda made us run, fight, something… Instead we stood there, triple stupe, slack-jawed like some buncha mutie inbreds. Easy meat, One-eye…" She stopped, gathering herself. Then, "Before any of us was smart and fast enough to react, he'd taken this big blaster rifle from the side of the bike.

"We were scattering. Some were firing as they ran, but we were spooked like horses. I guess most of the shots went into our own people. Nothing seemed to hit the rider. Calm, like nothing was happening—I saw him, like a stupe I couldn't take my eyes away—he turns around to the bike and reaches into the packs. Had this strange little blaster he took out, looked like it had tin cans in it. He pulled his goggles down, then fired the little blaster over our heads. It hit one of the buildings, side-on. Exploded like a gren, bits of wall flying all over us, but it was more than that. Gas—no, like gas but not like it. It was like there was gas but with liquid in it. Orange. Stained the walls, spread like an orange mist, and as it came down it burned those it fell on. Most of those burned by it have bought the farm, but some are still living. Better off chilled, if you ask me, but you can't just let them…"

She paused again, gathering herself. "I got lucky. The first gren of orange mist fell away from where I was standing. Shit, when I saw it burn, I ran. No way did I want that on me. I managed to get to cover, watched the rest. I shoulda done something, but I didn't know what. And I was scared. Like some fucking madman, he just stands there, saying nothing. Real careful, like he was totally in control, he fires at all the buildings, picking those on the corners of the streets with the most people jammed in 'em to start with. People falling over each other, pissing themselves with fear. Easy meat…

"When the mist is falling, and people are burning, and there's brick and stone and shit raining down, with all the buildings on fire, he takes the long-barreled blaster again and starts to pick off men at random. Then he stops, nods to himself like he's just been told to stop and gets back on the bike.

"No one's fired back, One-eye. No one. Can you believe that? All so…frightened? Froze in fear? I dunno… He just gets on the bike, revs the fucker up and rides out. Weaving past the bricks, the chilled, the orange shit on the ground, just like none of it's there. Just like he hasn't just taken out our entire ville.

"So he's gone, and we have to pick up the pieces and try to fix it as new." She laughed bitterly, hawked and spit.

"You wanted to know what happened? *That's* what happened, One-eye."

WHEN THEY RETURNED to the center of the ville, Mildred and Krysty had been able to start making some small difference. The path between the debris had also been improved by small teams under the direction of J.B. and Jak. They had only children to help them, the women being occupied in the infirmary, but the youth of the ville were wiry and strong. Doc, meanwhile, had continued his single-minded pursuit of his task, and his white hair was plastered to his scalp, his coat long since discarded in a heap, shirtsleeves rolled up.

Ryan paused for a moment, looking at the carnage with a fresh eye. The mystery rider had done this with no help, and with an armory that could comfortably be carried on a bike—a big bike, admittedly, but still one smaller than a wag. His words, which had seemed as so much stupe trash to the woman, made a kind of sense to the one-eyed man. The guy was crazy, sure. But crazy with a hell of an armory. That made him a triple-red threat.

Thing was, could they take him on? He hadn't promised the woman that they'd go after him, but if they were offered a reward? They were in no position to turn down jack or supplies. Moreover, Ryan had felt his instinct for self-preservation tugging at him. They'd already encountered the rider once, and by the sound of it they'd got lucky. Mebbe they wouldn't be so lucky a second time, and there was inevitably going to be a second time. Trouble followed them, there was no denying. So mebbe it would be for the best to hunt it down and face it before it came up behind and caught them unawares.

His reverie was interrupted by Jak.

"Ryan, careful orange dirt," the albino said without preamble. "Look…"

He held out his hand. There was a smear of orange mud against the white skin of his palm, and showing around the smear was a red weal, blistering at the edges.

"Get Mildred to look at that," Ryan said.

Jak grinned. "Gonna—not before show you, though. Some chem shit, stays burning a day after going off? Not seen before."

"Just got the story from her," Ryan said softly, indicating the woman who had returned to joining Doc's quest to deliver water. "Fill you all in later. This was our rider, and he's one mad coldheart by the sound of it."

Jak gave the briefest of nods, turned and went across to the infirmary. Ryan took his place in clearing rubble and caught the expression on Mildred's face as she examined Jak's chem burn.

There would be much to discuss later.

BY THE TIME THE SUN had sunk and the cold night chilled their bones, the companions were exhausted. They went back to where they had tied up the wag and horses.

Almost everyone else had stayed in the center of the ville. A few stragglers returned to their homes; most wanted the security of staying close together. The house where the wag was tethered remained empty. Whether the occupant had been chilled, they did not know.

And it didn't matter, except that it gave them the privacy they needed to talk about what had happened, and how it affected them. Ryan began by repeating what the woman had told him. They listened in silence. When he finished, and without comment, Mildred added her opinion of the burn she had seen on Jak's hand. She told them about napalm, and how she had felt when they first entered the ville.

When she finished, no one wanted to be the first to speak.

"I suppose the real question here is, do we see ourselves as knights errant," Doc said eventually. "I suspect that is what has been playing on your mind, Ryan."

"You're kind of right, Doc," the one-eyed man replied. "I feel like we need to go after this coldheart before he comes after us. And I feel like if we do that, we can mebbe get what we need from here…the things we came here for in the first place."

"There's not much left in the way of provisions," Krysty said quietly. "From here, the next ville is who knows where? We couldn't get far."

J.B. took off his spectacles and polished them. It was a habit, an indication that he was thinking. Eventually, he perched them back on his nose and started to speak.

"We got two separate problems here. First, we've got nothing in reserve, so we can't move on unless we trade with these people in some way. Now, they got jackshit, too. The only way they're going to give us what we need is if we can offer them something they want. Like revenge. Second problem is that this stupe is riding 'round at random, blasting the shit out of villes. Who knows where else he's been? Who knows where he'll stop? We stay in this area for any time, chances are we're going to run into him. So, do we do it now, or later?"

The Armorer paused, then looked steadily at Ryan. "Seems to me that the only way we solve one problem is by solving the other. That simple."

"Nothing to do with wanting to get your hands on his armory?" Ryan murmured.

A grin split J.B.'s face. "There could be that, too."

IT TOOK SEVERAL DAYS to help get the ville back into something approaching a functioning order. After the second day, the friends were offered food and water, so they could preserve their own. No mention was made of any condition. Rather, it was taken as payment for the work they were doing, which suited them fine at that point. The work was hard, and there was little demand beyond the immediate.

Soon the time was drawing near when the friends would want to leave. Question was, would they leave with renewed supplies and a mission?

The answer came on the fifth night. By now, the survivors had adopted a more communal style of living, pooling as they were their resources and their skills. It was while they were eating in the building that they'd adopted as their communal dining hall that Maggie, the woman Ryan had questioned on the first day, stood to address them all.

"You know what we all been through," she began with a halting tone, "and you know that these people—" here she indicated the friends "—have been a lot of help. But there's something else. Something some of you know about 'cause we've discussed it among ourselves.

"Ryan," she continued, "you said you'd help us get the coldheart bastard who did this if we'd help you with what you wanted. You still stand by that?"

"I do," he said slowly. "We all do. Happens that this mystery rider coldheart of yours might be a threat to others, might be a threat to us. That's no reason to go looking for trouble, but mebbe it'd be better to find it before it finds us. As well, you've been fair to us, feeding us while we've worked for you, so I figure you'll be reasonable about what we ask."

"Depends," the woman said, glancing at those around her.

Ryan's face twisted into a wry grin. "It isn't much. You know that when we arrived here we were looking to trade, pick up supplies as we were running low. You pay us in goods to go after this coldheart, and we will. We'll need more than we've got now if we're going to make a real job of it."

"How do we know you won't just go in the opposite direction fast as you can, forget about the rider as soon as you're outta here?" The speaker was one of the older boys, emboldened by the silence of expectation that had descended over the hall.

"You don't," Ryan said simply. "But you know what we're like. You've seen us work. We didn't have to do that. Weak as you are, we could have just taken what we wanted and already be long gone. So you think about that. Then you say yes or no to our terms. It's your choice."

Chapter Three

No choice at all. The people of the ville agreed to their terms. The companions loaded their wag and set off the next morning, before the sun was too high in the clear sky.

"I never thought I would wish for the toiling colors of a chem cloud, but then there are many things to which I thought the word 'never' would apply," Doc said sadly as he stared at the sky.

"Don't talk shit, save energy, drive," Jak muttered from the back of the wag. Doc, first on driving duties, spared himself a small smile and coaxed the horses onto the road out of the ville.

They could have taken a motorized wag, one that would have negated the need for food and water for the horses, one that would perhaps have been more reliable. But J.B.'s recce of the ville's resources the night before had revealed that their wags were old and in poor repair, and that their supplies of fuel were low. To take what was needed from them would have left the ville with next to nothing, while at the same time taking a big risk on being stranded in the middle of the sandy dustbowl that was their chosen route.

The lack of speed shown by the two stringy creatures pulling their wooden wag was a small trade-off against these risks.

But that was not the only reasoning that Ryan was using. The rider had seen them once before, using this wag. That time he had been friendly. If he saw them again in a motorized vehicle, would he be more likely to perceive them as a threat? If he saw them with the horse-drawn wag, would he recall seeing them once before and passing by? These questions were important. He was one dangerous coldheart, and to attract undue attention and hostility in tracking him was the last thing Ryan wanted.

Although they set out along the route by which they had entered the ville—tracking back along the trail left by the rider almost a week before—they had no intentions of blindly following it and hoping that they might just, conceivably, run into him along the way. It was purely that it was the only road in. After all, the rider was faster than them, and had days of start on them. The problem here was how to try to find him.

Wherever he was currently based, he could only travel as far as the fuel tanks on the bike would take him. A return journey, at that. He had, by all accounts, left the ville by the same road he had entered. So his base of operations was more likely to lay back in the direction from where he had come than it was to lay on the road on the far side of the ville. If he was triple smart and didn't want to be followed, Ryan thought, then he may have doubled on himself and circled the ville. But that notion didn't tally with their encountering him a day's wag ride along that return line.

Trying to get inside the mind of a triple crazie had given Ryan a headache. He'd discussed the options with the others, and it had left them with a headache, too.

Most crazies were easy to figure out. When he thought of all the madmen they'd come up against, it was clear that for most of them there was always one driving obsession that was at the center of their craziness. You find that, and you find the key to how to deal with them. Strategy was easier when you had something to go up against. But what did they have with the mystery rider?

Mildred and Doc were the most likely to have some idea of what might be going on inside the head of the rider.

"The things of which he speaks are very much concepts from before the nukecaust," Doc had mused. "There has been very little to survive that could have fully informed him of such notions."

"Particularly if he was out here living in it," Mildred added. "Let's face it, a lot of our notions about the law and justice lasted squat once we actually had to adjust and survive."

Doc gave a quiet chuckle. "True, my dear Doctor. Truer than you know...or maybe not." He gave her a quizzical stare. "We were soon disabused of such notions, even if we kept knowledge. Yet our mysterious friend seems to still have an intrinsic belief that such a thing is possible. Now that shows a peculiarly muddled sense of reality, does it not? Yet he seems quite rational in other ways."

"Doc's right. The rider has the ability to function to a high degree," Mildred mused. "So how could you get that combination? That isolation, and that knowledge, that would enable you to still function, yet have no real idea of the world in which you lived?"

"Lori…" Doc said softly.

Mildred looked at him, brow furrowed. Lori was before she had joined them, but she had heard tell of her. A glance around the others confirmed her suspicions— Lori Quint, the tall blonde with the short skirt. She'd been Doc's companion for a short while, until she bought the farm. She had been born and brought up in a redoubt, never seeing the outside world until Ryan and the others had landed in the redoubt by sheer chance.

"You think he may live in a redoubt? There might be one around here?" Ryan questioned.

"Perhaps. Not necessarily a redoubt, but maybe a base of some kind? Somewhere that would be protected against the nukecaust. Somewhere people could inter-breed without ever having to go outside."

"Wouldn't be the first time we'd found crazies living like that," Krysty mused. "But as you say, people rarely go outside."

So they reached a kind of conclusion. It wasn't much to work on, but it was the best they could come up with and it did give them a place to start. If there was a limit to the fuel his bike could carry, and he had a base some-where along a line from the ville to where they had first seen him, then it might be possible to narrow the search by drawing a circle that could encompass other villes in the area, and working in from there.

They had little in the way of maps to work from, but J.B. was an excellent navigator and plotter. Some judi-cious questioning of the people from the ville gave him the names and rough locations of other villes in the area, along with an indication of distance by the time it usually took to travel between them. Using old predark maps of the area leading to the Grand Canyon and New Mex that were among the papers he always carried with him, he was able to prescribe a rough circle, within which lay three other villes. It would take them several days to visit all of them, and the reception they would receive was a variable to be met with caution, but it was a plan that gave them somewhere to begin the search.

J.B.'s MAP AND ROUTE PRESCRIBED an arc that would take them a round 360 degrees back to their starting point. Along the way, they would hope to pick up more information about the mystery rider that they could use to pinpoint his base of operations. It would be a long, arduous task, but there was little else they could do to make it any easier.

As they made the tedious journey, under the boiling sun or the freezing moon, they looked across the desolate landscape for any sign of the rider, or for his tracks. There was none before they came to the first ville on their route.

Station Browns ville had no old predark rail depot from which it could have derived its name. There was little in the way of old railroad that had even traversed this section of the Deathlands, as they knew too well from past experience. The origin of its name was a mystery, except that it rang some distant bell in Mildred's youth.

It was of no matter. Like the ville they had originally stumbled upon, Station Browns was, in effect, little more than a way station for passing trade. And as there was little that passed this way, it was as dirt poor as its neighbors. The little they had gleaned about it indicated that it was little more than a pesthole ville, with a gaudy house that paid its way and a nice line in home brew that traveled well. There was a kind of rivalry between Station Browns ville and a ville called Casa Belle Taco, which had a similar trade. But there was enough distance between them for horny and thirsty convoys and travelers to keep both in business.

On the third day out, both Jak and Krysty felt prickles of unease within them.

The albino, his hunting senses as sharp as they were, could find no reason why he was feeling that way. There was no scent, no sound that he could put a name to, yet he could feel that out there, somewhere just beyond the limits of his senses, there was someone—something?—watching them.

For Krysty, it was much the same. Except that she did not have to rely on empirical evidence. Her ability to sense danger was almost infallible, and it was sounding alarms in her head that were impossible to ignore. Yet the landscape was deserted, and the sense seemed to fade in and out, like a badly tuned old transmitter picking up white noise that was almost—but not quite—decipherable. When it was strong, it was impossible to ignore it. Yet just as quickly it would fade out, before returning with a great intensity. And so she kept quiet about it, figuring she would wait until she could pin it down a little better.

It was nonexistent when they got their first view of Station Browns ville. Across the flat plain, it was still several miles away—a good two or three hours by horse-drawn—and the ville looked to be undamaged.

It was only as they got closer that the truth became apparent.

HIS SUSPICIONS HAD FIRST become aroused as he sped away from the folks in the horse-drawn wagon. Regular types, the sort who could help to build a new world. That was what had come to mind. But why? That was what had nagged at Thunder Rider all the way back to base. What had made him think that of a random encounter that lasted only a few seconds? He knew there had to be something else, a trigger that had started that thought. The question that faced him was how to discern what that trigger might be.

Back at base, he had the technology that could help him. In the lab, there was a brain wave decoder. It had been built for him, and in truth he did not fully understand the principles on which it worked; but in essence, it took his brain waves from the memory sector of his brain and translated them into images that were digitally recorded, so that he would be able to study them in detail. The persistent nagging made him hit the throttle even harder: there was no way he could rest until he had laid his mind to rest.

When he reached base, he docked the bike, leaving maintenance and refueling until later, and went straight to the lab. The LED was simple to set, and he selected the decoder option, plugging the headset into the jack on the console before carefully positioning it on his skull. Seating himself, he relaxed, taking deep breaths as he had been taught, before punching the key that would set the program in operation.

The trick was to think about anything else other than what you wanted to capture. If you tried too hard, and bought it to mind, then you would be dragging it from the memory center, making it hard for the computer to scan and collect.

He diverted himself by thinking about his favorite video. The one where the cowboy found the underworld kingdom ruled by the ice queen. She was merciless to begin with, but only in the protection of her people. She had taught him that to do good, you had to be prepared to sometimes do things that would be bad...unless, of course, you were doing them to people who would do even worse. His sister had told him of that old saying "you can't make an omelet without breaking an egg." He knew what they were, of course, but he wondered what they tasted like. He had never seen one, other than in pictures.

The console hummed and a monitor screen flickered to light, a message appearing to tell him that the scan of the area was complete, the images captured. Letting his mind wander had worked, as he hoped it would. Sometimes he found it hard not to think of the things that concerned him.

He took off the headset, unplugged it and put it carefully away. He was mindful of the fact that he was fortunate to have this legacy of equipment with which to execute his mission, and he did not wish to waste or damage it with carelessness.

The computer program did it all for him. He had

merely to key in the sequence to play, and then watch. The events of the past two days played out before him. He hit the key to fast forward to the relevant section, not wishing to view all of his life over again so soon. When it came to that section, he marked it on the toolbar: where it began, where it ended. He cut it out and played it over and over again, switching the angles, enhancing the image, zooming in and out. He wanted to try to catch as much of a view of the inhabitants of the wagon as he could.

It was far from easy. They had adopted defensive postures that were so accomplished that little of them could be gleaned. However, he could tell that there were six of them. One of them was small, pale. He had white hair, as did another. One was dark-skinned. And one… For a moment his breath was taken away. A flash of hair, a brilliant red, waving in a nonexistent breeze, as though alive of its own accord.

It could not be… He saved the best images he could and left them on screen. Each of the six images centered on one of the people hiding behind the wagon.

Swiveling in his chair, he went to another monitor. This archived all the reports, visual and verbal, that had been collected by the base's intel-gathering equipment since the time of the Long Night. There was, in truth, very little. This system had been designed for use in the days before the darkness, and it had a vast capacity for memory. It was a sign of how things had degenerated that only a fraction of its vast storage capacity was in use. This made it simple for the search facility to scan intel for correlation with the people on the screen.

The search bought several matches, recorded over a period of time. There was precious little to go on, as there were very few facilities capable of broadcast and communication technology in these days. But these sparse mentions added up to a picture, one that Thunder Rider had noted while he had scanned the outside, preparing for his entrance.

This group of people—who seemed to have added and lost a few members over time, but remained with the same core nucleus—had, like himself, been pillars of right. They were the kind of allies he sought.

More… The vision of the red hair floating in a non-existent breeze stirred something within him. It was something new, something that he had never felt before.

He was determined. When he had completed maintenance and refueling, when he had rested himself, then he had to find them.

He had to find her.

THEIR FIRST INDICATION that all was not well came with the burst of fire that seemed to erupt from nowhere, kicking up the sandy soil a few yards ahead of them. The horses reacted, moving erratically enough to throw off balance those who were in the back of the wag. It was as well that the horses had proved themselves calm to the point of stupidity under fire, otherwise Jak, currently at the reins, would have dropped them with a slug to each head. As it was, he was able to pull them around, giving those in the back the chance to find their feet and grab their weapons.

The burst of fire was followed by silence, the echo on

the still air, mocking them. With the wag sideways-on to the direction the burst had come from, they lined up behind the shelter of the vehicle, just as they had when the mystery rider had skirted them. There was no other cover in this barren landscape.

"What do you reckon?" Ryan asked J.B.

The Armorer scanned the land between the wag and the horizon. Only the first few buildings on the edge of Station Browns ville broke the unrelenting flat.

"It didn't sound like serious ordnance, or rip up much dirt. It had to have come from someplace between here and the buildings, some kind of hide or shelter. No way something that weak got that distance otherwise."

Jak had been scanning the ground ahead of them, blotting out the conversation beside him. If there was anywhere they could hide, then he was determined to spot it. With no cover, it had to be some kind of dugout. Even the best-made hide would show somewhere against such a featureless surface.

It wasn't well made, and it didn't take him long to locate it.

"Ryan, there. Forty degrees," he whispered, directing the one-eyed man's gaze along a line prescribed by his bony white finger. Ryan followed and saw it immediately. Once you knew where it was, it was obvious: raised by the side of a cactus, dust- and dirt-covered canvas over a hole with a built-up ledge. Just enough of a slit between dirt and canvas to see out of, to direct a blaster.

Ryan beckoned Mildred and indicated the hide. "Just frighten the fucker out," he said simply.

Mildred nodded and focused her aim. Her Czech-

made ZKR was a specialist target pistol, and she had
once been a specialist target shooter. This was simple.
She placed three shots around the lip of the hide. One
kicked up dust in the center, while the others knocked out
the tiny supports that gave the hide its view of the world.
With a puff of dust, the hide closed up.

"So we know where you are, you know where we are.
We could have taken you out, but we didn't want to. You
come out, we won't shoot. We aren't your enemy…but
we might know who is. We're chasing a coldheart with
a freaky motorcycle—"

"That fucker. Okay, I'll trust you 'cause I'm pinned.
Don't let me down."

The woman was an unlikely sec sniper. Dressed in a
dirty camisole top, shorts and combat boots, long blond
hair tied back, the large-busted and curvy young woman
looked more like a gaudy slut who'd been given a blaster
and thrown into the wrong job.

Showing good faith by holstering his SIG-Sauer and
walking out into the open, Ryan prompted her to introduce herself.

"Name's Anita. Long time since I hefted a blaster.
More used to handling other kinds of weapons," she said
with a grin, "but I figure that we need all the skills we
can get after what happened."

"Which was?"

"Bastard you described…" Briefly, and with more
cursing than even Jak would have thought possible, she
outlined a situation similar to the one that went down in
the last ville. By the time she had finished, the others had
joined Ryan in front of the wag.

"So where the fuck do you fit into it?" Anita asked in what they had discovered to be her usual forthright manner.

Ryan told her briefly about their experiences, and about the pact they had made in the last ville.

"Should be glad we aren't the only ones," she said at the conclusion, "but then I wouldn't wish that asshole on anyone. So I guess you'd better come on back with me, see if mebbe you can find out something else that would help."

"You think there could be something?"

She shrugged. "Dunno. Can't hurt to ask. 'Sides which, we're pretty much on top of clearing up now. Weird fucker thought us girls were all prisoners. Didn't touch any of us, just chilled all the men and blew up a lot of shit."

"Where did a gaudy slut learn to shoot like that?" Krysty asked her.

The smile vanished. "My daddy."

"He was a good shot?" Krysty prompted.

Anita sniffed. "Fucker wanted me to be mommy to my new little sister. Would have been if he'd got his hands on me. Sweetest shot I ever made, right through the bastard's dick. Now, you gonna give me a ride back, or do I have to walk in front of that wag of yours?"

Doc gathered the horses and drove the wag into the ville, Anita sitting beside him to indicate that all was well. They made the short journey in silence, the friends gleaning what they could from the view out the back of the canvas wag cover.

There was little to see that wasn't familiar to them. Station Browns ville was almost too small to have a center as such; rather, it had a few buildings that radiated from the hub, which was a cluster of about five buildings. It was difficult to tell, as they hadn't been well-constructed, and the rider's ordnance had wreaked more havoc here than the ville they had recently left.

The ville had looked fine from a distance: no smoking wreckage, and now they could see why. Any fires had long ago burned themselves out. The flattened center section of the ville was nothing more than rubble and corpses. Some of the gaudy sluts, incongruously still dressed for trade, were working to clear the corpses.

"How many of you are left, my dear?" Doc whispered.

"No more than fifteen, all women and girls. Every male, young or old, is chilled. Criminacs, or somethin', that was what he called them."

"Criminals, my dear. An old word, of no real meaning now."

Anita sniffed. "Figure it must mean somethin' if it makes him chill all our menfolk. That what he did where you come from?"

"Almost. A larger population, perhaps not enough time for him. We must find out all we can, I think, and quickly," he said over his shoulder at Ryan.

The one-eyed man was in agreement. They had another two villes to get to. Chances were, on this evidence, that the coldheart rider had already paid them a visit. It was not a time to stand on ceremony.

Their approach had attracted the attention of those still left alive, and it was no problem for Anita to gather them together to explain who the strangers were and what they wanted. There was no shortage of information. What emerged was that the mystery rider's visit to Station

Browns ville followed the same pattern as the other event: ride in, speak of arcane things in a strange pattern, and when he didn't get the reaction he wanted, he started firing—except that he refused this time to fire on any women, believing them to be innocents. As employees of the gaudy house, they weren't allowed to carry blasters. A pity, as his leaving them alone would have given them a clear shot at him, and maybe avoided this destruction…and the destruction where they had come from, as it seemed that this attack had occurred before the one they had stumbled on.

The only other thing of note was that there was no sign of the napalmlike substance in this ville. Had he considered this ville too small to make that necessary, or was he limited by numbers as to how often he could use it? That question would only really be answered if they found the next ville had also been attacked.

There was little they could do to help here. The women had the situation as under control as was possible, and there was little medical help needed. The stark truth was that those who would buy the farm had already done so by this time.

There was little else they could do but leave, with the words of the gaudies ringing in their ears—pleas to wreak revenge.

It was when they were out on the empty expanse of desert once more that Krysty started to get that sense of being watched.

IT WAS WITH A SINKING HEART that they made the slow trek across the wastes to their next destination. The ville had been wiped out. No survivors.

But at least one important thing was evident at their last stop: this ville had been attacked in the time between the other two attacks, which meant that the rider wasn't working his way around an arc, but was more likely to be at some point equidistant to all three villes.

Two down, one to go. They set off with a little more information, but not enough to reach any real conclusions. After a two-day drive across the desert and dustbowl, they found themselves with a ville that had been the first to be visited by the rider. Those that had been chilled had been disposed of. The infrastructure had been restored as much as was possible, and there had been no orange chem here. Again, the people talked of the rider's strange language and undreamed-of ordnance. Their descriptions were sketchy, as had been those of the other villes, but they were enough to tell J.B. that the man had been using a limited range of weaponry so far. It didn't mean he didn't have a wider range available, but it did say much about his thought process.

They left the final ville on their arc with a little more information than when they had started, but not as much as Ryan would have wished.

"Not much good," Jak commented tersely.

"On the contrary, dear boy, I would say that we have something that John Barrymore could work with," Doc commented.

J.B. grimaced. "Okay, so if he starts from one point and attacks them, but not in any order of progression, then if we drew a line from the villes, we might get a central point, but only if the four villes form enough of an angle from which—"

"Yeah, okay, I get it—it won't be accurate. But it would give us an area to start looking," Ryan pointed out, "and that's better than where we are now."

"Mebbe," J.B. breathed, "but you figured how big that area could be?"

Ryan sighed. "It's about all we got right now."

Jak exchanged a look with Krysty. "Ryan, head right direction, figure scum look for us. Knows where are," the albino said.

"You sure of that?" Ryan questioned, dividing his gaze between them.

"Oh, yeah, I'm sure of that," Krysty said with a shiver, her hair flicking around her shoulders nervously. "I don't know where he's hiding out there, with no cover, but he's been watching us. All the while. I can feel it."

Ryan nodded, almost to himself. "Okay. Let him bring it on, then. We plot a rough course, and we start out first thing. If that's how it's gonna be, let's draw the bastard out."

Chapter Four

"I am on a line going thirty-three by seventeen. The fourth quadrant. They are at rest for the evening, operating a watch rotation system. They seem to be very lightly armed, which has surprised me given their reputation. However, I shall still use long-distance search and recover tactics, and take no chances. Further reports after operations commence, which should be at 0400 by my chronometer. Message ends."

Thunder Rider flipped up the slim mike that came down from his goggles and adjusted the long-range infrared recon scope before lifting the eyepiece to his left eye. The darkness of the surrounding desert now became a relief in grays and greens. The figures and the wagon in the distance, barely visible by the naked eye even in the light, now came into sharp focus. He adjusted the range with the slightest touch of his index finger, and the figures grew larger in the scope. He could see that the small albino and the famed Armorer were on watch. The others were sleeping, clustered around the fire. The red-haired woman was close up against the one-eyed man. For a moment, Rider felt a twinge of something in his chest, and was baffled. He truly had no idea what bothered him, only that something did. No matter, it did not fit in with the plan.

The scope had a long-range directional mike attached. Thunder Rider activated the facility. The receiver was attached to a small speaker in the goggles, relaying directly to his ear all that could be heard from such a distance. Not that there was much. The old man and the black woman were snoring. The albino was silent, and prowled like a wolf ready to spring. He was the most immediate danger. Not relevant now, but a point worth noting. The Armorer was muttering softly to himself, possibly as an aid to concentration. It was almost inaudible, and certainly under his breath. Rider doubted that the others would be able to hear him. It was testament to the power of the recon equipment that he was able to discern this.

So: two on watch, the others sleeping. Reflex times would be reduced. They would, of course, know before the strike hit. In this silence, even the best of stealth weapons would be detected, certainly by the albino. Even with an advanced warning, there would be little they could do against the weaponry he chose to use. However, no one won a war without caution and care. Preparation, thinking ahead, and the ability to be flexible. It was easier to do this when training than out in the field, as he had discovered. There were aspects of his recent activities that needed review and improvement.

Nonetheless, that made him all the more determined to be precise in this operation. To get it right.

The chassis of the bike was made of a polycarbon fiber, surrounded by titanium supports. The polycarbon enabled the frame to be strong and lightweight, the titanium supports forming an exoskeleton over the top to which were attached the pods that contained equipment, and the holstering that held his ordnance.

Thunder Rider crouched over one of the pods, snapping it open. All of the pods were self-contained, ready to be attached and removed to the frame as necessary. Their interior design was specific to whatever they were carrying, enabling him a secure storage system for ordnance and equipment that could be easily changed on the bike at a moment's notice, back at base. He had thought long and hard before preparation for this mission, and as he inspected the contents of the pod he had just opened, he had no regrets for his decisions.

He had chosen the recon equipment from the stores with care. Knowing the reputation of the people he was about to trail, he wished to ensure that he would not have to engage them in direct combat. He had a twofold purpose in this: the first was that he had no desire to fight those he would wish to make his allies. The second was that he was outnumbered by six-to-one: not odds that would bother him in the usual run of things—had not his missions to those small towns shown this?—but when he was against an adversary with such a reputation as this group, it would bode him well to show some caution.

His basic plan was to take the redheaded woman, show her the base and support systems, and discuss with her the basic philosophy of his mission. He felt sure that if he were to do this, then she would help him convert the others to his cause. There were other, stranger feelings that he could not explain coursing through him. He chose to ignore them for the moment.

He focused his mind on the task in hand. The recon

equipment had served him well so far. He was pleased by that as it was the first time that he had been called upon to use this in an operational capacity, and it had proved as effective in the field as he had hoped. The night scope was augmented by a long-distance digital imager for use in daylight. Between them, these two devices had enabled him to keep a close watch on the group without going too close. Similarly, the long-range directional mike had helped him to try to understand what was going on in the dynamics of the group, the better to adapt his tactics to the situation. In truth, there were certain elements of this operation that were completely new to him, and as such he was treating this as an exercise that would make him a better operative in the future.

The recon equipment was one thing: what lay in the pod in front of him, nestled comfortably into its protective fittings, was another matter entirely. It consisted of a series of small polycarbon rods that fitted together to form a barrel of variable length. There were overlapping supporting rods to reinforce the barrel when assembled. A small, electronic sight and laser target finder sat within a soft protective base, ready to be switched on and attached. The battery unit powering the target finder had a half-life of five hundred years. A triggering mechanism was also comfortably fitted into the pod, ready to be attached and deployed.

Most important of all were the small black eggs that sat in a line, snugly arrayed in a rack fitted into soft material. From the computer files back at base, he knew that these had been derived from a prototype that had never been called into commission. The design had been perfect, but the costings had been deemed prohibitive at the time. The report on file had been sidetracked into a rant about the wastage in military spending. The gist of the report had, however, been clear: this was a highly effective weapon, to be used sparingly and with great caution.

Again, he took this to be a good thing. Not only would it achieve its purpose, but he would be learning as he progressed in the mission. Thunder Rider was always looking to be better.

Dismissing such thoughts from his mind, he set to assembling the weapon. Using the range and directional finder on the recon equipment to set the coordinates on the directional and firing unit, he attached it to the long barrel he had constructed. The trigger unit came next, and remembering what the files had advised about caution, he did not deploy it until he had taken one of the small black eggs and inserted it into the chamber that was formed within the now fully assembled weapon.

He turned to the direction of his target. From the files, he knew that the dispersal of the gas was rapid, and that its effect was virtually immediate. That would give them little to no time in which to deal with the attack.

The effects of the gas would last for several hours, which gave him more than enough time to disassemble the weapon, take the bike across the desert surface, check their status and take the redhead. He would have no need to hurry, which was good. Hurry was the mother of panic.

A wireless unit on the recon equipment would feed exact coordinates into the directional unit. One touch, and it was done. A shielded light on the directional unit blinked once, paused, then blinked twice. A signal that the information was received, processed and the weapon was primed for deployment.

All he had to do now was to attach the trigger unit and point the weapon in the right direction. He smiled to himself, thinking of some of the old videos he loved, and the difference between the quality of weaponry used by those heroes and by himself. What they could have achieved if…

He pursed his lips, shook his head firmly. This was not the time to enter into such a reverie. He attached and deployed the trigger unit. Another shielded light, blinking once, pausing, then twice. Ready.

He nestled the weapon into the hollow of his shoulder, setting himself, then put the eyepiece of the directional unit to his goggles. An infrared grid, switching automatically as it read the light levels, showed him the campfire and those gathered around it. On the periphery of the scope's vision he could see the Armorer and the albino, pursuing their separate circuits. It was surprising how clustered together they were, really. The range of the gas once the egg had burst was such that it would touch them easily.

Flickering figures in one corner of the eyepiece recorded time and distance. Coordinates appeared, and it told him how long it would take for the grenade to reach the target area once fired. He set the crosshairs to one side of the campfire. For want of anything else, it seemed an obvious target point. He squeezed gently and the egg was expelled with a recoil that jolted at his shoulder.

It had taken him by surprise. It was, after all, the first

time that he had fired this weapon. With an ordinary piece of ordnance he would be cursing the fact that his shot would now be off target. But he had the satisfaction of knowing that a laser directional beam had locked on to the coordinates and once the egg had been sent along this beam, the smart circuits in it would keep it on target.

He brought the weapon back in line, using the direction unit to see what was occurring. They were momentarily unaware, and then he could see the albino turn, could hear him yell through the mike link.

They had quick reactions, as he had expected. But not quick enough. With a small nod of satisfaction, he turned away and began to disassemble the weapon. Swiftly, but without hurry. He had the time, now.

JAK WAS STARING into the dark. He knew that the bastard was out there, it was just a matter of where. He could almost sniff his scent on the cold night air. But it was as if he was just beyond reach. Still, every fiber of his being was screaming triple red.

Red. Something had brought that phrase to mind, something seen from the corner of his eye and registered only on the most subconscious level. He turned and looked toward the fire, which was still burning bright enough to cause him to squint at the contrast in brightness. Not a contrast so great that he could not see what had registered in his mind. A small red dot on the sandy soil, almost invisible in the glow of the fire, just to one side of it. It was steady on the ground. A laser of some kind. A marker?

Every nerve in his body jangled, his stomach flipping as the first wave of adrenaline began to rush through him.

"J.B.! Look! Incoming—everyone..." he yelled, words coming out in a jumbled bark.

On the far side of the circle cast by the fire's light, J.B. whirled and was heading toward the albino even before his Uzi had come to hand. He didn't waste time with words. A quizzical glance, answered by Jak's own gaze, was enough, directing him to the red dot on the ground.

"Pathfinder," he whispered to himself, knowing as he did that their only chance was to move quickly out of the immediate area, then try to locate where the attack originated. To do anything else except run would be to ask how much jack the farm cost.

Both men, despite having weapons to hand by reflex, showed no concern with following the direction of the beam. That would have been fruitless, anyway. It was little more than a red dot, with no chance of ascertaining direction by the naked eye. No, the only thing to do that would be of any practical use would be to rouse the others, get them out before whatever was heading their way hit.

Jak's shouts had already awakened them. Ryan and Krysty were bolt awake, on their way to being on their feet before his words had even died away. Mildred was a little slower, having been asleep longer and much deeper into her rest. She was bleary, but under the fog of sleep her reflexes were forcing her to the surface. She was stumbling to her feet even as she felt J.B.'s hand under her arm, lifting her as if she were no more than a feather, his wiry frame lent strength by urgency. She wasn't too sure where she was, but every fiber of her being yelled danger, her own adrenaline rush forcing her back to full consciousness.

Doc was the only one who did not respond with the necessary urgency. The shouts, the pounding of feet on the soil and sand around the campfire, all of these served to bring him out of his slumbers. But it was a slack-jawed Doc, eyes open but blank and uncomprehending, who greeted the night. His sleep, as ever, had been disturbed by nightmare visions. Sleep was a necessary evil, where pale demons emerged from the recesses of his mind to torment him, to remind him of that which had tortured him, of that which he had lost. On waking, he was never sure if it was still part of a dream or whether it was little more than an extension of the hellish vagaries of his own mind.

"Doc," Mildred blurted, sleep clearing from her eyes, mind racing, catching sight of the disoriented man. She stumbled toward him, pulling at his arm to try to lever him up. He yelled incoherently, pulling himself away and stumbling from his half-standing position so that he sprawled back on the ground, raising a cloud of dust.

"Jak—" Ryan barked. The albino knew the one-eyed man's query before he even voiced it, and pointed to the red dot.

"Coming fast," he added, indicating to his rear.

With a speed far in excess of the time it would take to voice such thoughts, Ryan realized that whatever it was that was coming for them, it would be locked onto the laser dot, and it would be quick. It had to be from a great distance, otherwise they would have seen their tracker—

for he had no doubt that whatever it was, the source was the mystery rider—but it was likely to be traveling at great speed.

So if it was locked onto the dot, then they needed to get as far away from that bastard red mark as possible. He knew that Krysty, Jak, J.B. and himself stood a chance if they set off at a run, but he could also see that Doc was still on the ground, and Mildred was slowed by her efforts to aid him. Run, or go to her assistance. There wasn't time to think about the choice, just act. He took a step toward Mildred and Doc, could see that J.B. was doing the same.

The gas egg wasn't visible in the darkness until the last moment. As it entered the ring of light cast by the fire, its dark shape was thrown into relief. Even then, it was hard to track as the speed at which it descended made it little more than a blur. It was audible from farther out, a high, whistling scream in the air as it was propelled at great speed toward its target. In what seemed like time slowed to an almost infinitesimal degree, all who turned their gaze could see the egg fall toward the red dot on the ground, the smart circuit in the gren making it follow the perfect arc to land and impact. It seemed to slow from its great speed until it was almost possible to see the rotation in flight that guided its direction. It fell toward the red dot with an inevitability and slowness that made Ryan feel that he could dive across the sandy soil between his feet and the red dot and pluck the gren out of the air, stopping it from hitting the earth and exploding, letting out whatever lethal load it may carry.

The one-eyed man tried to carry the thought through, forcing his sluggish limbs to move, feeling his muscles tense and wobble as though pushing against quicksand rather than air. In a flash of insight that was faster than real time, he realized that it was only normal air resistance that he felt, that, in truth, his danger-honed mind was trying to make him move faster than was humanly possible.

It had to have been imagination or hallucination, but he was almost sure that he saw the gren take one final wobbling turn in the air before hitting the sand. Felt sure that he saw the puff of dust raised by impact before the gren splintered into a thousand pieces, unleashing the payload. He flinched, squinting his good eye for fear of flying metal.

But it was no frag gren. A puff of smoke—or so it seemed—was all that issued forth, a white that shone incandescent against the red glow of the fire before spreading and dissipating into a mist that seemed to fade and die before it reached Ryan.

He was aware of a numbing that spread from his chest outwards, and a faint smell, sweet but with a bitterness underlying it. The two were connected, he knew, but it was hard to work out how, hard to work out why he should be bothering to ponder this, hard to…

He could breathe still, but everything else was becoming numb. His chest felt empty yet heavy at the same time. His shoulders were reduced to lumps of flesh with no movement, the numbness spread down his arms as though carried in his veins, trickling into his fingers, down to the very tips. He could feel the same happening in his legs, the lack of feeling spreading down to his groin and then down each leg, knees buckling as the muscles supporting them went dead.

Ryan felt himself tumble as his balance was unable to account for the lack of feeling and support from his body. He could not control the fall. He teetered, then pitched forward, landing full-length with a thud on the densely packed, sandy soil with a reverberation that seemed to resonate through his frame. He could sense this, and yet not feel it, almost as though he was detached from himself.

He could see nothing. The light from the fire was too slight, the ground in front of him too close to his face. He could hear little else but the crackle of the fire. Then, in the distance, approaching at speed and growing louder with every breath he took, the sound of a motorcycle engine.

Somewhere, deep in the recesses of a momentarily clouded mind, he knew that the gren had contained some kind of nerve gas. He had heard of such predark relics, had on occasion witnessed examples of them that had chilled on contact.

He hated being at the mercy of whoever—the mystery rider, he guessed—had fired the gren. The coldheart bastard could do anything he wanted to them, and they could not fight back.

Although Ryan could see nothing, falling as he had, there were others who had a better view of what was about to occur. Doc had fallen onto his back, staring up at the night sky, uncomprehending. No sooner had he managed to focus in some manner and realize where he was than the paralysis had hit him. It bewildered him as he had still been too befuddled to notice the gren. He was only aware of the numbness, the inability to raise himself up as he fell backward, and of the fact that he was flat to the ground without feeling it beneath him. As though he were floating above it, just hovering, and yet unable to move through any direction. In this state of disconnection, he heard the engine's roar as the sound of his own approaching doom. Tears prickled at his eyes.

The vagaries of Doc's imagination were as far away from what went through the head of Mildred Wyeth as it was possible to get. Caught trying to help the old man to his feet, Mildred had seen the gren impact from the periphery of her vision, and the first scent that hit her had told her that it was some kind of nerve gas. She tried to hold her breath for a second, then realized that it would probably be able to absorb through the skin, and so holding her breath was useless. She exhaled heavily as the first wave of numbness began to spread. For some reason that she could not explain, it seemed to take hold on her left side first, dragging her in that direction so that she toppled on her side. Her vision was partly obscured by the plaits that fell across her face, but in the far distance she could see a shape move across the landscape in sync with the sound of an engine. It was just beyond the circle of light cast by the fire, but as she lay immobile, wondering if she was going to be conscious and helpless at the moment of her death, she saw that it was the mystery rider. Something told her that their chilling was not on his mind…which led her to question what, then, his purpose could be in doing this.

J.B. and Jak were, in their own ways, cold and dark with impotent rage at what had happened. It was their watch, and they had failed. More than that, they were both now on the ground, twisted at odd angles because of the speed with which the gas had taken effect while they tried to rally the group, both struck down within yards of each other. J.B. could see Jak's legs, above his head now that he was horizontal. Both could see the bike approach, and cursed the mystery rider. Coldheart bastard could do what the hell he liked with them and they would be unable to take revenge or even put up a fight.

Chapter Five

The motorcycle ate up the distance. Thunder Rider had carefully dismantled the grenade launcher, packing it away in the pod and securing it. The surveillance equipment he had also packed away. The nerve gas was such that he knew there would be no further need for it. As he'd mounted the bike and kicked the starter, feeling the powerful engine rev up beneath him, he'd known that he had turned a corner in his fight for justice. He would have one ally before the night was through. He would take her back to base, show her the extent of his operation, persuade her that his fight was her fight.

How could she not be won over by his persuasive arguments? She would obviously want to join in his fight, and stay by his side.

Strange. He had not really considered that before. Not seriously. But the more he considered it, the more obvious it became. Of course she would persuade her companions that it would be in their best interests to form an alliance with Thunder Rider, and to use their knowledge and ability along with his technology in the fight to bring justice back to the land. But why, then, would she want to rejoin them when she could be at his side, his partner...

He felt the surge of the engine between his thighs and a

tingle of excitement ran through him. The beginnings of a dynasty of crime fighters, perhaps?

No. It was too soon to think of that. To think of anything at all, other than the matter in hand, was inadvisable. If there was one thing that he had learned in the short time since his mission began, it was that his ability to stay focused was in need of honing.

No. It was too soon.

He shook his head to clear his mind, looked ahead of him. Through the infrared of the goggles he could see that the nerve gas had taken effect. The six members of the group were arrayed around the fire, twisted into contorted positions, trapped by the gas in the attitudes in which they had fallen. As he neared them, he could see that the albino and the Armorer were closest. Their eyes were open, and even at this distance he felt sure he could see the hostility in their glares.

He couldn't blame them. In their position he would have felt exactly the same. The only thing he could do was to hope that when they saw the complete picture, they would understand that it had to be this way.

He slowed the bike, steering its thick tired wheels between them. Farther on, he could see the black woman and the old man. The one-eyed man—named Ryan Cawdor if intel reports were correct—was just to one side of them. He was facedown…could be dangerous. Thunder Rider could not let this man perish in such an ignominious manner. He would attend to it shortly.

But first, his eyes sought his prey…

There she was, on her back, staring at the night sky. He walked over to her, leaned over and looked into her eyes, seeing only incomprehension by the light of the campfire, not fear. That he would have expected, in such a situation. Good. It showed her toughness.

Leaving her for a second, he went over to where the one-eyed man lay on his front, face in danger of being buried in the sand by its own weight. Thunder Rider leaned over him, grasped him firmly by the shoulders and heaved him over onto his back. The man was no fool. He should realize that Rider was saving him. Not that he would expect him to be grateful. No, he would still be angry. But perhaps he would wonder why Thunder Rider had done this, and it would give him pause for thought.

Thunder Rider was surprised by the feel of the man's body as he turned him. The skin of his arms was leathery, the muscle and sinew beneath the clothing was hard and compact. So different to Thunder Rider. He had trained hard, or so he'd thought. Yet compared to this man he was soft and flabby. That was something he would have to attend to, and soon. A bout of more rigorous training in the gym would be in order.

As Ryan Cawdor fell onto his back, his single orb glared up into Thunder Rider's face. Despite his own righteousness, Thunder Rider was for a moment glad that he was wearing goggles and that Cawdor could not see into his own eyes. For the single orb held such barely contained fury, such malevolence and anger, such desire for revenge, that it sent a shiver down his spine. A small, quavering voice at the back of his mind told him that this man would take much in the way of placating and explanation before he would understand the mission, or even be willing to understand.

He left the one-eyed man staring malevolently up at him. Backing away, wondering if it would be of any use to offer placating words, he opted to deal with the real reason for his actions. She lay, still breathing with a gasping shallowness, a few yards away.

He had to collect her and take her before the others began to recover movement. Without a word, he leaned over and gathered her inert frame in his arms, lifting her effortlessly off the surface of the desert. She was lighter than he had expected, although in part her body was as hard and toned as Ryan Cawdor's. Other parts of it were softer, and this was a sensation that he found appealing. For a moment, it almost distracted him again.

He looked down into her face as he lifted her, and could see confusion writ large in her expression. Perhaps it was time to offer a few words of comfort. He spoke, keeping his voice low for now.

"There is nothing for you to fear, Krysty Wroth. Yes, I know your name. I know who you are. I know who your companions are. I have a mission for you. One that I think I share with all of you. But I am only just come into this world, and so have no alliances. I want you to be one of those alliances that I seek, but I would understand your mistrust. The weeds of crime and injustice grow rank on the surface of this world. Their fruits are bitter for those who taste them. Together, you and I—and those who are your fellow travelers—could make a difference. But I know that you would not trust me without proof. And I know that you would not give me the chance to prove myself of your own free will. I understand this. So I have been forced to adopt measures that may seem to you to be intrusive and villainous. For this I can only apologize, and hope that you will soon come to understand the reasons for my actions."

Saying no more, Thunder Rider carried her over to his bike. Her form was inert, but with a slight stiffness and inability to bend, her muscles tautened in paralysis by the effects of the nerve gas. So it was with slightly more difficulty than he had anticipated that he maneuvered her onto the pillion of the bike, using synthetic fiber ropes to secure her in an upright position, using her own inertia and balance against her.

Feeling slightly more awkward than he would have wished, he turned away when he had finished and, raising his voice slightly, addressed the others as they lay motionless. It seemed strange to talk to people who were so apparently unresponsive, even though he knew that they could understand his every word.

"People, I regret the measures that I have had to take. And I apologize for the seeming abduction of your companion. I realize that this may seem to be an act of hostility, but I hope that in the long term you will understand my reasons for acting as I have, and will realize the necessity if my aims and plans are to be implemented swiftly.

"Although you are all currently immobilized, and have been for the past hour or so, the effects will begin to wear off after a maximum of three hours. By this time, I will be too far away for you to trail me. Rest assured that I will contact you when I—and Krysty—are ready. You will experience no ill-effects from the gas, and will be able to move and act normally within a very short while.

"I will leave you now. Krysty is in no danger. Nor are you. I hope, I say again, that you will understand shortly why this was necessary."

Without pause, feeling that he had said all that he could, Thunder Rider turned and mounted his machine. Tying Krysty's arms around him, for extra balance, he kicked the engine into life and slowly piloted the machine out of the fire's glow and into the darkness of the desert night.

He did not look back as he opened the engine and roared across the sandy soil. The feel of the redheaded woman against him was satisfying yet also disturbing and confusing.

It was a feeling that he enjoyed.

ALTHOUGH SHE WOULD NOT HAVE cared to share their suffering if she had known the mental torture, at that moment Krysty would have given anything to have been there rather than here. Still paralyzed, her nerve endings feeding her nothing, she was reliant only on what she could see, hear and smell, and on the workings of her own mind.

Where was this triple-crazy stupe taking her? And what did he intend to do with her when they got there?

She felt like she could vomit. The effects of the gas had left her with little strength, and it was only because of the way that the mystery rider had secured her that she could be sure she would not fall off, even if she passed out. And, frankly, consciousness was flickering in and out as she saw the sun rise. The words the man had spoken to her, and then to the others, whirled around her head, and she tried to understand them. This was a person who had a completely different way of looking at the world.

She knew that if she was going to survive, if she was going to bide her time until she was in a position to effect an escape, then she would have to understand that way. It was crucial to her survival.

Survival.

She wondered, with the last thought before she passed out, if the others would survive long enough to try to follow her.

J.B. FELT IT FIRST, A TINGLING at the extremities, spreading with a warmth that soon turned to agonizing cramp. It came to rest in the chest cavity, where it felt as though it had gripped his heart and lungs like a vise at full screw.

He gasped, yelled and sat bolt-upright, clutching at his chest. It was only after he had gulped down several lungfuls of air and the pain had started to subside that he realized he was able to move once again.

He tried to get to his feet. It took him falling back down three times before he made it on the fourth. He felt weak and defenseless still, but he was on his feet at the very least. Staggering, he made his way over to Mildred. She was still immobile, but behind him he heard Jak scream as the cramps started to spread through his body.

"Millie… It hurts like fuck, but once…" He could read incomprehension in her eyes. Then she, too, screamed in a high-pitched wail, her torso coming up at an odd angle, her head cracking against his, bright lights going off in his brain. He fell once more, a wave of nausea sweeping over him, bile gagging in his throat. He hawked and spit it out. He was quicker to recover his equilibrium this time. Mildred was on her feet, as unsteady as a newborn foal. She clung to him for support.

By the time they were both able to stand unsupported, Ryan and Doc had also experienced the intense agonies of the gas wearing off. The five friends were now tottering around the dying embers of the fire, not knowing what they were doing; what they should be doing. The pain, the weakness, the disorientation. It felt in some ways as though they were more vulnerable now than they had been when they were paralyzed.

Gradually, it subsided. No one spoke, each wrapped in his or her own thoughts. What to say and where to begin? Come to that, no one yet had the strength to talk. They drank to rehydrate, ate for the salts and sugars they had lost during the paralysis and the rising of the sun. Eventually, after what had seemed like the longest few hours they had ever lived through, Jak finally spoke, quietly but with an unmistakable venom.

"Catch bastard, chill slowly. Enjoy it. Not want hurt us. Lucky night critters not interested."

No one had any real argument with that. A lengthy silence ensued before Mildred spoke.

"What did that half-wit think he was talking about? Why the hell did he take Krysty away?"

Ryan shook his head. "Figure you'd know better than me. He was using language like I've only heard in predark vids. Tell you something, though. He'd better not harm Krysty."

"She can look after herself," J.B. commented.

"Mebbe normally, but not if she's as fucked as we are," Ryan muttered.

"I suspect that she may be all right, at least for the time being," Doc said with some reflection. "If I understood our enemy correctly, he thinks that we are his friends—or at least, could be. I surmised that his intention is to convert Krysty to his cause, and use her to persuade us of the rightness of his."

"But why, for God's sake?" Mildred exploded.

Doc gave a sad smile. "Because, my dear Doctor, I fear that like so many of us, he may not be exactly of sound mind."

"Crazy. Great." Jak snorted.

Doc's smile broadened. "I think you may have missed my point, dear boy. If he has this one aim in mind—that Krysty become converted to his cause in order to convert us—then he will do all within his power to keep her alive and well. It is in his best interests. And, of course, he is unwittingly buying us time to find and destroy him."

Ryan nodded. "I think you might be right, Doc. The question is, how long have we got, and are we in any fit state to fight?"

"Maybe not now, but we've no injuries to recover. Just the remains of that damn gas to get out of our systems," Mildred mused. "And that can be happening while we're on his trail."

"Besides, he's going to be looking for us sooner or later, right?" J.B. pointed out.

"Exactly, my dear John Barrymore," Doc agreed. "The irony is that he has mistaken our pragmatism for a sense of spurious justice, and faith in a law that no longer exists. A misunderstanding that will lead him straight back to us. In a sense, we have no need to chase him. He will come to us."

Ryan's face split into a grin for the first time in hours. "Guess you're right, Doc. But let's give him a little surprise. Let's go after the coldheart bastard anyway, and meet him halfway. Full-on."

Chapter Six

Unconsciousness had at least given her a respite. To be dragged from it and thrown into a world of pain and confusion was not how she would have chosen to have surfaced. She was still on the bike, still secured to the mystery rider, and the wind chill from their speed was freezing bones that had only just regained the sense to feel.

And how. The cramps that the others had felt on their recovery were intensified for her by the weakness she still felt, and by her restraints. She was unable to move with the spasms, and did not have the energy to fight against the painful contortions of her muscles. The agony ripped through her head in a welter of flashing lights behind her closed eyes, like synapses exploding and splattering her brain against the insides of her skull. She opened her eyes, hoping that light and the sense of where she was would somehow still the waves of nausea that welled up in her throat, pressing against the sore hollow of her breastbone.

Her eyes were immediately hit by brilliant sunlight, strobed by the movement of the rider's broad back as it moved on the saddle in front of her. The movement also broke up the wind that whipped over and around the man.

He sheltered her from the worst of the buffeting, but this only had the effect of making what did hit her seem all the harder. It sucked the breath from her mouth and nose, making her gulp for air when all she wanted to do was to take a deep breath.

The convulsions caused by the cramps made her twitch uncontrollably on the pillion of the huge bike. She was grateful for its size as, even though the rider still had to adjust to the way in which she momentarily threw his balance, her convulsions would have thrown them from a smaller machine.

She knew she was going to puke. If she did it all over his back it would stink, maybe even splash back on her face, which would make her puke some more. Frankly, she doubted that she had the strength in her to heave more than the once. She was more likely to choke herself. If she had to go out, she wanted to go out fighting, not choking on her own spew while she was tied to a captor.

She hung her head out to one side, hoping that the convulsions wouldn't be so strong as to overbalance her, throwing her from the bike. The wind from their speed blew her hair out behind them like the clouds of dust that rose in their wake. The chill was such that the heat of the sun didn't even register for her. She could have done with it at that moment, as a cold shiver swept through her, the sweat on her back like ice.

She opened her mouth, surrendering to the reflexive cramps in her stomach that rippled up her esophagus, forcing bile into her throat, deep poison following...

Her stomach felt like it was turning over and over, trying to flip itself inside out as she emptied everything inside her in a stream that trailed out behind them, the wet sound of it hitting the desert dirt lost in the roar of the bike and the distance that was eaten up at great speed.

She hawked and spit the last remnants from her mouth before righting herself. The sour taste was unpleasant, and she could feel it running down her chin, the stench drifting up to her nose. But the cold sweat had passed, and the muscle cramps were subsiding. A little taste and smell she could take for a while.

She was weak, like a newborn. She felt physically defenseless. But she knew that would pass. There were other ways of defending yourself. Like being prepared.

She tried to piece together what had happened. She felt as though she had once had a grasp on it, but now it was foggy. She tried to pull the pieces out of the mist, tried to make sense of it.

She could remember the confusion before the incoming gren. The numbing paralysis. The man at whose back she now traveled, speaking words that made sense and yet did not. And then passing out...

Shit—the others. Unable to move, it occurred to her that they may have just bought the farm before they'd had a chance to regain use of their limbs. There were so many dangers they had been left open to, yet that had not seemed to be the rider's intent. Alongside her fear for her friends, Krysty's brain registered that her enemy may not have the wit and intelligence he would have wished for.

Okay, then. She could not take it for granted that they were coming in search of her. If they were able, then they would, but she figured that she couldn't count on it. She would have to rely on herself.

The mystery rider obviously meant her no harm. Quite the opposite, from what she could remember of his words. In truth, there was something about that which made her skin crawl. But no matter. She couldn't think about that now. She was too weak to attempt an escape, and out here it would be pointless.

Best to just play possum, as the old predark phrase went, and see where the rider was taking her. Once there she could see his strengths: personnel, equipment, tech. She could see how crazy he was, whether there was anything in his makeup she could use against him.

And she could recover her own strength while working out a way to wipe the triple-crazy bastard off the face of the earth.

THINGS HAD NOT, perhaps, gone quite as he'd wanted. All had been well up until the moment Krysty Wroth recovered consciousness. The file, he knew, had said nothing about the spasms that seemed to follow recovering from the gas. Her body was racked by them, and it made him wonder if there would be a similar risk of neural damage. It would be a shame if he had gone to so much trouble, only for the woman to be reduced to a vegetable. She would be of little use to him in such an event. Nonetheless, he would look after her. She would live out her days at the base, wanting for nothing in the way of care. It would, frankly, be the least he could do. He felt a responsibility to her.

Strange. This was the first time that he had felt such a thing. True, in a general sense he felt that he had a responsibility to the human race. But this was a very different feeling to that which had powered his forays into the field so far. He would have to record this later, discuss it and what it meant.

Meantime, he had distance to cover. He felt her move behind him and adjusted his balance accordingly. He could not see what she was doing, but he was sure it was not escape. The feeling was confirmed when an unpleasant sour odor assailed him. She had vomited, another side effect of the gas that the file had not mentioned.

In truth, he was beginning to wonder how accurate the files were—how much was evidential, how much supposition and how much was a sin of omission. There was a lesson to be learned here. Not to trust the computer systems a hundred percent, and to test equipment more thoroughly before use in the field.

There was something good to be drawn from any situation.

Meantime, he had other matters of more immediate importance. He took one hand from the bike's handlebars and flipped down the mike at the side of the goggles.

"Thunder Rider reporting in. We are now approximately fifteen minutes from first defense lines. Please disable as approach registers. Estimated time of arrival at base, twenty-one minutes. Message ends."

He flicked the mike back up and returned both hands to the handlebars. The farthest reaches of the border fence were now in sight. The ranch building was nestled in a small, man-made valley in the center of the compound. Those who had come before had made it this way. Finding the ranch from the ground without falling foul of the defenses was nearly impossible. He remembered

Jenny's words: "Nothing is ever fail-safe. Caution is the best word in the language. The most useful. Learn not just the word, but its real meaning."

Air attack would be dealt with by long-range, radar-guided missile defenses. In many ways, these were much easier to deal with, as nothing could truly hide in the open skies. But it was—what was the word she had used?—"academic" now that there were no planes to take to the skies. Still, he was glad the systems were there, as one day, perhaps...

He snapped out of his reverie. The boundary was approaching. Time to concentrate.

Thunder Rider and his machine were almost as one as he guided it through the boundary defenses. Invisible to the naked eye, undersoil detectors registered movement within two square yards, and would detonate fragment grenades. The motion sensors would also send back to base details on the weight and bulk of any vehicles that came close. From this, the computer would estimate the probability of the grenades alone securing the base. If the calculations proved that the next line of defense was necessary, then digital imaging equipment that was in place around the land surrounding the ranch would kick into operation. Trackers would mark the intruders, and smart missiles would seek and destroy.

If, by any chance, an attacking force should get beyond this, a wall of chemical fire would be triggered. A particularly good tactician, or perhaps sheer weight of numbers, may get an enemy this far. The possibility of them getting beyond the chemical fires was very slight. However, while there was still the smallest possibility then it was politic to have a last line of defense. The ranch house itself was circled at a distance of five hundred yards by rapid-fire automatic heavy-caliber ordnance. Anyone who got past the fire, by some amazing quirk of chance, would surely fall at this stage.

No matter. The ranch house itself, merely a shell these days, was also booby-trapped. After the days following the nuclear winter, those left in the base had emerged to maintain the weapons and defense systems, considering these to be top priority. The wreckage of the ranch house itself had been left as it was. The disrepair and damage would act as a diversion. Besides, they had long ago opted to live belowground rather than try to rebuild on the surface.

So it became the perfect disguise for the base, a fortuitous act for which he could only thank those who had come before.

To gain access to the base, anyone approaching would have to steer a course between the triggering devices once they were in operation. This was a labyrinthine route that had to be intimately memorized by those who sought to use it. It was of a narrow gauge designed to be negotiated only by the bike. Any larger vehicle, even assuming they should accidentally stumble on the route, would overlap the safety zone and trigger the defenses.

Despite the almost nonexistent margin for error, Thunder Rider took the route at speed, such was his confidence. Why not? It was something that he had been learning from a young age. He had always been prepared for this moment.

PUKING HER GUTS UP had cleared Krysty's head, if nothing else. Although her body still felt weak, she was starting to think a little more like her old self. She could have done without the twisting and turning of the bike, as the rider seemed to pilot it on a completely random course—it made her already weakened body feel even more fragile—but her mind was sharp enough to figure that there was a reason for this action.

It had to be that there was some kind of hidden defenses in these parts, and that the evasive course of action was to drive a course through them. Concentrating, no matter how hard it seemed, she scanned the area. To take in the terrain at the kinds of speeds they were using was almost impossible, and as far as she could see there was nothing to mark this area of wasteland as any different from that which they had traveled straight. But there had to be something…

It was when he veered to ninety degrees for a short stretch that she realized why here, why now. She caught her first glimpse of the ranch house, hidden in a small valley but with the roof just showing above the slightly raised level of the ground. Before, any indication of it had been concealed both by its own location and by the broad back of the rider, her primary view during the journey.

This had to be his base. Where it was exactly in relation to where they had come from, she had no real way of telling. She squinted up at the sun, hoping that she could deduce something from its position in the sky. But given the twists and turns of their course, the most she could get from the position was that it was now past the middle of the day, which, she wryly reflected, was next to useless.

Instead, she concentrated her attention on where they were headed. Moving as much as she could behind the rider, not wanting to attract his attention, and also mindful of the fact that she had no goggles, and it was his back that had protected her eyes from the onrushing wind resistance, she tried to look around him as he righted direction and drove head-on for the ranch house. It was almost impossible. The briefest of glances gave her a fleeting impression of a building that showed only a roof gaping with holes, the upper story barely visible but seemingly stripped of paint and stucco, weather-beaten, with the frame of the ranch house showing through in places.

That was all she could get before the solid wall of air drove dust and bugs into her eyes. Dipping back behind the cover of his back, she blinked rapidly, her eyes streaming. She desperately wanted to wipe, no, to claw at them and stop the irritation, but her arms were too secured around the rider to allow her to do this.

Still, this brief glimpse had been enough to make her wonder. There was no way that anyone could live in a building like that, especially if the rest of the building was as derelict as the top sections. So why head for it? Perhaps it was just a marker on the route?

No. That wouldn't account for the strange maneuvers he had indulged in with the bike. The building had to be the key. Her mind raced. If there were a number of defense systems that couldn't be seen, then that would suggest a survival of predark tech. And if the ruined ranch house was a front, then that would suggest something hidden, like a redoubt. Gaia alone knew that they had encountered enough of those over the past few years; some other hidden bases, too.

The mystery rider obviously knew enough about the tech to work it, and there were others where he came from. She wondered if he was in some way allied to the tech-nomads, the elusive and loosely knit bunch of travelers she had encountered after meeting the rail ghost, Paul Yawl. They liked to keep themselves separate from what passed for civilization out in the Deathlands, so it would be unlikely that they would have wanted anything to do with the rider. The last thing he could be accused of was keeping himself apart from the rest of society.

She was guessing that he wasn't military. He wore no uniform as such, and remnants of old military had a way about them that he didn't. Whitecoat survivors like those freak mutie crazies they had once encountered at Crater Lake? Perhaps, but he seemed a little too proactive for those types: they liked to keep themselves apart, like the tech-nomads. So was he, perhaps, part of a group that had stumbled on old tech, much as they had soon after she had first met Ryan and J.B.? Sure, they had used it mostly just to move on from place to place, but what if some bunch of mercies or coldhearts had decided to use it to gain power and jack?

No, that didn't make sense. Despite all the damage he had done, the rider hadn't taken anything. And the way he talked was odd, old-fashioned. He didn't speak like a mercie, although he did act like a coldheart. But even then, it was like there was some kind of twisted logic at work. He was a coldheart who wanted to do good things. That crazy talk about justice and crime, concepts that she, like Ryan, had heard of only in things that survived from before the nukecaust.

No, whatever was going on here, it was unlike anything they had ever come across before, which made it even more dangerous for her. There would be no second-guessing and no second chances. If she was to get out alive, then she would have to get it right first time.

In the time it had taken her to think this through, they had crested the small rise that ringed the valley holding the ruined ranch house, and were now descending toward the building itself. Every part of it looked derelict, and the outbuildings were little more than matchwood and rubble. No one would ever think of looking twice at this place. It looked as if it had been empty since skydark.

But it wasn't. She knew this was their destination, and she figured she'd find a few answers before too long.

Whether she wanted them or not.

THE FIVE COMPANIONS HAD BEEN traveling in silence for some time. There was nothing to say, and idle talk would only have cost them energy that they needed to conserve. So they traveled, wrapped in their own thoughts.

The horses had been affected by the nerve gas, but had recovered before their human masters. They had been at a greater distance from the point of impact, and by the time the gas had reached the point where they were tethered, its worst effects had been dissipated in the air.

While the friends were still weakened by the time they had gathered the horses, the wag and set off, the horses showed no signs of wear, and proceeded at their usual dogged pace.

All within could have wished for greater speed, but it was the same old trade-off they had lived with since coming back to this region—they had no real idea of the kind of distances involved in their chase, and they had only limited supplies of food and water. Food could be overcome to a degree. There was enough game emerging at night for Jak to make them a meal, although keeping the horses fed would be a problem with the lack of grass.

But water: this was both friend and enemy. Friend because it was all that kept them alive. Enemy because they only had the supplies they carried. A trap to catch the cold air deposits of the night, the dew of morning, would not give them enough should they run low. The cacti would not yield enough, in a similar manner, although this carried with it the additional problem of not knowing if the mutated cacti carried water without taint.

So it was important that they keep their expenditure of energy to a minimum, to make the most of their meager rations. The horses could not be driven too fast, because they might use more than could be allocated to them. Here, in the wastelands of dustbowl soil and desert sand that comprised the territory, the worst thing that could happen would be the demise of the horses. Without them, a draining trek carrying supplies that would be eaten up all the faster by the energy used to carry them was a certain way to buying the farm.

So it had to be slow and steady, slow and sure. Slow, with nothing to do except dwell on what had happened to them.

It could take days to catch up, even if the tire tracks remained visible. Perhaps they never would.

Would they find the mystery rider? Would the trail just end? If it didn't, then would they find Krysty alive at the end of it? Would she have been hurt, damaged, harmed in some way? Not just physically?

Every dark imagining that could lurk in the recesses of the mind kept welling up to the forefront of Ryan's imagination as he sat in the back of the wag. The bond that existed between himself and Krysty went deeper than the bond between himself and any of the others. Even though he would buy the farm to fight for them, and they for him as he knew, there was something deeper and more intimate between himself and the flame-haired woman. If such a concept as love could find a home in the stony soil of the postdark world, then it existed in what he felt for Krysty, just as he knew it existed between his oldest friend, J.B., and Mildred.

His mind went back to the last time they had been in this part of the Deathlands. The time when he had been shot, presumed chilled, and the others had been captured. All except Krysty, who had evaded capture and had then single-mindedly pursued the coldheart responsible until her actions had resulted not just in his demise, but in the collapse of the plans that had powered the man's existence. Her vengeance had been total.

She had done that for him, even when she had assumed that he was no longer alive. It was no more than he would have expected of her, in truth, knowing her character.

Just as she would expect that he would do the same for her. They had never talked of it. There had been no reason, and to even broach the subject implied the threat of it occurring, which is something that neither of them would wish to contemplate.

Well, he was doing it now. Except that it didn't feel like that. At this plodding pace, with her how many miles ahead of them now? If that coldheart bastard had harmed her, she would be avenged. But that wasn't enough. He wanted to get to her before she was harmed. The question was, would he be able to?

His brow furrowed as he remembered something. Reaching into a pocket in his combat pants, his fingers searched until they found a delicate chain. He extracted it and looked at the locket that dangled from between his fingers, so small and delicate at the end of the chain that it seemed absurd between his scarred and calloused knuckle joints.

Krysty had given him this locket when she had found that he was alive. It had been given to her, in turn, by a man who had helped her in her quest.

He fervently hoped that he would be able to give it back to her, yet again in turn, when they found her alive. She would know they would come looking for her if they could. That he would. But could she assume that they would be able to do this?

He just hoped to hell that she wasn't going to rely solely on them.

THE RUINED RANCH HOUSE showed no indication of being anything other than that. The rider circled it, almost as if giving her the chance to scout the territory. Parts of the walls had collapsed, the interior floors and ceilings were patchwork constructions, sometimes held together by only one surviving beam. And original decoration and furnishing had long since been stripped bare or reduced to wormwood. A couple of metal objects, corroded and covered by debris until they bore no resemblance to anything she could name, stood out from the sea of trash that littered the ground floor. A staircase stood, half demolished, leading to nowhere. The bottom section seemed to have suffered little damage, suggesting reinforcement. There was a door set into the staircase. Stripped of its wooden facade by time, she could see that this bottom section had survived as it had a concrete surround, the inset door being of steel, showing signs of wear but no corrosion. No ordinary household metal.

It was the briefest of glimpses through a tumbledown wall, but it was enough for her to realize that her suspicions had been correct. There was more to this site than just a ruined predark dwelling like so many that had housed farms and ranches before skydark.

So they had arrived at the place the mystery rider called home. She had been aware, over the roar of the engine and the rush of the wind, that he had been intermittently speaking to someone on a headset. The extraneous noise had precluded her making out the nature of these brief communications, but now that he had eased the throttle, and their decreased speed cut out the roar of onrushing air, she was able to half grasp what he said.

"…approach…research file. The gas…prepare for entry…"

She knew that she was about to find out the extent of the rider's resources. Part of her was glad. Now she could start planning for her escape. Part of her was terrified. What if the odds were overwhelming, especially as she still felt weak?

Determined to note every detail, she kept herself focused as the man guided his vehicle around the rear of the ranch house and toward what had to have been a barn. It was little more than a few sticks of wood marking out an area of dust slightly different in hue to the land around.

She was impressed, but not perhaps as surprised as he would have liked, if he but knew, when a section of soil and sand raised up slowly on hydraulics. It rose at an angle until it was standing about six feet off the surface of the ground. The topsoil remained, only some dust falling from the edges, running backward. Perhaps sheer weight kept it in place, as the ascent had been measured. Perhaps it was secured in some way. Whatever, she could see that something kept it in place so that the hydraulic platform would descend with no indication that this piece of land had ever been moved.

Beneath the platform, a concrete slope led down into the earth. Lights were inset in the walls, providing an illumination that was less than the sun, but still more than enough by which to see your way.

The rider guided the bike down the slope and into a tunnel. She immediately felt the coolness of an air conditioner hit her, something she had not felt outside the redoubts they had visited. There was something about the quality of the air in these places: a kind of dryness, a lack of any scent or musk that was natural, that maybe the regular inhabitants had never noticed but was startlingly different and alien to her. She felt it every time they had landed in a redoubt, and this place was exactly the same.

The motorcycle slowed to a glide, taking the curve of the tunnel with ease. It was a shallow incline, but the curve told her that they were circling to go deep without a steep gradient. So the rider's base was far below the surface. That figured. How else could it have survived so long? She tried to work out the circumference of the spiraling circle they were circumscribing, but she was still too weak and disoriented to get a real impression. She did know that the deeper they went, the stronger the lighting. She didn't notice it at first, but she realized as she was forced to squint that the wall-mounted lights gained in power as they descended.

The bike suddenly came out of the mouth of the tunnel and into a long, wide, concrete-lined bunker lit by fluorescent tube lighting that made her momentarily squint her eyes, preventing her from getting a good look at the surroundings. Her eyes were still screwed shut when the motorcycle slowed to a halt, and she felt the rider flick down the stand. Carefully, he untied her arms from around him and dismounted. She felt as though she might fall without his help, as she was so weak. It was only when she didn't that she realized how well he had secured her to the vehicle.

Gradually, the light through her lids became less painful and she carefully opened her eyes. The rider was standing in front of her, his hands behind his back, observing her…impassively? It was hard to tell, as his goggles were still in place, and so his eyes gave nothing away. His body language and posture were unthreatening, but she was still wary.

Besides which, she was trying to cast a glance around her without giving it away, looking over his shoulder rather than at him, hoping that he wouldn't notice.

The long bunker was well-equipped, looking for all the world like a mechanic's wet dream. The motorcycle she was still secured to was one of three such vehicles. And the tools: she had never seen the like outside of military redoubts, which this wasn't—there was none of the insignia, none of the signs, the rules and regulations that came with such places. The vehicles weren't painted in camou colors or a uniform shade. In fact, a nearby armored wag was a bright scarlet, the like of which suggested that this had been a base with no military affiliations.

She knew enough about the jack before skydark to know that this would have cost big. So if not remnants of military, who were these people?

There were five doors at points along the walls. She would have loved to know what lay behind each. Maybe later. For now, she had to find out more about the crazie who stood watching her. Were the rest of the people here like him? Or—Gaia forbid—worse?

A thin smile cracked the face of the rider. It looked sinister, but was belied by the warmness of his tone.

"Good, good, you are awake. I trust you have recovered from your illness as we journeyed here. For that I must apologize. I have had no call to use the gas before, and that was an effect that was not on the file. I shall have to see if this unfortunate effect can be remedied before any further use."

Nice—so he had every intention of putting others

through that less-than-charming experience. She felt that she had to choose her words carefully.

"That's…good. Yes, it's good that you want to avoid anyone experiencing discomfort…"

He inclined his head. "You seem a little upset, a little less than reassured by my assurances. I know that it was neither the best nor the friendliest way to introduce myself, but as I stated, it was the most expedient. And that is my priority right now. The notion of having to do what may not necessarily be the right thing per se, but is the right thing for that moment, must surely be something with which you are familiar, Krysty Wroth."

Gaia, but she was having trouble following his arcane speech. However, she had been able to follow it enough to make her point. Looking down at the bonds that held her secure, she said, "If you know who I am, and you want to gain my trust, then the first thing you'd know is that I don't take kindly to being tied up like this. You can explain anything else you want in whatever way you want, but it isn't going to mean shit while you've got me trussed up like road chill."

The rider shook his head and moved toward her. "Please forgive me, that was most remiss," he said hurriedly. "You are, of course, correct."

He took off his goggles and hung them over the steering column of the bike. Taking in as much as she could quickly, she saw that the goggles were high tech. It looked like a scope, a speaker and a mike attached to it, and she caught a glimpse of some other circuitry, the purpose of which was beyond her, before the rider moved in front of her and blocked the view. As he leaned over, she also caught a brief glimpse of startling blue eyes—not just the color, but something else that she didn't have time to fully absorb.

With a tenderness that she would not have expected given her perception and slight knowledge of him, the rider loosed the bonds and took her weight as she swayed, weaker than she thought. He picked her up gently.

"Please. You are still weak, and your circulation will have been momentarily impaired by the bonds and the journey. Allow me…"

He carried her across the floor of the bunker toward one of the five doors. Part of Krysty balked at letting him do this. He was the enemy, and she felt that could in no way let him gain the advantage. Yet, at the same time, she could feel how weak she was. Anything that would let her regain her strength, give her time, was a good thing. Besides, she figured that she could fake being more exhausted than she was, and take the opportunity to try to observe as much as possible of the complex in which she found herself.

"Sector Three, open door two, please," the rider said, seemingly to no one.

Still, one of the doors glided effortlessly open, with no human hand to guide it. The whole area of the mechanics bunker had to be miked up; probably cameras, too. She was triple glad she had been too weak to try anything. An attempt at escape would likely have brought a whole sec squad down on her. She was going to have to watch every word and action.

He exited into a corridor that was noticeably more ornate than the bunker. The walls were painted in an eggshell-blue, and the lighting was concealed. A soft-hued tone lit the corridor with a less harsh glare, and the doors leading off this corridor—all, frustratingly, closed—were made of old wood, varnished, polished and ornate. The floor was actually covered with an old, predark-style carpet. In a shade to match the walls, no less.

Hell, this was certainly no redoubt. So what was it?

She allowed herself to be carried, taking all this in—even though, in truth, it told her very little.

Even so, it was a surprise when the voice seemed to slip out of the walls around her. She looked around as surreptitiously as she could, but could see no sign of the speaker, or even of a remote speaker from which the sound could emanate.

"Howard, your request for addition to file 444/720G has been noted and attended to. Work is currently taking place on synthesizing an element to eliminate the noted effect. Until this is achieved, the remaining grenades will be removed from the Ordnance Depot."

"Thank you, Sid. Would it be possible to have records of the missions available by 0700?"

"This can be done. Is there anything else?"

"Inform Hammill that I would like schematics for the cruiser available first thing. There's still a lot of work to be done, but I think it may not be too long before we have allies in our quest."

"That is excellent news, Howard. I shall refer the request immediately."

"Thank you." He looked down into Krysty's eyes, reading the question. "Sid is the hub of this base. Without him, the whole Thunder Rider project could not have been launched."

"'Thunder Rider'?" The name bemused her. It seemed to have no meaning that she could discern. And what was with this Sid and Hammill that he had mentioned? Names and voices but no sign of the people?

He smiled. "Don't concern yourself at this stage. It will all become clear to you soon. But first, you must rest. I fear that the effects of the gas are more wide-ranging than the files would have led me to believe."

They had reached the end of the corridor. A staircase wound around an elevator shaft. It looked something like she had seen in old vids or photographs. The stairs were carpeted like the corridor, and the elevator was of open ironwork, the cage decorated in a design like leaves and flowers, while the cage within was open.

No, certainly no military redoubt. What the hell was it? Krysty's mind raced as she tried to piece together what she knew…which was very little, but was beginning to make an intriguing picture. From the old vids and photographs, she knew that only people with a lot of jack lived in places that looked like this. She also knew that anyone nonmilitary with this much tech would also be loaded with jack. Put that together, and you had someone who had serious power and influence before skydark. That would also account for the staff—the invisible staff. She'd feel happier when she'd seen them, had some idea of what they looked like.

So you had people with a lot of power who'd taken to their bunker when the nukecaust happened. And Howard—which didn't seem somehow threatening enough for such a coldheart—was the result of several generations underground. There had to be a bigger gene pool down here than she'd reckon, as he was nowhere near as inbred as she would have figured. No drooling, stunted stupe. But there was something about the eyes, a kind of coldness that made her hair curl around her protectively, made her wonder what was going on behind those ice-blue orbs.

While this had been racing through her mind, and she had been doing her best to keep it from her face, Thunder Rider had entered the elevator, and they had ascended two floors. They were now partway down another corridor, decorated in a similar style. He paused outside a door.

"Level Four, door seven, please."

The door clicked softly before opening. He carried her inside a room that was lushly decorated in pinks and oranges, and placed her on a bed covered with a richly decorated pane.

"This was my sister's room," he said softly. "I think you will be comfortable here."

Krysty didn't know what to say. Thankfully, he turned and left before she had need to frame a reply, leaving her lying on the bed, staring at the ceiling.

Where, she wondered, were the monitors? What was the Thunder Rider project he spoke of? Where was his sister? And most of all, what was lurking behind those eyes that made her skin crawl?

There was nothing she could do right now except get some rest. Until she'd had a chance to find out more, any thoughts of escape would have to wait. She turned onto her side and tried to sleep, but the knowledge that something in the room was watching her made that far from easy.

Just like everything was going to be far from easy.

Chapter Seven

Day two, coming up for thirty-six hours since they had lost Krysty. A day and a half. That was without the added time it would take them to catch up. And there was nothing they could do about it. Their pace was fixed by the horses and couldn't be increased.

There was nothing to do. Nothing except watch the wastelands up ahead, and the territory they had already covered to their rear.

Ryan had never felt so frustrated, so helpless. It was a feeling he didn't like. He was used to taking action, to being in charge of a situation…or at least trying to take that charge. Now he could do nothing, and the tension and frustration was like an itch under his skin that he could not scratch. It crawled in his gut, making him edgy. It had no release: there wasn't even anything he could do to take his mind off the nagging doubts. Could he have done something to protect his people back at the camp? Could he be doing something now?

His frustration was nearly boiling over, waiting for an outlet.

"Incoming, eleven o'clock," J.B. muttered. Those three words, said in a laconic tone, referred to something so far away that Ryan couldn't even, at this point, hear it. But it was enough. Galvanized, he felt like a coiled spring given release.

He had been brooding in the back of the wag, J.B. taking the reins while Doc stared out the back, trying to stop his mind wandering more than usual. Jak and Mildred were trying to sleep, but in the silence of the seemingly endless wastes even the murmur of the Armorer was enough to rouse them.

Ryan was out the front of the wag, crouching beside the Armorer, before his words had even had time to die away. Following the direction of J.B.'s gaze, Ryan could see a cloud of dust on the horizon, seemingly floating in midair as it hovered at the point where sand and sky meet. But with a rapidity suggesting great speed, it moved away from the vanishing point and became a much more corporeal figure on the landscape. The cloud billowed, and even at such a great distance it was possible to make out the rough impression of a wag.

"Our coldheart?" Ryan mused.

"Figure not," J.B. replied. "Our boy's trail leads more one o'clock, and this isn't any kind of a bike. Even a big fucker like his."

"He could have more than a bike," Ryan cautioned, "but I take your point. So someone else, then. Question is, are they looking for him, too?"

"Mebbe. Not our problem if they are, though," J.B. drawled.

Ryan nodded. "Exactly. They're just gonna see this wag, see the horse, and think easy meat."

J.B.'s mouth quirked. "Better advise them of their error, then...."

The others had been listening to this exchange, and as Ryan turned to them he could see that they were already going through the routines of checking and preparing their blasters. Truth was that they were always combat ready. It did no harm to make triple sure.

"You heard that, right?" He looked at them, could see he was correct, and continued without pause. "We don't know who these people are, but they're better protected than us in that wag, and they'll see us as easy. I want them to think there's just J.B. and me on board. You stay here, stay down, and get ready to move out the back and adopt firing positions at the least provocation."

"Think you want much as me, Ryan." Jak grinned, his teeth showing in a vulpine leer.

Ryan shrugged. "Glad I'm not the only one feeling it." He looked over his shoulder. "Shit, they've got some speed... Get ready."

He moved to the front of the wag, settling himself beside J.B. The Armorer had kept up the same pace and direction as before. Anything else would have been noted by the approaching wag. No way did he want to give them any cause for suspicion. They were bigger, and they were better protected. He didn't want them to start blasting from distance, or else the companions were really screwed.

And the wag—whoever was in it—was definitely taking an interest in them. While their course had remained constant, the wag had deviated from the line it had been taking from the horizon, so that it arced around to come closer to them. It was still throwing up clouds of dust to its rear, but from the front they could now see that it was an old military armored wag. It had a gun turret with a front-mounted machine blaster, with two ports below, under the windshield. Most of those old wags had originally had comp equipment so that they could drive blind. J.B. would guess, from the slightly erratic line, that the driver was having to rely on visual alone. A bubble-mounted blaster on each side, with a full 180 rotation; two wheels on each side at the front. He couldn't see the rear, but he was guessing caterpillar tracks.

A formidable vehicle against five people with a couple of horses and a hunk of wood.

It sped toward them with no sign of diminishing its speed. It was fortunate that the horses had their remarkable placidity, or even a more experienced horseman than J.B. would have had trouble controlling them. As it was, they showed no interest in the approaching wag, and the Armorer was able to handle the reins with one hand while slipping his mini-Uzi from his shoulder so that it rested by his hip. Similarly, Ryan had slowly dropped the Steyr from his back until it rested casually across his lap. The two blasters wouldn't be much good against the armor-plated wag, but both men figured that whoever was inside would feel just confident enough against a horse-drawn wag to want to show their faces. They'd seen enough sloppy fighters in their time to lay odds on this.

The wag continued until it looked as though it was prepared to drive right through them. J.B. kept to his course, kept his nerve and hoped that his judgment was sound. As the roaring, whining engine approached them, and the dissipating clouds of dust started to reach them in choking waves, the Armorer wondered momentarily if he'd picked the wrong moment to make a bad call.

But no. At the last, the wag skidded on the sandy soil and turned side-on, the braking throwing up even larger, denser clouds of dust that temporarily blinded them, making them choke. In the rear of the covered wag, Jak, Mildred and Doc were partially protected from this, but were still denied the clear sight they needed.

The reason for the move became obvious when the dust settled. Between tear-filled, blinking red-eye stares and coughs that yielded dust-flecked sputum, both Ryan and J.B. could see that two men had emerged from the wag. One was standing in front of it, pointing an AK-47 directly at them. The other was half-hidden by the turret of the wag, from which his upper torso projected. He was holding them in the sights of a scattergun. He was older than the man with the AK-47, with a gray beard covering his grizzled face, a dusty stovepipe hat topping his long, gray hair. The younger man had no beard, and his long black hair was tied back in a ponytail. Both men had the same long, hooked nose and protruding front teeth. They had to be kin, probably father and son.

Their clothes were old and patched. Their blasters looked pretty much the same to J.B.'s practiced eye. Because of this, and because of the way they had turned the wag side-on, the Armorer figured that however they had laid hands on it, they either hadn't got ammo for the mounted blasters, or else they hadn't maintained the ordnance properly and it no longer worked.

Which was good. If they were the only two in the wag, then it more than evened the odds.

"G'afternoon, gentlemen," the older man said with a twang in his voice that told them that, like themselves, these were not natives of the area. From farther south, Ryan would guess. Not that it mattered. Coldhearts were coldhearts, and from the shrewd stare he was getting, Ryan knew these men for stone chillers.

There was a long silence. The older man had obviously been expecting a reply, maybe even a capitulation.

It wasn't going to happen. Ryan and J.B. could outwait any bastard they encountered. And so it was this time. The silence hung too heavy for the old man.

"So mebbe I was thinking that you were gonna be in the least bit curious as to why we've stopped you like this," he said. "Mebbe you are. Mebbe you're smarter than two dudes trying to cover this land with horses have any damn right to be. Mebbe you're mute retards who can't speak 'cause you got no tongues. Makes no difference to me."

He waited again for them to break their silence. When they remained silent, he sighed and carried on.

"See, me and my boy here—" he indicated the younger man "—we been traveling across this here stretch of useless shit for some time, and we're running a little low on the necessities of life. To be blunt, gentlemen, we ain't got shit in the way of water or food. And when we saw your wag in the distance, we said to ourselves, what kind of damn fool is gonna be rumbling across this land at that speed? And we kinda knew what the answer might be—a damn fool who's at least smart enough to make sure that they've got enough water and food to stop themselves from buying the farm halfway across.

"And so you see, gentlemen, we want you to hand over everything you've got. Now, we ain't nasty types. We ain't gonna chill you. We're fair men. You hand over your blasters and your supplies, and we drive off, and you take your chances out there. Now, I'll admit that it ain't much of a chance. But it's better'n being chilled.

"Course, you don't wanna do that, then we got no choice other than to blast the living shit out of you right now and just take it all anyway. See, either way you lose your blasters and your food and water. But do it our way, and at least you get to live a little longer…mebbe a lot longer.

"So how d'you want to play it, gentlemen?"

Ryan and J.B. exchanged glances. It seemed to them that these coldhearts were bluffing. No one was given a chance in these kinds of circumstances. The blasters had to be empty, and they were desperate enough to try to con what they wanted. From the way that the old man spoke, it was also pretty clear that there was only those two traveling in the wag. So perhaps they could just bring up their blasters and fire now, calling that bluff. Sure, there was a chance that it could backfire and they could get fired on, but…

There was no need for that. They had three blasters in the back, just waiting to spring. This was going to be somebody's lucky day, and it wasn't going to be the two men facing them.

"Okay," Ryan said simply, "we'll take our chances. That we can survive, and that you won't just chill us anyway."

"Boy, you can take my word on that," the old man said in a voice that sounded sincere.

Yeah, sure. Sincere because they were right. The two men wouldn't fire on them because they had no ammo. This was going to be easy.

Ryan shrugged. "Take your word for it. We're going to throw down our blasters on the count of three, then start to unload. That okay with you? You got the cards."

Don't overplay it—he could almost feel J.B.'s thoughts. Too easy to give in, and these coldhearts would be suspicious. There was still the chance they weren't bluffing.

The old man nodded his agreement, and Ryan counted out loud. On three, both he and J.B. took the Steyr and the mini-Uzi, holding them barrel-first, and threw them past the horses so that they landed with a dull thud in the sand, puffing up dust around them. They waited until that dust had settled.

This was the crucial moment. If the younger man collected the blasters before they had a chance to move—to clear the shot for the trio of blasters at their backs—then there was a chance he might be able to snatch at one of the blasters on the ground and return fire before he had been chilled.

Ryan's eye locked with the old man. An almost imperceptible nod as a signal, and Ryan took this as his cue to turn toward the rear of the wag. This was the moment when he figured that, if they really meant to chill them, the younger man would make his move.

J.B. anticipated his friend's action. He delayed his own turn the merest fraction of a second, enough to see that the younger man darted forward for the fallen blasters.

"Now!" he yelled, diving off to one side and rolling under the wag, his arm shooting out as he did so to push at Ryan, give him more momentum.

The one-eyed man was grateful for that. Not very often would he be glad to fall face-first into a pile of less-than-soft sacks, but this time was different. He heard and sensed, rather than saw, the action above his head. He felt Jak brush against him, heard the deafening roar of the .357 Magnum Colt Python, so close to his head that it drowned out even the elephantine roar of Doc's LeMat.

As J.B. fell sideways, and Ryan fell in front of them, the three friends who had been listening from the back of the wag took their cue. Regardless of whether the men in the wag had been bluffing, they knew they only had one shot. One shot, one chance: the difference between life and a long time chilled.

Jak was nearest to the younger man, had been able to tell this by the sound of movements across the sand. Even as he was rising from his position crouched in the back of the wag, he was bringing up his blaster and drawing a bead with one fluid motion, his finger already squeezing on the trigger. As the blaster exploded, the recoil made him rock on the wag's unsteady wooden floor; but it didn't affect his aim. The powerful slug took off the side of the young man's head as he bent down, an eye socket, an ear and part of his skull exploding in a mulch of blood, brain and bone. The slug continued into his shoulder, gouging out flesh and bone. Not that he felt it. The initial impact had taken away all consciousness and life.

The older man would have been shocked by the sudden chilling of his son if he had been given the chance

to even register it. Instead, he was hit by a double blow.
A dead shot from Mildred's ZKR drilled a small hole
between his eyes, neatly piercing his brain. That was
followed in less time than it took to blink by a hail of shot
from the LeMat, which obliterated not just the neatly
drilled hole, but most of his head. His body, topped only
by a bloodied mass of pulp, slumped in the turret of the
wag. If, by chance, there had been anyone inside, they
would have been trapped by the inert corpse.

As the burst of fire echoed and evaporated over the
wasteland, there was a moment where no one dared to
move. Then it became apparent that the threat posed by
the two men had been eradicated, and Ryan and J.B. rose
to their feet.

The one-eyed man jumped down from the wag and
joined the Armorer as he collected their blasters from
beneath the body of the son. As the others dismounted
and joined them, they strolled over to the armored wag.
The tension in the air had dissipated with the blasterfire,
and they now felt at ease. If anything, they felt better than
they had for the past thirty-six hours. Now, perhaps, they
may have found themselves a faster form of transport.

First, though, they had to check over the wag, which
meant moving the old man's corpse. It was difficult, as
his deadweight had slumped in such a way as to jam him
in the hatch. Doc and J.B. shifted him after a lot of sweat
and more cursing. The Armorer then descended into the
body of the wag, still cautious lest anyone be lurking.

In truth, all that was lurking was the stench of filthy
bodies, excreta and the remains of rotting food. It was all
he could do not to retch. How the previous owners had

managed to bear it was beyond him, and he was a man who considered he had a strong stomach.

Swallowing hard and biting down on the bile that rose from his gut, he adjusted his eyes to the interior gloom. There had been a light in the cab of the wag at one time, but the bulb had long since blown, and these stupes either didn't have a replacement, or had been unable to work out how to fit it. No matter. As his eyes grew used to the feeble light, he was able to make out the control panel of the wag without too much effort. So, if necessary, they could drive without any extra illumination. However, there was no point straining his vision unnecessarily. He took out his flashlight and switched it on, directing the beam in a slow sweep over the interior.

It was much as his nose had told him. The floor of the wag was sticky with something that could have been shit, could have been blood, and was probably a mixture of both, along with other bodily fluids. Not necessarily those belonging to the chilled coldhearts, either. The sweet and heavy stench of decaying meat that had hit him was explained by the pile thrown into one corner. Some of it was animal, the fur, heads and paws still attached in places, empty eye sockets filled with dark masses of flies that buzzed greedily and possessively around their prize, their low hum becoming clear to him only when he could see them. The heated interior of the wag was buzzing with metal expansion and contraction, and he had unconsciously attributed all noise to that.

Some of the meat was patently not animal in origin. Pale skin showed on some roughly hacked pieces, skin that had not been shorn of fur. Bone showing through with jaggedly cut edges had shape that came not from a quadruped. J.B. didn't want to touch the rotten, diseased pile, but he had to know. Gingerly, with a tentative prod of his boot, he shifted the bulk of the pile. It moved with a slithering, sucking sound that made him gag, and the flies hummed and buzzed angrily when disturbed at their task. In the slithering morass, a hand fell out, the fingers limp, blackening at the ends, the skin grayer than other human-seeming chunks. The hand was small, though: it was difficult to see if it had been that of a child or a woman at that advanced stage of decay.

The Armorer turned away. He had seen things that were in some ways worse than this—people burning alive, tortured and slowly chilled, disemboweled while still conscious. Yet somehow this was worse. It wasn't just that someone who had once had a life, however hard it had been, had been chilled and then chopped up for meat. It was that the sicko crazies who had done this had then carried it with them: living, sleeping, shitting and breathing next to it as it started to rot away; and then casually eating it as though it were nothing more than the jackrabbits and rats that it lay with.

It was the simple matter of the hand lying limp next to the empty-eyed stare of a rotting jackrabbit as just another game tidbit that made him lose the contents of his stomach, the acid bile splashing on the floor of the wag, hot stink rising as it mixed with the fetid layer of mulch on the floor.

Taking a deep breath—and regretting it as the stench made him gag again—J.B. hawked up the last of the bile and phlegm and spit it out, sparing a mouthful from the canteen of water he carried with him to rinse the taste away before spitting that out, also.

Dark night! he thought. The wag had better be worth cleaning out after this…

He turned the flashlight and his attention toward the control panel of the wag, dismissing the images still seared on his retina, and instead focusing on the matter in hand.

The wag was a military vehicle, as he had known. The control panel was mostly useless, the equipment to which it had been connected taken out to give an optimum of interior space. The steering system left in place was sturdy and in good repair, considering who had been in charge of the wag of late.

It would take some cleaning to get the interior into a condition where they could all comfortably sit inside, but there was space. And when he checked, there was a good fuel supply and an air con system that coughed into life when he switched it on. It would use fuel, and would be wasteful over a long distance, but would be useful in the short term to drive out any remaining stink.

Like all such wags, there were sluices for cleaning, and these looked as though they would be relatively easy to clear of any blockages. And there was plenty of water. These coldhearts hadn't been so crazy that they hadn't provided for themselves after their own fashion. They might have wanted to scavenge from the friends, but their need had—and no surprise here—been nowhere as desperate as they made out.

Water was one thing of which the friends were short, but the notion of using it for anything other than cleaning out the wag stayed with him for only a second. Just a moment's thought of what the crazies they had just chilled may have done in the water supply, and where they may have got it from, dissuaded him of this notion.

Finally, J.B. was ready to climb out of the cab and tell the others of what he had found. As he emerged from the snub turret of the wag, it was obvious to all of them that what he had seen down there had been appalling. His face, in the bright light of the sun, was pale and drawn, and his eyes had the puffy, strained appearance of one who has recently vomited heavily.

Before he even began to outline what was within the wag, they could guess. He finished his report and added his own views on cleaning and using the wag.

"We'd take a few hours to clean it out so that it's usable, and mebbe we think that'll be wasted time. But once we start, the speed we'll gain will more than compensate," he finished.

Ryan gave a wry grin. "Just got to keep patient while it's being done," he said with a dry humor, knowing that he would be the one most likely to need keeping in check.

"It sounds less than ideal in there, and we will have to take our time, I know, but the benefits accruing will be more than worthy of the delay," Doc mused.

"Shit, understand half that. Getting better, Doc," Jak murmured. It was the closest to humor that the dour albino would ever get, and was a reflection of the manner in which their mood was beginning to lift.

Not wanting to waste any more time than was necessary, they began the task of clearing and cleaning the wag. With the flies already beginning to gather on the corpses of the coldhearts, it was time to get busy. Doc volunteered to clear the rotting meat from the interior. With a grimness that he tried to hide behind a jaunty mask, he reasoned that he had seen things far worse in his time—had been treated almost as badly as he imagined the people whose remains now littered the wag's interior had suffered. He was still alive. There were times when he regretted it. But it meant that although a feeling of being scared could overtake him in panic, he no longer feared anything. It was distasteful, but that was all.

As Doc began his task, Ryan and J.B. took the corpses of the coldhearts and dragged them across the sand, leaving two blood-soaked trails, until they were bundled together. They would form the basis of a fire. There was little chance of anyone noticing out here in the wastes, but such a store of raw decaying meat would surely attract predators and call attention to their trail. The last thing they wanted was another encounter with anyone other than their target.

When the interior had been cleared, Doc—at J.B.'s behest—took a can of fuel from the store of the wag and poured a little of it over the rotting pile, touching a flame to it and watching it catch in black, gasoline-assisted smoke. The smell was appalling to begin with, but the gas and the acrid odor of burning fur began to swiftly eclipse the fatty, sweet tang of flesh.

This dealt with, Jak and Mildred clambered into the wag's cab and used the water inside to wash as much of the filth from the floor and other surfaces as was possible. Again, a little of the gas helped to shift some of the encrusted dirt. The smell of the gas also, despite its own sharp tang, aided in covering the charnel house smell of decay in the enclosed space.

While the interior of the wag was cleaned, Ryan and J.B. unloaded the friends' supplies from the covered wag and carried them to the armored wag, ready to be loaded when the cleaning had been completed.

The horses, unhitched, wandered only a few yards away, and watched the proceedings with bland disinterest. As with everything they had seen since they had first been hitched to the wag, they seemed unconcerned almost to the point of catatonia. It had been a positive when they had been hitched to the wag, but it didn't bode well for their survival. Would they wander off in search of food and water, or would they just stand there until they died slowly of torpor as much as starvation and dehydration?

Jak walked over and led them toward the blazing fire. They followed him without complaint, and he maneuvered them so that they both stood at a right angle to the fire, staring at him with large, brown, uncomprehending eyes.

The albino drew his Python and without hesitation fired a shot into the forehead of each horse, so quick that the second animal had no time to even register what had happened to its mate before its own brain had been pulped. The two corpses fell into the fire, sending up showers of sparks and momentarily damping it before the flames started to lick around and take hold of their fur.

Ryan raised an eyebrow at Jak.

The albino shrugged. "Never find way back. Better quick."

It was an inarguable point, yet unusual for the albino to waste ammo on such a humane act.

Ryan walked over to the wag. Water was leaking from the sluices, heavily discolored and smelling as bad as it looked as it soaked into the sandy soil, leaving behind pools of fetid sludge. He climbed up and stuck his head into the turret. The smell was still pretty foul, but nowhere near as bad as that which had greeted J.B., or indeed Doc when he had climbed in to begin the cleaning process.

"How long do you think?" Ryan asked shortly.

"Not long," Mildred replied, her voice tight as she tried to avoid breathing in too deeply. "I hope John's right about the air-conditioning," she added with an even tighter smile.

By this time, everything was ready to load. Ryan joined Jak and J.B. while they waited for Mildred and Doc to finish. They tried to judge by the amount of water coming from the sluices, but the openings were so small that it was hard to tell if the flow was abating. Eventually, Doc's head appeared and with a brief nod he signaled that all was ready. It was only when they were loading the last of the supplies that J.B. noticed the water flow finally slow to a trickle.

It had ceased entirely by the time that they had all descended into the wag and the turret was closed. Even with the apertures for ordnance, there was little air within. The smell of gasoline, underpinned by the still-lingering scent of decay, would soon be overlaid by the smell of their own bodies as they clustered within the tight space.

"Let's hope we don't have to spend too long in here," J.B. murmured almost to himself as he hit the ignition.

The engine of the wag coughed into life, spluttering as it turned over. He knew from past experience that this kind of armored wag was a fine piece of machinery, and the sound of the mechanics bespoke of neglect. If he'd had more time, he would have felt comfort in stripping the bastard down and making sure it was tuned. Lurking at the back of his mind was the possibility that it could get halfway to wherever they were going and then just buy the farm on them, which would be just great.

He tried to dismiss this worry from his mind, hitting the air-conditioning switch. A deathly rattle started up, and they could all feel the cold air begin to circulate within the heated confines of the wag. The rising heat of their bodies, crammed together, had started to make the smell of rotten flesh creep up from beneath the top note of gasoline. J.B. had hit the switch not a moment too soon. There was almost a collective sigh of relief as air sucked from outside and fed through the cooling plant began to drive out the fetid air that was gathering within.

"By the Three Kennedys, I am grateful for such small mercies," Doc murmured.

Ryan said nothing, but kept his eye fixed on the trail ahead as he sat by the Armorer's side. The desert atmosphere out here was so airless, and the chem storms that raged in waves had been quiet, so the trail left by the mystery rider's bike was still visible to the naked eye, even at some distance. The delay in setting forth had been added to both by the relative tardiness of the horse-drawn wag, and then by the delay both in being held up by the coldhearts and the time it had taken to clean out the armored wag so that it was habitable.

None of these things had been of any great duration in its own right, but cumulatively, had taken one hell of a chunk out of the day. By the sun, he could see that it was now edging toward late afternoon. Soon, the darkness would begin to descend. If the exterior lights on the wag were working, then maybe they could travel all night and make up some time. He didn't hold out much hope for that, seeing as the dim glow of the instrument panel was all that lit the interior.

The mystery rider and Krysty had been given a major head start. The rider's speed would have been consistent, and he would not have been held up on his way.

Ryan chewed on his lip, cursed to himself. They didn't know how far this bastard had gone, and he had an advantage over them when it came to speed. At least until now.

Even if they rode this bastard all night, pushing it to the limit, there was no way of knowing whether they could find him before it was too late for Krysty.

It was the helplessness that chilled Ryan to the core. He wasn't in control. There was nothing he could do.

That was the bastard feeling he hated.

Some fucker was going to pay.

Chapter Eight

"Good morning, Krysty Wroth. We hope you slept well."

The voice was calm, assured, sibilant and not the rider's. The lights, which had dimmed almost to blackness when the door had shut on her the night before, were now raised to a level where they penetrated almost painfully through her eyelids. She opened her eyes, squinting blearily at the surrounding room, ready to hit out blindly if the voice came too close.

She hadn't meant to fall asleep. She'd wanted to keep awake, ready to meet any challenge. But the fatigue of the journey, the toll that the gas had taken on her body, had made her unable to resist the weariness that seeped through her bones. At some point, lulled by darkness, she had drifted off. A dreamless sleep, so deep that she wouldn't have known if someone had crept in and chilled her. She hated to be so vulnerable at the best of times, let alone in a situation such as this.

And the voice. It had seemed so close. She could have... Ah, there was no reason to worry about that now. If it had been her time, it would be too late for regrets by now.

She sat up, shaking her head, using the seemingly half-awake, still-bleary motion to take a surreptitious look around. Perhaps the cameras and speakers were visible, and she had just missed them in her tiredness of the previous night. But no. The room just looked like a garishly decorated bedroom. What had he said to her? It had been his sister's. Presumably the woman had bought the farm.

So how many people lived down here? She needed to find out as soon as possible.

"You may speak, and your voice will be picked up by our monitors," the voice prompted.

"That's sure nice to know," she muttered to herself, then added in a louder tone, "Breakfast would be good. And mebbe seeing who you are."

"Food will be provided. I shall not be able to attend to your request personally, but I am sure Howard will be with you soon."

She had to hand it to whoever the voice was: equable, even, and not showing the slightest sign of being riled. And keeping well out of the way. So it was only the rider she was being allowed to have contact with right now. She wondered why that was. Could they be worried about her carrying disease from the outside? Perhaps they figured she could be dangerous, and they were paring down the risk? After all, they knew her name, so they had to know a whole lot more. Hadn't Howard the rider said something about that last night? The Thunder Rider project? What the hell was that?

Whatever, it didn't sound good.

She sat on the edge of the bed, waiting. The good thing about her sleep was that, now she had adjusted to the lights, she felt better than she had for what seemed like forever. She sat, head down, seemingly still in a state of fatigue. In truth, as her hair hung down over her face like a curtain, she was peering from beneath it, using it as a mask, marking all the points of the room, anything that she may be able to use as a weapon.

Not that she intended to do any such thing until she had seen what the coldheart Howard had to offer. She wanted to know more about this place, if possible.

She didn't have long to wait. Within a few minutes of the anonymous voice, the door to the bedroom opened automatically and Howard came through bearing a tray. It had a plate piled high with food she didn't recognize, and a steaming cup of what smelled like coffee, but somehow richer than the freeze-dried granules she knew from redoubts. Richer than the odd brews passed off as coffee she had tasted on the outside, too.

"I didn't know what you'd like, so I've guessed," Howard said with a smile. He was dressed today in a one-piece worksuit covered in oil stains, and looked slighter than in his "Thunder Rider" costume. She could see that he was still wiry and tough, though perhaps not as muscle-bound as she had at first thought. He wasn't much bigger than her.

But despite her best intentions, she was distracted by the food. She hadn't realized how hungry she was until the smell of the food and the coffee had made the hunger begin to gnaw at her stomach.

He placed the tray across her knees, and in leaning in so close would have made it easy for her to take him out. Now was not the time. Especially when her hunger was overwhelming her.

She began to eat greedily. The flavors were rich and full, suggesting to that part of her mind not occupied with the task in hand that this base had one hell of a stockpile, and one hell of a way of maintaining that pile. The coffee, when she took a mouthful, hit her tastebuds like an explosion. For a second, it was easy to forget exactly how she had got here and what her intention of only a few moments ago had been.

Then the caffeine buzz hit her, and her head cleared. She could see him standing just a few yards from her, watching her with a smile playing about his lips that didn't touch those dead eyes.

And she remembered.

When she swallowed again, it was as though she had to force it down past the lump of bile in her craw.

"Good?" he prompted.

"Sure is," she said as sincerely as she could. It sounded false to her ears, hollow and ringing, but Howard didn't seem to notice.

"Excellent," he said happily, clapping his hands. "Then when you have freshened up, I will give you a brief tour to familiarize yourself with the complex. It won't be the full tour, as I have work to do—as you can no doubt tell," he added with a grin, indicating his clothing. "However, I shall leave you in Sid's capable hands while I proceed with my task. Now then, I shall leave you to your repast, and the bathroom is over there—" he waved to his left "—and I shall see you in about half an hour."

He turned and left, leaving Krysty more than a little confused. There she was, thinking that it was going to be a struggle to find out what was going on here, and he was offering it to her on a plate, same as the food in front of her. Well, one way or another she would soon be able to size up her enemy. She shrugged, and returned to the breakfast—the repast?—he had given her. Still slipping those odd words into the conversation, which suggested to her that the people here hadn't been out since skydark. That was if you could call it a conversation. There was something about the way he spoke to her that suggested social interaction beyond the level of blasting the shit out of people was an unfamiliar concept, too.

What the hell. The food warmed her belly, filled the gnawing hunger. The coffee buzzed, made her feel alive again. Unwittingly, he was giving her just the boost she needed to face him, and whomever he had with him. She could feel her old self returning, the Krysty drained by the nerve gas and the misfiring Gaia power being replenished.

She placed the tray on the floor and stood, surreptitiously testing herself in case of residual weakness from the gas. But no, her legs felt strong, her steps firm as she moved across the room to the door he had indicated. She cast a glance at the door to the corridor as she passed it, wondering if she should try it, see if it was locked. Mebbe not. She was sure she had heard the soft click of the locking mechanism as it closed behind Howard, and she was aware of the hidden cameras monitoring her every move.

She felt uncomfortable as she entered the bathroom. Was there a camera here, too? The idea of stripping naked for some hidden guard to get his jollies watching her wasn't something she relished. On the other hand, a spell under the hot jets of the shower would do her a lot of good. She still felt dirty and sticky from the journey, and the shower almost called out to her, it looked so good.

Trying not to be too obvious as she tried to scan for cameras, she opened the mirrored cabinet on the wall. Whoever Howard's sister had been, she had used a hell of a lot of creams and lotions. The cabinet was rammed full of bottles and jars, most with odd-sounding names and no obvious function. She took a few out at random, examining the writing on the labels. Some of it she could read, and some of it she wasn't sure about, strange words she couldn't get her tongue around, which she guessed had to be chem names that Mildred or Doc might know. The idea of putting chem stuff on her body without any worry was an odd one for Krysty. Still, whatever Howard's sister had been like, she had obviously not bought the farm too far back. Opening those jars at random, she could see that the stuff inside was still fresh.

She found toothpaste and a brush, and swilled out her mouth. It was odd to have such sharp flavors back in her mouth, and again it reminded her of the things they found in deserted redoubts. Again, it was still fresh.

She turned to the shower, fiddling with the faucets until the water was hot but not scalding. Steam filled the small bathroom, and as she stripped she was consoled with the thought it might obscure the camera as it had the cabinet mirror. Krysty had no problems with being naked, except that it had to be when she wanted, and for who she wanted.

The thoughts were banished from her mind as she stepped beneath the jets and felt the water wash the sweat and dirt from her. She turned her face to it, eyes closed, and felt each individual jet as its constant pressure cleaned and stimulated her skin, the pummeling of the high-pressure jets seeming to massage through to her brain. Her hair was plastered to her skull, clinging to her neck not through fear but through the weight of water it held.

She stepped out of the shower, the steam now dissipated, but making no attempt to hide herself. So what if some stupe guard got a hard-on looking at her? It was the closest he would get to the real thing without being chilled. She toweled her hair, dried herself on the towels that were on a wall-mounted rack. They were softer than anything she had used before, seeming to soak up the excess liquid rather than rub it away. If these bastards lived like this, then chances were they were as soft if you rubbed at them.

She dressed rapidly, her only regret being the lack of a change of clothes. No matter. Her annoyance at the filthy clothing on her newly clean skin was something she could channel and use to make herself sharper.

She was sitting on the bed, waiting with the outward appearance of patience, when Howard returned.

"You're ready. Good. I would have offered you some of my late sister's clothing in exchange for your own dirty apparel, but I fear that the styles would not impress—she was something of a very 'girlie' sort of woman—and also she was very petite. She was neither tall nor muscular enough for her things to fit you. But no matter, I'm sure we can get something appropriate for you from the stores. Over the years, we have been col-

lecting a variety of sizes, so it should not be too hard."
He held out his hand.

"Over the years?" Krysty repeated as she rose to her
feet, making light of ignoring his outstretched hand.
"That kind of implies that you've been down here a long
time."

"Ah, such impatience and yet such a desire to know
more. Both, in their way, admirable traits, but not perhaps
well-timed. Follow me," he continued. He then realized
his hand was still outstretched and being ignored. With-
drawing it with barely concealed embarrassment, he said,
"Your tour begins."

And it did, though it was not, in truth, exactly what
Krysty was hoping for. Howard instructed the hidden Sid
to open the door and to prepare a clear path through
Sector Two. Immediately, the Titian-haired woman knew
that she was getting the safe and trusted route. She would
only see what Howard wanted her to see.

And in truth, it wasn't much. Sector Two seemed to
consist mostly of the living quarters for the compound.
There were a number of bedrooms that she was shown,
none of which showed much sign of habitation. They
passed rooms that Howard dismissed as "not interesting,"
which she took to mean that they were inhabited and
therefore out of bounds in case they gave too much away.
She noted the locations of these rooms for when she was
able to explore alone and unnoticed.

They reached a general quarters area. As with the
bedrooms she had seen, this showed signs of being originally decorated by an individual or organization with a
possibly endless amount of predark jack. The carpets

were thick and plush, as were the furnishings, in rich, dark colors that had not faded or frayed with age. The temperature control from the air-conditioning, which seemed to be set at a cool constant, probably helped. There was a large vid screen here, and a wall of old vid cases, some covered with dust, others obviously much fingered. Some of these were piled on the floor, gaps in the wall announcing their original home.

One was playing as they entered.

"I love this—one of my favorites. A real influence on me," Howard murmured. He watched the screen. On it, an old black-and-white movie from way before skydark played. It was hokey and cheap—even Krysty, with her extremely limited knowledge of old predark vids could tell this. In truth, the way the people on the screen were acting reminded her of children back in Harmony, playing in the dirt, chasing one another and yelling as they play-fought. Men in really old wags were chasing one another, firing blasters that were heavy antiques, revolvers for the most part. One of them was dressed in a just-as-heavy black coat, his face shrouded by a wide-brimmed hat, the lower half covered by a scarf. In between bouts of firing that looked to her, frankly, to be really poor examples of marksmanship, he made pronouncements about justice and crime that sounded all too familiar.

Some of it could have been said by the man who stared, openmouthed, at the screen, lost in a world that was a million miles away from the woman standing next to him.

Krysty reached out and touched him. He looked

around, his blank eyes seeming even more distant, and then gradually seemed to become aware of his surroundings. His face broke into a grin that was almost bashful, and for the first time she saw it reach his eyes.

"Sorry," he said eventually in a small voice, "this always has this effect on me. It's all I've been striving to be. But I don't expect you to understand this quite yet. Most of these old tapes are too fragile to play now, but fortunately my predecessors transferred everything to computer, so it can be accessed. I just like the feel of the tapes…to look at them, to read the boxes. It's as though… as though I was back there, I guess. The same goes for the books and comics," he added, indicating the shelves behind him that were jammed with old volumes and thin paper magazines. "I like to get them down and look at them, feel the paper and think about the people they recorded. They were more just times, and these people made it so. That's so very important, don't you think? But all the same, when I read them I do so from the computer screen, as I'm so very scared of damaging them. It would be like losing the past. And that's all I have until I've built a new present. Come…"

He beckoned to her, not making the mistake of trying to touch her or offering her his hand. This way, she figured, he wouldn't feel embarrassed, perhaps felt more in control.

And she had a nasty feeling that control was a big part of what made him tick. And that meant that, at some point, he would want to control her.

And that moment would be decisive.

She took a deep breath and smiled at Howard, following him as he led her out of the general quarters and into the kitchen area. It was sparse and clean. The food, he explained, was stored in vast freezers and airtight containers. He went into a long explanation of how the air was sucked from the airtight rooms every time they were opened and then resealed. Machinery was obviously a fetish with him. Krysty pretended to listen attentively, but all the time her attention was flicking around the room.

It seemed as though no one ever used the kitchen. The surfaces were gleaming, the tools hung from the walls and ceiling in serrated rows of knife edges. Weapons, if necessary. There was no sign of any food preparation. No sign of habitation.

"It's all so wonderfully clean." She burst in on his monologue with a faked ingenuousness she hoped sounded more real to him than it did to her.

Howard stopped, looking momentarily puzzled. "I suppose, from what I've seen so far, this level of hygiene is probably unheard-of on the surface world as of yet. Hammill and Sid have a team of workers who deal with this. They're extremely efficient. I prepare all my own meals, you know," he added in a boyish tone. "I haven't had to rely on any help for a long time. Not since my sister—" He broke off, looking away. "Anyway, in time… Meanwhile, there is still much for you to see."

Krysty followed him as he left through the far door, thinking that perhaps he had given away more than he wanted.

How many workers, for Gaia's sake?

The tour continued. They went through labs with closed-off Plexiglas partitions. It was here that his chem weapons were synthesized from existing stocks, or premade and stored. There were two armories that would have made J.B. faint with pleasure, weapons that she sure couldn't identify, along with a lot that she could and that she knew to be deadly in their effect. And there was ammo for all that ordnance.

The odd thing was that she was used to seeing labs and armories in the harsh sodium glare of fluorescent lighting, with bare concrete floors and functional walls. This was weird. All that she had seen so far was like some opulent mansion from one of those old vids that lined the general quarters. The walls were in pastel shades, a thick carpeting in contrasting hues dulled their every footfall, and there were pictures on the walls. Some were paintings that she recognized from books, and others were photographs. A number of them featured individuals or groups that had people with a resemblance to the man in front of her.

"Howard, what are these?" she asked eventually. He stopped, looked back at her with the mildest of puzzlement on his face. It was hard for her to keep in mind that this seemingly childlike figure was also a coldheart chiller.

"Some of them are individual family members, others are groups. As you can see," he added with a grin. "What I mean is that they are those who went before and made all this possible. It was their efforts, and the efforts of those who worked for them, that ensured our survival after the nuclear winter."

"Those who worked for them?"

"Oh, yes—they were plenty smart, but they couldn't

have done this alone. They recruited the best brains of their generation to assist them in this project. Their reward was to be that they, too, would survive. And they did. Without them I would not be here now, talking to you. And the work goes on."

"But there are no pictures of the others here," she said.

He looked at her as though she were a stupe child. "Of course not. They aren't family," he said simply. "Now, if we continue, we'll come to the motor bays. You saw one of these yesterday, when we arrived. That's where I was this morning, before Sid informed me of your waking. And I hate to be impolite, but I must soon return to my work if I am to keep to my schedule."

He led her through to the bays, but his last words were preying on her mind. What was the schedule? How short was it? And what the hell was the aim? There were too many questions, and although she'd had hints of answers that he'd unwittingly given away, there was still far too much that she needed to find out before she could work out a course of action.

The bays were much as she would have expected from the night before. They housed a variety of vehicles, in states of repair and maintenance. Heavy tools and equipment littered the bays, and she was pretty sure that if she could get down here on her own she could hot-wire one of the wags, fight off any opposition and…and what? Until she could study the sec systems in any way, there was no guarantee she could get out of the exit tunnel in one piece.

And where was everyone? This, like the other sectors she had seen, was deserted except for the two of them.

He was keeping her apart from the others he had spoken of, and she didn't like the idea of going up against an unknown quantity. Another thing she had still to find out.

She feigned interest in what he had to say, waiting for the moment when he would leave her and she would be able to work out her own plan of action. He spoke at length, saying nothing that made any sense to her, before indicating that it was time for him to return to his work. If she followed the same route back, she would be able to find her way to her room—as it was now designated. She could stop and look at the books and vids if she wished, but if she had any requests she was to ask Sid, who would relay them to the computer terminal in her room, as the originals were too fragile.

That caught her attention. She couldn't remember seeing a terminal in the room. Perhaps if she used that for the innocuous business of watching old vids, then she might be able to access the mainframe and find out a little more about what exactly was going on here.

She waited until he had finished, signaling this by turning to the mechanics he had been working on earlier that morning, and then made to leave. She walked directly to the door from which they had accessed the bays, yet all the time she was scanning the area, noting other doors, positions of possible weapons. She left Howard to his task and retraced her earlier steps.

Sid—whoever he may be—automatically opened doors as she approached, signaling her path. She wanted to detour, to try one of the other doors along the way, one of those that had been locked or closed to her.

She couldn't make it look too deliberate. She had

noted the doors that had been unlocked previously, and she made for one of them.

"What are you doing, Krysty Wroth?" Sid's unseen presence asked her in the mildest of tones.

"Just curious," she replied in as offhand a manner as she could muster. "It must be okay, I was shown this before." She opened the door and looked in on the plushly furnished room. After a pause, she said, "Sid, Howard ran through things a little quickly, and I think I must be a little confused, still. I can't remember whose room he said this was?"

"He did not say," Sid replied with the mildest note of censure in his voice. "In point of fact, it belonged to a now deceased family member."

"Just like my room," she murmured. "How many of the family have bought the farm, then?"

There was a pause.

"Sid?"

"I'm sorry, Ms. Wroth, I was not immediately familiar with the term. I understand you to be asking how many of the family are now deceased. Am I correct?" She nodded, knowing that he could see her. "The numbers are unimportant. What you have to remember is that we have been down here for several generations, so many have passed naturally."

"'We,' Sid? Are you one of the family."

"No. I am one of those who serve."

She waited, but the voice was not forthcoming with any more information. Like it was going to be that easy.

She continued on the route back to her new quarters, stopping a couple of times to look at unlocked rooms.

"What is it you require?" Sid asked.

"I'm just acquainting myself with the place," she answered in as neutral a manner as she could muster.

The distant voice did not reply. She took that as a good sign. He wasn't actively dissuading her, so if she made an error of some kind…

She continued down the route until she had looked in another two rooms, then went to a door she knew was locked, or at least had not been actively opened to her the previous occasion. She tried it and was less than surprised to find that it would not budge.

"Ms. Wroth, what are you doing?" Sid's voice carried the mildest of rebukes. That was no indication. She'd met many a coldheart who sounded as soft as summer rain yet would chill you without blinking.

"My mistake," she replied. "I thought this was one of the rooms that I saw earlier."

"Please do not lie to me, Krysty Wroth. Just because I am not with you in presence does not mean that I cannot tell what is going on. You are attempting to gain access to rooms that were not on the route given to me by Howard. Please explain yourself."

"Why did Howard only allow certain rooms to be opened to me?"

"You have not answered my question."

"And you haven't answered mine."

"Very well," Sid intoned after a pause. "There is a simple and innocuous answer to your question. Howard wished you to see family rooms, as you will become part of the family. The other rooms are of no concern as they are worker rooms."

The phrase about becoming part of the family caused a cold chill to run down her spine, but she elected to ignore this in favor of pressing home the fact that she had got Sid to reveal something.

"Why can't I see workers' rooms? In point of fact, why haven't I seen any of these workers who Howard talks about? Where are you? Why am I being kept from you?"

"Really, Ms. Wroth, there is little I can say. Howard would not be pleased with this discourse as it stands. All I can say to you is that there has been no reason for you to encounter any of us. Howard is our master by birth, and we must obey him."

"Why? Your ancestors built this base for his ancestors. You were the brains and the hands. His people were just the jack." She was taking a chance here, and she knew it. But she had to test the territory sooner or later.

She thought she'd blown it, as Sid was quiet for some while. Then, when she was sure she'd pushed too far and sec guards would descend on her, he spoke.

"You do not understand, Ms. Wroth. I could not expect you to. Howard is not a bad man, so please do not judge him as such. Indeed, compared to some members of the family who have come before him, he is positively saintly. Yet consider this—would it be possible to be born, live down here, and come from a limited gene pool without being in many ways incomprehensible to such as yourself? Howard is good to us, to what we have become. He does not abuse his powers when it comes to the workers. Certainly not in the way that many who preceded him have done."

Krysty frowned. "I don't think I understand you. Not

completely. I think that your boss is completely mad, and probably very dangerous. Not bad. To be bad he would have to know what was good, and I don't think he has the capacity for that. But that doesn't make me any the less easy about being down here. And I still don't understand why I haven't seen anyone else. Why are you being kept from me?"

"Perhaps for your own peace of mind, Ms. Wroth. Had you considered that?"

Krysty gave a dry, humorless laugh. "It's hard to consider anything when I'm standing out here talking to a voice without a face or body."

There was a long pause. "Those are, perhaps, unfortunate choices of words, Ms. Wroth. But I feel—and I suspect that those of the others who are capable of such feeling may share this—that you can be trusted. Not, perhaps, in the way that Howard thinks. But maybe in a more real way. I will show myself to you. Please go to the fifth door on your left."

Krysty looked back along the way she had come. One of the doors gave a soft click, although it did not open.

With measured tread, slightly apprehensive at what she may have put in train, Krysty walked toward the door. It did not open, not until she was right in front of it.

"I hope you are ready for this, Ms. Wroth. I know from intelligence sources that you have seen many things. Hopefully, this will not be too big a shock."

As the door opened, she could see the length of one wall. It was painted white. A simple bed and a tiled floor. The bed was dusty, as though it had not been used for many years. There were no decorations on the walls, no pictures to relieve the white. As the door swung wider, she could see a long-unused desk and chair, both empty for many decades.

It was only when the door opened to its full extent, back against the wall, and the whole room was revealed, that she understood what Sid had meant.

"Gaia!" she exclaimed before a string of curses escaped her lips.

HOWARD HAD EXPECTED many things from Krysty Wroth, but her behavior still baffled him. He had shown her respect and hospitality, and yet she had repaid him with fear. Her reluctance to touch him in case he hurt her had shown him this. It was a pity. He had a great desire to feel her skin against his as their hands touched. Human contact was painful and odd to him after this time, and he desired to rectify that.

But as he busied himself on preparing the land cruiser so that it could augment the bike, and act as a vehicle for them both, he felt more reassured than he had just a short time earlier. It was the living shadows of the old movies that had brought them together. For his own part, he knew that the records of those times before the nuclear winter never failed to entrance and inspire him. It had been that way since Jenny had showed them to him when he was young. But he had not expected the same from Krysty.

And yet she had joined him, watching the course of justice follow its natural path. She had said nothing, had not questioned… It was more than he could have expected. She knew! She instinctively understood what motivated him, as it motivated her and her traveling companions.

Ah, yes, the others. That was why he was preparing the land cruiser, after all. The idea that she should be shown the way and understand it—as he felt she did—and then help him convince the others to join him. That had been the plan, and a good one. A task force for justice. But now, it seemed to be…not so good. Why, he couldn't quite tell. Only that there seemed an imbalance to it. The idea of Thunder Rider and Storm Girl, though, that had a certain symmetry to it that he found appealing. For that was what she should be called. All across the lawless wastes would know her name, and tremble in fear if they were wrongdoers. For she was wild, like the storm that swept over the land, cleansing the earth. That hair, a red fire that…

He shook his head. He was getting too carried away. For all he knew, she would wish to be reunited with her companions, especially the one-eyed man, Ryan Cawdor.

The nut he was tightening with a wrench sheared from its mount, spun across the floor. He watched it, aware that it was an extra turn from him that had done this, aware of the anger that had built in him with a rapid rage, boiling over into that one violent action. And he knew why that was: Ryan Cawdor. He was not worthy of one such as Storm Girl. He was a good man, admittedly, but no crusader for justice and truth.

There was only one who was right for Krysty: that was Thunder Rider. They would be the perfect team.

He had only to make her see that. He returned to his work, selecting a replacement nut to tighten on the underside of the chassis. He felt sure that she was already seeing this. That was why he had allowed her to return on her own.

He could trust her.

"SWEET GAIA, what have they done to you?"

Krysty walked closer to the metal lab table, breathing shallowly and quickly, trying to come to terms with what she could see.

"And the other workers? Are they...?"

"No. Myself and Hammill are like this. We were, perhaps, the lucky ones."

"How can you say that?"

For the first time since she had been in the complex, the omnipotent voice of Sid showed some emotion. He laughed, a low chuckle that gave her a feeling for how he had to, at one time, have looked.

"It must seem strange for you to hear me say, Ms. Wroth. I'll admit to that. But the others have lost far more than I. They may be ambulatory, but they have lost that vital spark."

Krysty looked at Sid—or what was left of him—and frowned. "Say that plain. There's a lot of words there that haven't survived outside."

"Ah, I see. I apologize. It must seem some time as though we speak a different language, even though it is on the surface the same. Although what you see before you is but a pale shadow of the man I once was, at least I am still myself. I have memory and character, though sometimes it fades in and out. Hammill is the same. Though we cannot leave our rooms, and serve only by remote means, we can still talk to each other, can still share, and not feel alone. The other workers were placed in moving canisters to enable them to respond physically. Somewhere along the way, something left them. They have no memory of why they are as they are. No indication that they are anything other than automatons."

"But to exist like this—" She put out her hand, trying not to recoil at the touch, as it felt like nothing she expected.

"Is often better than no existence at all."

The container on the lab table looked solid. Yet it yielded to her touch, the slightest amount of give. She expected it to be cold, but it was warm. It was semi-opaque, but she could still see what was within. The liquid surrounding Sid was greenish in hue, though she couldn't be sure that it wasn't due to the membranous container. It seemed too still in there for something that was alive, and spoke to her. She'd seen old whitecoat stories from before skydark, and in them disembodied brains were attached by wires in tanks of bubbling liquid, and they pulsed in time with the rhythm of their words.

Sid did none of this. He—and it was, in truth, hard to think of that thing as a him, as the voice that had spoken so warmly to her—sat inert in the middle of the tank, suspended in the thick, viscous gloop that was contained by a tank that was not the Plexiglas she would have expected, but something that resembled a living organism.

"You have nothing to fear," Sid said with an undertone of amusement. "As you must have guessed, I can only hurt you through the use of the complex's facilities. But I realize how strange, and perhaps frightening, I must look. Oh, I have eyes. Not in the sense that I used to, but

I have signals from all cameras fed to me. There is one in this room, as in all others. Myself and Hammill, we know what we have become."

"But how—"

"How did this happen? How can I still be alive? And yes, I do call this alive. I still know, think, feel. But I digress. To answer the second question, it would be difficult to explain to someone like yourself, who has only known the world after nuclear winter. If I tell you that scientists before that time had developed a genetically made material that is tough and allows me to 'breathe,' then would you understand that?"

She nodded.

"I communicate via the liquid in which I am suspended. Workers replace it to feed me the nutrients that enables my brain tissue not to decay. In this liquid are small circuits—what we called nanotech before the war—and these are intelligent and tiny. They fulfill the function of wires and cables." He chuckled. "I can see you are still unsure. Would it help if I said they were like mechanical insects that carry information to and from me, enabling me to operate the complex?"

Krysty sighed. "*Understand* isn't the word I'd use, but I can see how it works, at least. Whoever your original boss was had to have had serious jack, as this is up there with the best tech we've ever seen in old sec redoubts."

She could swear he was smiling as he answered. "It has been a long time since someone like yourself talked to me. You know that we have intel about you, know some of what you have experienced."

"The way Howard talked to us, to me, was kind of a giveaway."

"You are right in your assumptions in many ways. Howard comes from a family that wielded both great wealth and great power in the times before the holocaust. They were people who had contacts in every level of both the government and the military. He comes from a line that started with a namesake of his, a man who, in his time, had the kind of fame about which people in this new society can have no notion. He was feted—" Sid noted her growing incomprehension "—I'm sorry, it's easy to forget that this is the same language and yet not. I should say that in the days of global videos, everyone had seen and knew the name of this ancestor. The industry he established, the money and contacts he made, these were continued after his death.

"Many people knew what was coming with the holocaust. If you have ever seen any remains of preholocaust history in book or on video, then you may know this. For the ordinary people, it was a surprise, but for those with the kinds of contacts this family had, it was something that was common knowledge and accepted as an inevitability. So they had to plan.

"Their businesses supplied arms, technology and the service industries that, in turn, supplied other sectors of these industries. How can I explain in terms that you could easily grasp?"

"I'm not that stupe," Krysty replied wryly. "I can get the meaning of what you're saying, even if some of the details are—"

"No, you misunderstand me," Sid broke in, his tone

seeming incongruous as he was nothing more than a brain and stem floating in a tank of gloop. "I know you can grasp the essentials, but the extent of this family's influence in this place you now call the Deathlands, I don't know if… Let me put it this way—imagine the man you knew as the Trader. Imagine that his trading network extended the breadth of the land. Further, imagine that all other traders relied upon him, so that if people were not bartering and buying from him, then they were doing it from traders who then had to go to him, with a percentage of their jack going into his stockpile. Imagine this, and that not another soul except Trader, perhaps yourself, and your friends knew about it. A network that was all-encompassing and also mostly a secret."

He waited a second, pausing to see if Krysty grasped this. Finally she said, "That would make Howard's family one of—mebbe the—most powerful on earth, and also the most private. Right?"

"Yes, I think you have it," Sid affirmed. "Imagine that extent of power, and how you could use your contacts, those who owed you, and the technologies you had helped develop and have access to, to secure a future for your people."

"I don't have to imagine, do I? I'm standing in it."

Sid chuckled. "Correct. You know of the Totality Concept. Your friend Dr. Tanner was a victim of one of its divisions. Much of the knowledge behind the execution of that concept came from people controlled in one way or another by Howard's ancestors and their businesses. They were able to cherry-pick—ah, to choose the best parts, those that both worked best and served their purpose best—and then utilize them. They were also able to use the pressure of those contacts, what they knew, to keep this a secret."

"So where did you fit into this?"

"I was what you call a whitecoat. My speciality was guidance and security systems. The defense technology around this complex is my work. I warn you, Ms. Wroth, that if your friends come looking for you, as I am sure they will from my knowledge of them, they will find it impossible to get near here without being fried."

"Can't you turn the systems off, or at least alter them so that the attacks would not be direct, give them a chance to escape."

There was a pause. When he spoke again, Sid's voice had changed in tone. There was a weariness of someone who had been alive longer than they wished, and felt trapped by existence itself.

"Krysty, if I could do this, I would. There are many things I would do if it were possible. But although Hammill and myself retain some essential part of ourselves, so that we have at least a semblance of something you would call a life, we do not have control over that."

"Sid, is there anything I can do for you?"

The question remained unspoken, unfinished. But she knew that he divined her meaning.

"No, Krysty, I don't think that it is possible. I will try to help you if you want to escape, but it will not be easy. I would advise you not to, knowing the complex as I do, and also how powerless both myself and Hammill are, ultimately. But from what I know of you, I think that will not prevent you from trying. If only I had that courage when I was able."

"You've got courage. To continue as you are—"

"You know," he said hurriedly, cutting her off, "I never really knew Hammill until this happened to us. Why we were selected for this task, I don't know. I suspect that we were not only the right experts, but the right kind— we were both weak men, when we were men. And there were many workers down here in those days. But in the long, long years since this happened to us, I have got to know him better than anyone I ever knew when I was whole. I think I could say the same of him."

"Where is he?"

"In another room. We talked, and I said I would face you. He is more ashamed of this than I am. I was always able to escape facing the reality of a situation," he added wryly. "We have a pact. We are fed images from security cameras across the complex. These are always with us. But I do not look at him, and he does not look at me. We have those cameras blocked. We prefer to think of each other as we were."

Krysty felt an overwhelming sadness washing through her. There had to be something she could do to help them both. That was even assuming that she would be able to help herself.

Sid broke into her thoughts. "You should go. Howard has finished in the mechanic's bay. He will probably be looking for you. Go to your room, say you have been sleeping. I can loop footage if he wants to check records. There's not much I can do, but there is that. If you want to know more, I can also allow you access to the mainframe from the terminal in your room, removing some of the security codes. But this can only be done temporarily. Now go."

It was strange, but Krysty felt reluctant to leave the brain. It looked more alien than human, yet it was more human that Howard would ever be able to know. She wanted to stay—Sid needed her, had fed off her for a humanity that he had missed for so long—but she knew that he was right. At all costs, she had to keep Howard sweet until she had a plan of action.

She left without another word, returning to her room without pause. Her head was spinning with what Sid had told her. That people could do this to each other... The world she lived in was brutal and harsh, but no one had ever taken some poor bastard's brain and left it to an agonizing half-life, or put a man's brain into a machine. She had seen and heard of such things during their encounters with the remnants of the past, but had never been face-to-face with the consequences and realized what it truly meant.

As she lay on the bed, she looked at the room around her. The pastel colors, the predark feminine flounces, all seemed to be mocking her. They were the tainted remnants of a corrupt culture. Maybe skydark had been a good thing, if it had cleansed the world of people who did things like this. Then she thought of the people they had crossed. The only thing separating them from the likes of Howard and his ancestors was access to technology.

She lay back to wait for him, and to try to work out what she should do next.

HOWARD DISCARDED his coveralls and stepped into the shower. It was not something that had ever occurred to him before, but he knew as if by some kind of instinct that he had to look his best for his Storm Girl. Neat and groomed. That was the way the good guys always made an impression on the girl of their dreams.

Was that what she was? He hadn't considered it before. He had always seen them as partners in the fight for justice; first with her friends, and latterly on her own. But the girl of his dreams?

As he soaped himself in the shower, perhaps lingering too long over areas that he would previously have washed in a perfunctory manner, he considered why his feelings had changed in this way. In the old tales of those who had gone before, the fighter for justice had a girl to whom he could return at the end of the day. Whether she knew the truth of his whole identity, or just as the man in the mask, or even his cover without knowing his mission, she was always there. She was more than just a girl, more than just a love interest. She was also a representation of all those good things that the fighter for justice was searching for.

He frowned. For a moment, images and words from the intel reports he had gathered came into his mind. It was hard to reconcile those women of story and legend with the woman in the intel reports, but these were harder times, a different land. People had different standards. It was not her fault that she came from an age where there was less justice and goodness. She had proved herself to be worthy in her fights against evil. They all had.

Again the picture of the one-eyed man came to mind.

Fury built in Howard until he had to release it. He punched the tiled wall of the shower unit. Blood from his skinned knuckles trickled down the tiles, red on white, turning pink as the water from the shower jets diluted it, washed it away, just as his anger and frustration ebbed away with the pain he could feel in his hand. He looked at the knuckles of his fist, unclenched his hand and flexed his fingers. There was no pain except where the flesh had been exposed.

There was no pain except when he thought about Storm Girl and Cawdor together. Even the realization made the fury begin to rise within him again. It was a revelation to him just how strongly he felt about this. He had read of such things, but had assumed that in this world they would not happen to him.

And yet, it nagged at him. Why, then, had he chosen to take her out of all of them? Logically, now he stopped to think about it, he should have taken old man Tanner or Dr. Wyeth. They had knowledge of the world before, and they would be more likely to understand with greater ease. Yes, you could say that the old man was on the verge of madness. That was reason to leave him. But there was no reason that he could think of to choose Storm Girl over Dr. Wyeth.

Except for one.

He looked down at his naked body, water running over it, dripping off his flesh.

Yes.

There was a reason.

Chapter Nine

"There is one thing that occurs to me," Doc mused as the wag steadily ate up the miles. "Our friend the mystery man seems to have access to a lot of technology. So does it not follow that he will have good defenses around wherever he hangs his hat?"

"His what?" Jak frowned.

"His home," Mildred explained. "Don't worry about it," she continued as she saw his puzzled expression. "It's just a old saying from when I was young—though God knows where Doc picked it up," she added, raising a brow to the old man.

Doc smiled, his white, even perfect teeth looking sinister in the red glow of the wag's emergency lighting. "My dear Doctor, I may have been incarcerated during my time at the end of the world, but there were such things as televisions, radios, newspapers and books. My guards were not averse to my having those things."

"Will you stop talking shit?" Ryan barked. "Bad enough that we're still on the trail. I've been hoping that we'll run across the bastard when he's out on that blasted machine. I haven't been triple stupe, Doc, I have thought about what the hell he could have waiting for us wherever he's based."

"My dear Ryan, I was only voicing a question that I knew we had all formulated," Tanner rebuked mildly.

Ryan turned around so that he faced Doc, Jak and Mildred, seated behind the driving positions occupied by J.B. and himself.

"Shit, I know, Doc. Guess it's getting to all of us. Not knowing where we're going, what we'll find."

"Way I see it," J.B. said, without taking his eyes from the road ahead, "our real problem is that we won't know what this stupe has for us until we hit it, so we don't know what we're dealing with. And, more to the point, we don't know when we're going to hit it."

"Meaning?" Mildred asked.

"Think about it. This coldheart has to have a base. Chances are it's old military. Most of them are pretty well disguised."

"Most of the redoubts we've ever known didn't have exterior offensive weapons, though," she pointed out.

"You saw the bike he had. You ever seen anything that looked like that where we've been? I know I sure as hell would remember it. So mebbe this base isn't like any of the others we've ever come across."

"And so perhaps we should be expecting the unexpected," she finished. "Guess it's a fair point, John."

"Don't know about that, but it might just stop us buying the farm before we're ready," he replied in a dry tone.

They had been driving for hours that seemed like days. Even with the air-conditioning, there was still a lingering undertone of stink that each of them was trying hard to ignore. The fact that they were also tight in the space, under the red glow of the emergency lighting, was also beginning to tell. The air-conditioning was good enough to stop them sweating from the heat, but the incipient claustrophobia was another matter. The cabin was not made for five people, and in the well behind the seats for the intended two-man crew they had been forced to find positions where they could sit or squat with, if not comfort, then with a relative ease.

At least it wasn't dark. J.B. had not been able to fix the wag's lighting system, but he had discovered that the crazies who were the previous occupants had been unaware of the emergency electrics powered off the engine, which was just as well, as they would probably have driven these to destruction, as they had much else. As it was, J.B. discovered on checking that the system was intact, and so they at least had some light in the interior.

For some time they had driven across the wasteland in silence. Each person had been grimly aware that, although they now had the means to make good time and distance, they had lost so much. So, despite the speed at which the wag could now take them, each of them was silently urging it to go faster, and feeling frustrated that it was not.

The feeling of helplessness was not doing much to abate the rage that each of them felt, and the growing frustration at not gaining ground.

SHE WAS IN HER ROOM when she heard it, a two-tone siren, distant from the living quarters, coming from another level. She had been accessing the historical files on the mainframe, trying to piece together the chronology of this place, to get an angle on understanding Howard so that she knew how to deal with him. As soon as the siren began to sound, the comp closed down the terminal.

"Sid?"

"An emergency. Breach of security sensors on the far eastern reach of the defense ring."

"What are you going to do?"

"There is nothing I can do. Howard is in the shower and is making his way to the main console room. When he arrives, I shall not be able to converse with you. He will have complete control of both myself and Hammill, and we will not be responsible for the course of action."

"What do you mean?"

"You asked me why I had not tried to end this. The simple answer is that I cannot. Once myself and Hammill were…changed…we became to a great extent part of the computer mainframe. We have no override powers. In effect, we are slaves. The mainframe is geared to answer only to someone with the genetic imprint of the original owners. Only Howard can actuate certain procedures. And if he does, the mainframe programming does not allow any other intelligence to interfere."

"So if the incoming were to be friendly to me, you would not be able to prevent yourself from firing on them, even if you did not wish to?"

"No, Krysty. Neither myself nor Hammill would be able to prevent ourselves from instigating such actions. I'm sorry."

"It's not your fault. You're a prisoner here much more than I am. At least I could set myself free by buying the farm. You can't even do that."

"I would not recommend such a course of action. I confess, Krysty, that we may be using you as much as Howard would wish to. You could set us free, if you could find the key."

"You mean if I can find a way to destroy this place, then you would be willing to buy the farm?"

"Ah, I still have enough humor and humanity left in me to cherish those strange phrases… But yes, we would both be prepared to end these lives that are not, if we could be at peace. And I have a suggestion for you. I have been monitoring the files you have been studying, and I think I see your reasoning. In which case, may I recommend that you skip forward to the file I will make available to you."

"My terminal has shut down, Sid, I can't—"

"Don't concern yourself with that. It's nothing more than a standard procedure when the perimeter is breached. Until Howard comes and inputs his code, the system is in stasis. As soon as he does this, I will send the file to you. He will not know that you have this on your terminal, and he will be too occupied to care about your movements. This is the first alarm that has been anything other than a test procedure. Please, try not to think about your friends. We will do all we can within our limits, but mostly I feel you can trust Howard's lack of experience. Meantime, study the file when it arrives. I'm sure it will hold the key to all our freedom."

HOWARD'S TRAIN OF THOUGHT was interrupted by the clarion call of the siren. An invasion: something, or somebody, was attempting to breach the defenses on the outer perimeter. This had not happened before. The drills had been regular, and the procedures were as rote to him. And yet he was unsure for a moment, frozen in the excited expectation of action. It was a delicious feeling, part ripple of fear, part surge of adrenaline, that coursed through his body. It was this surge that galvanized him.

"Water off," he barked as he strode from the shower, his anger of moments ago, and the pain in his knuckles caused by that anger, now forgotten. He grabbed a towel and dried himself quickly, dressing in the Rider costume he kept in the lockers. All the while, his mind was racing. Who was the intruder?

It had to be Krysty Wroth's companions. They did not realize that she was no longer their Krysty, but about to become Storm Girl, companion to Thunder Rider. They had come to—as they saw it—rescue her, which was a noble act, and not without merit. It showed their honor and loyalty. And for this, at least, he could not bring himself to simply eliminate them. Whether he would wish for them to join him and Storm Girl in his mission, he could not, at this moment, say.

One thing for sure, he would not wish Krysty to turn against him because of his actions. He had to be very careful about what he did. He wanted to keep them at bay for now, but the defenses were geared toward the annihilation of any who should attempt to breach them.

"Hammill, status report," he commanded as he strode down the corridor toward the command complex.

"Armored vehicle thirty-three degrees east, passing vector seven of the ring. It would appear to be a military vehicle of the preholocaust era. Condition poor. Scanning reveals a low radiation level indicating that it carries no warheads, and that it is run from conventional plant. Scanning for life and ordnance… Readings are not clear. Four, maybe five people within, and nothing that registers on any data base as coincident with conventional ordnance for such vehicles. It has been refitted, but probably at a lower level. It represents no discernible threat and can be eradicated by a level-one strike."

"Do not instigate at this moment. If necessary, cover fire to drive it back, but do not aim for the vehicle. I don't want it damaged, or the inhabitants harmed at this stage. I want to have a look at it, so I need it contained."

"Very good, Howard."

"Thank you, Hammill."

"Sid?"

"Yes, Howard?"

"Ms. Wroth—where is she?"

"She is currently in her quarters, Howard."

"Does she know what the alarm means?"

"She asked me, and I informed her of its purpose. I did not, however, inform her of the possible identity of the vehicle making the breach. Rather, I implied that it was a routine drill by reference to past events."

"Good. I would like you to keep her in her quarters for the moment. If necessary, lock the door and tell her that it's part of standard security procedure during such a drill. I don't want her to know what's happening until I've worked out what exactly I'm going to do."

"Very good, Howard."

By this time, Howard had reached the command complex. A long desk set with terminals and monitors took up one side of the room. Screens relaying images from all cameras in sequence flashed in front of him, covering one wall. A chair on a sliding track enabled him to move with ease from one end of the desk to the other. He slid into the chair and automatically set the chair in motion until it had arrived at the section of desk he required. An inset panel, oval and with an indent shaped like a thumb, was in front of him. He put his right thumb in, felt a slight tingle as it scored a small piece of top skin layer for analysis.

"DNA check. Authorization approved."

The automatic lock on the control complex, which came into operation every time the alarm sounded, was now off. He—as the last of his line and the only man with the correct genetic code—was now in sole charge of all systems.

"Status report, Hammill."

"The vehicle is another mile farther in. Range on missiles and lasers locked and approved. Mines armed and on link response."

Link response. If the wheels of the vehicle passed over one and triggered it, then any four in a surrounding arc would also be automatically triggered. It enabled a vehicle to be destroyed rather than merely disabled.

"Disarm link response."

"Disarmed, Howard."

"How far are they from the edge of the minefields?"

"Five hundred yards, Howard."

Only a few seconds for him to consider and act. He did not want them to be injured. Not yet. However, he did wish to keep them at a safe distance. Perhaps...

"Trigger eight mines in a random pattern around their projected path. Let's give them fair warning."

"DARK NIGHT! What the fuck—" J.B. yelled, and felt the pull on his arms as the steering of the vehicle bucked and wheeled in his grasp. It felt like an immense force, but it was hard for him to tell as, in truth, he was more concerned about the fact that his vision had been impaired by the sudden rain of sand and dirt flung up by the deafening explosions that had erupted just in front of the wag.

Explosions: more than one, but how many none of them could tell, as they were so close together as to sound almost as one continuous blast. One moment they had been traveling at a constant speed across what seemed like empty waste; the next, the sun had been blotted out by the mountains of dark debris flung up by the explosions. Ripples of impact under the ground had made the unstable topsoil buck and weave beneath the wheels and tracks of the wag, giving it precarious purchase, throwing the front and rear in wildly diverging directions.

Within, the shock to the vehicle had made the emergency lighting black out for a few seconds before the circuit kicked back to life, and in the darkness they had all been thrown around the tiny cabin by the violent impact. J.B. and Ryan, the only ones on secured seating, had just about managed to stay in enough of a position to keep control. Doc was dazed, as his head struck metal, and Mildred and Jak careered into each other with a bone-crunching impact lessened only by the confined space.

Inside the hollow metal shell, the sound from outside as it struck the metal walls caused reverberations that made teeth rattle, that made skulls pound. It was hard for any of them to concentrate, to focus on what was happening.

Part of J.B. wrestled with the wag, tendons and sinews standing out in stark relief on his arms and shoulders, the force of the wag's skidding trajectory almost wrenching his arms from their sockets. A section of his mind coolly assessed what was happening.

If they had found the edge of the redoubt where the mystery rider was based, then it had shit-hot defenses, and was going to be a bastard to crack. What they had on their side was the probability that the rider did not want to chill them. Otherwise, why issue a warning and not finish them off? His mines had been so well disguised that J.B. would have driven them to their doom without even realizing what he was doing.

Something the rider had said to them while they had been paralyzed came back to him—the coldheart crazie wanted to enlist their help in his mission. Of course he didn't want them to buy the farm. Part of taking Krysty had been to help persuade them.

J.B. was damned if he could understand the reasoning, but he was willing to go along with it if it gave them the edge.

The torque on the vehicle became easier to handle, the pressure on his aching shoulders began to decrease and the reverberations within the vehicle lessened. His ears were still ringing, but the pain was less. His vision wasn't blurred by the pressure and the movement. His teeth didn't feel like they were being shaken from his jawbone. The whine of the engine under pressure became the predominant sound as everything outside returned to quiet. He was aware that he had the wag in the wrong gear, and that he had run into a sandbank thrown up by the upheaval of the explosions. The front wheels of the wag were deep into the pile, and were running without purchase. But at least he could now see calm sky over the top of the piled sand.

He killed the engine. It was a risk that it would not start again, but one worth taking rather than burn it out.

In the sudden silence, no one moved for a second.

"You thinking what I'm thinking?" the Armorer asked Ryan.

The one-eyed man fixed him with a stare. "Warning rather than attack? Keep us at bay but still alive? Mebbe make us wait, then make contact and bargain? Yeah, I'd guess that. Also guess that we found the bastard's redoubt."

Ryan turned to take a look at the others. Jak was nursing a cut on his temple from the collision with Mildred, a crimson streak visible on the pale white skin, matting the lank strands of hair that fell over his face. His red eyes were unfocused, but he still managed a grin.

"Need better driver," he said shakily.

Mildred was bent over Doc, who was moaning softly. In the red light, J.B. could see that the skin on her cheekbone had been broken in the collision with Jak, but she had been luckier. It was a part of the skull less likely to lead to a concussion. Instead of worrying about herself, she was tending to Doc.

Ryan moved from his seat and crouched beside her. There was no blood, no cut that was visible, but a contusion was already spreading darkly from under his ear down to the point of his chin.

"What happened?" the one-eyed man asked.

"Not too sure, I was kind of occupied myself, trying to stay upright," she answered wryly. "But from the look of it, I'd say that the old buzzard fell onto that edge—" she tapped the metal surface above him "—and got himself just at the hinge of the jaw. Looks like it was a hell of a blow, and he might be a bit concussed, but there doesn't feel like any major damage."

Doc's eyes fluttered open, staring blankly. He muttered, "Major Damage? Sure, did I not serve under him at Gettysburg? Always so accident prone…"

"Must be okay, talking shit like usual," Jak said.

Ryan looked around at him. "You want to watch for concussion yourself."

Jak shook his head, looked like he instantly regretted it. "Just get Mildred dress it."

Ryan rose to his feet and turned to look at J.B. "Figure it's safe we take a recce?"

The Armorer grimaced, massaging one bruised shoulder while feeling the pull on the other. "If we're careful."

"Never anything else," Ryan said, shrugging.

J.B. frowned in thought. "No follow-up blasts of any kind. No incoming. Wherever they are, doesn't seem like they want to finish us off…not yet, anyway. Can't do any harm to see if we can get some kind of location for them."

Ryan nodded, looking at the others. "You stay here, Mildred. Look out for Doc and Jak. I don't want them moving until they're right. Same goes for you."

"You got it. Hell, always thought you and John should be first in the firing line." She grinned.

The two men left them, climbing up the turret ladder

of the wag, Ryan in front, opening the hatch and tentatively looking out.

He was greeted with a vista of perfect calm. The only sign of the recent violence came from the small splashes of sand that had landed in a fan pattern from the blast, and the craters left by the mines. Now that the dust and smoke had settled, even these looked as though they had been there for an indefinite amount of time. It was a tableau that may have existed since the days of the nuke-caust, untouched, and just stumbled upon.

Ryan climbed out and slid down the side of the wag, making sure that he took cover in the hollow formed by the body of the vehicle and the bank of sand into which it had plowed. He moved over to allow J.B. the room to slide down at his side.

"Shit, it doesn't give us much to go on, does it," the Armorer said softly.

Ryan stretched out an arm to indicate the sweep of the craters. "Look at that arc," he murmured. "We must have been driving right into that, heading that direction. They've been set off to send us back this way."

"Worked, then, hasn't it?" J.B. commented dryly.

Ryan's mouth quirked. "Yeah. But the question is, why?"

"Because the redoubt lies in a straight line from our course at an indeterminate distance," J.B. mused.

"I'll go with that," Ryan agreed. "Question, again, is, how far?"

"Look at it," J.B. commented, screwing up his eyes against the horizon. "Flat. Unless it's a concealed tunnel entrance, and even then…"

"Yeah. It ain't anywhere we can get to in a hurry. If they knew we were coming they have much better recon than we have. Probably know we're standing here talking about them."

"It's a big place—the area they cover," J.B. said. "You see those old fence posts rotting away about half a mile back?"

"Yeah. If that was a boundary to this place, and the defenses don't even start until here, then we've got some serious opposition."

"So what we're saying is that they can see us, we can't see them, that they have a massive area around their redoubt that is well protected, and that if we take so much as one step they can fuck us up before we even have a chance to know it?"

"That's about it, as far as I can see," Ryan stated. "How wide and deep is that minefield, for instance?"

"So what the fuck do we do about this?" J.B. questioned.

Ryan thought for a moment. "Nothing. Not yet. Doc, Mildred and Jak aren't exactly combat ready right now. Give them some time to stop seeing double, mebbe puke a little. We've got no choice but to wait."

J.B. frowned. "Think that'll work?"

Ryan grinned. "Hell, yeah. If we just sit here, it's gonna drive the coldheart bastards mad. They'll have to come and get us eventually. Right now, there's no opening for us. Mebbe they'll fuck up and give us one. It's all we've got, right?"

J.B. shrugged. "I'll be a stickie rolled in honey if I can think of anything else."

Ryan nodded. Yet, even as he did so, there was something nagging at the back of his brain. There was another option, but he was damned if he could bring it to mind right now.

"STATUS REPORT, Hammill," Howard demanded.

"Systems primed, on red alert. The objective has not moved for the last thirty-one minutes. The two men designated Cawdor and Dix have remained in station. The other occupants of the vehicle—sensors have a ninety percent probability of three—are also stationary. Nothing's happening, Howard. Analysis suggests that they are waiting for you to make the next move."

"I would if I was them, I guess," Howard said softly. "What on earth could they do, right now? They're not stupid. They wouldn't have got this far and been through what they have unless they were smart, so they're waiting for me to make the next move."

"Which is, Howard?"

The young man sighed. "I don't know, Hammill. I haven't decided as yet. Two can play the waiting game."

"But for how long?"

Howard smiled. "That's the sixty-four-thousand-dollar question, Hammill. Or it would be if there was still such a thing as U.S. currency."

He slid his chair along the track, checking the monitor screens in front and above his head. Krysty was in her quarters and seemed unconcerned by what was happening. In truth, she seemed absorbed in what she was watching on the terminal in front of her.

"Sid? What is Krysty doing?"

"She has one of the old videos online, Howard," Sid's smooth tones replied.

"She seems very interested in it," he commented. "Have we got audio as well as visual?" he continued, frowning as he tried to bring up the sound on her monitor, and was met with a fuzzy blur of white noise.

"There seems to be a minor malfunction," Sid answered. "Perhaps it has not been noticed before as the room has not been in use for some time, and resultantly the equipment has not been called into use."

"Hmm… Get a worker in there to effect repairs next time the room is vacant," Howard commanded.

"It has already been logged, and will be realized at the earliest opportunity," Sid replied.

Howard sat back. If she was that absorbed in an old video, then so much the better. She would not notice what was going on, and she would be immersing herself that much more in the culture of Thunder Rider, becoming Storm Girl.

IT WAS TRUE to say that Krysty was absorbed in an old video, but Sid had not revealed the whole of the truth to Howard. He could not lie. Part of the computer programming that had become melded with his identity over the past century had made this an impossibility. But Sid and Hammill still retained enough of their humanity, despite the gross physical distortions they had become, to be able to think outside of the box, to defy the logical paradigms of the machine. They were able to exchange ideas and thoughts and, at the same time, to bypass the memory of the mainframe that would record those exchanges and make it possible for Howard to stumble upon them if he should ever suspect.

They knew that they could "lie" to Howard when necessary not by telling mistruths, but by an assiduous pruning of the truth: by omission. If they did not tell Howard the whole truth, if they were selective about what they said, chose their words with infinite care, then it would enable them to only let him know that which they wanted him to know.

Of course, for the vast majority of the time, while he was alone in his bunker, this was not necessary. But they had both known that such a time would come. They had been ready for it, and had been prepared to test their theory to the limit, whichever of them had been called to task.

It just so happened that it was Sid. For instance, the question of the lack of sound on the monitor from Krysty's quarters. Sid had not lied to Howard when he told him that there seemed to be a minor malfunction. He knew this to be the absolute truth. He knew that for one simple reason: he had sent a worker in there earlier to cause this malfunction. But as Howard had not asked him that, and he had chosen his words with care, he had not lied. Sid and Hammill knew that they were trapped. They were in a half-life, in thrall to the man who was now the last of his line. After him, as things now stood, there would be nothing. They would be left to their half-life existence in the twilight world of the empty bunker forever...or at least for the thousands of years it would take for the nuclear-powered facility to finally die. Even if they were to be invaded by outsiders, they would be inactive as none would hold the genetic key to open up the system. But at least in such an instance they could hope for a frustration-fueled destruction to take away their torment.

But now they had another way. Sid had genuinely taken a liking to Krysty Wroth. She had divined the sadness and dilemma that lay at the root of the surviving souls of both Hammill and himself. She did not blame them. She also realized that Howard was not responsible for who he was, while at the same time realizing the threat he could represent.

Sid felt sure that she could be their salvation. She could end their suffering and eliminate the threat that Howard could represent to the outside world. From their intelligence, they knew that it was a far from perfect world. But Howard was not sane. He had access to weapons that could cause far more harm than good.

That was why Sid had downloaded the file now playing on Krysty's terminal. It was an old video, as he had told Howard. It was not one of Thunder Rider's favorites, as he had assumed.

It was the last sane testament of the intellects that had built this place before it had become a travesty.

KRYSTY HAD BEEN WATCHING the vid play out for she knew not how long. She had almost forgotten that something in the outside world was happening that had caused Howard to want her isolation. She did not know how much time had passed, she only knew that she was transfixed by the woman on the screen in front of her. She had a slight figure, her thin limbs and painfully twisted torso belying the porcelain-perfect features and the cultured, fluting voice. She sat uncomfortably on a chair in this very room, at some time in the recent past, speaking directly into a camera as though she were speaking directly to Krysty—though, of course, she could have been speaking to anyone who viewed this, even her own… what was he? Brother, son of her sister?

The woman had chosen her last few days alive to record, in a series of sessions, her personal history, that of her family and her concerns for the sole survivor she was soon to leave behind. And to do it in a manner that left Krysty in no doubt as to what she had to do.

The woman began by revealing that her name was Jenny, and that she and Howard were the last ones left alive of what had once been one of the most prosperous, powerful and influential families of predark times. This much Krysty knew from what Sid had told her. But what she hadn't realized was the extent of that influence.

"OUR FAMILY HAS MANY antecedents with what are these days disparagingly known as WASPs. 'These days.' In truth, I feel sure that the savages above the surface no longer have any idea that a wasp was an insect, let alone that it means White Anglo-Saxon Protestant. Nor what that means. Lord, it becomes hard to rid oneself of such assumptions, and to seek to explain for any who may see this. Even if you are what I have just termed a savage. Perhaps you are not, but you see, to myself and to Howard, trapped down here since long before our own birth by fate and accidents of that very birth, that is what you are. Different standards, ways of viewing the world. That is what… No, I must do this in the right order.

"As you can see, I am soon to die. I know this, and in

truth I am afraid of it only in one way. Not for myself, but for the poor boy I'll leave behind. Whatever he has done to lead you to this recording, it is not his fault. He cannot be held responsible for the actions of many previous generations.

"Our family had a lot of power in the old world. It's hard to explain to those of you who have no reference. Some records have survived, so perhaps you will know. Howard is named after one of our family who had no children acknowledged in his lifetime. However, genetics are strong, and this man who was a pioneer of air travel and weaponry, and owned studios that were dream factories, left a strong imprint on all of us. The family was good at making money, and was good with technology. In times when war is rife, these are good gifts. And, as I'm sure you have found in the outside world, even though there is not so much in the way of money and of technology, war is always rife.

"Money and technology make contacts. Our family was thus aware of what was about to happen long before it was actualized. Our companies, and those that were at least in part owned or who relied upon the contracts supplied by our companies for their own existence, were pressed to action. Much of our work was sanctioned by governments, utilizing technologies that were developed by their military arms. This made our own defense and safety simple. In the longer run, because we were able to call upon that expertise in order to build this underground complex in which you now sit. In the short term, because we were able to quell any opposition by using the power and influence we held. And where that did not work, well, it is probably nothing to be proud of, but man is a venal beast. Bribery and blackmail have been tools throughout history, and I suppose it is no different on the surface now.

"The family owned a vast amount of land in this state—or should I say, what used to be this state—and we had many of the elected officials who owed their very election to our power and patronage. So it was easy to avoid too many questions as this place was excavated and built. Many of them probably thought this was a government project, anyway, and so were afraid that too many questions would lead to them being taken away in the night, never to be seen again.

"So this place was built. One of us, in a spirit of fun, named it Murania. That was an underworld kingdom in an old film. We have it on video. Howard loves it dearly, and if that fool ancestor had known what he had set in motion, he would have been ashamed to have chosen such a name… No, perhaps not, shame is not something that has ever come easily to us, if I choose to be honest. So we were named after a joke. A prophetic one, as in the film the kingdom is destroyed by its own hubris. Much as we have been.

"We had family and servants. To ensure the maximum use from them they were dehumanized into the worker robots you may see, and Sid and Hammill, the living elements of the computer. They know how I feel about this. It is something that has tainted my life, that I can see the awful existence they have to endure because of the arrogance of my ancestors.

"But, having said that, has the fate of those of us who have followed them been any better? They were not stupid people, but they did not believe in diluting the family. The consequence of this, of course, has been shown over the last century. Children were born as lust ran riot. There was, after all, little to do in the long night of the nuclear winter. There were plenty of diversions, but nothing can replace the need to be outside of this box. And so the children begat children. Inbreeding…I know from intelligence reports that filter in via our systems that this is a problem for isolated communities. We were just as isolated, albeit in greater luxury.

"The children had things…wrong. They were deformed, prone to illness, mad. Miscarriage became more common as the combinations of family members became more labyrinthine, our DNA more entwined. Or do I mean our genetics? I suppose it doesn't matter if I have that correct. It's the results that matter.

"And the result was that life cycles became truncated. Gradually, deformities and illness claimed us before old age. As you can see, I have many things physically wrong. I count it as nothing short of a miracle that I have made it this far. I have, thankfully, not been blessed with issue, as they used to say. But my sister was—she was impregnated by our father, shortly before he died. Howard is the result.

"And this is what you must know. Howard is the first of us to look physically perfect for some time. And he is. For in him the taint is not visible. But it is there. He is, in many ways, a sweet and innocent boy. He watches the old videos, reads the old stories, and he is immersed in a world that takes him away from the sterility of our reality. But that is what I fear.

"When I am gone, there will be none to temper him. He has no notion of reality and fantasy. He believes only what his own insane logic will lead him to believe is the truth, no matter how much he has to bend what is before him. He has no idea what the world is really like out there. You do. You must, as to see this you would have had to… I'm sorry, I'm beginning to ramble. My illness is growing worse. My body is as twisted inside as it is on the outside. Every breath has always been a battle, and now it grows more and more a battle that I cannot win.

"But Howard… Since he was a small boy, and so strong and virile, I have always counseled that he should not be allowed outside. There was talk between my sister and father that he should go, as he was strong, and the surface is now relatively safe. They may have been insane and inbred, as possibly am I, but they were lucid enough to realize that I could not conceive, and any hope for the future line lay in Howard going beyond and of necessity tainting the bloodline. I wonder, am I the mad one in this setting that I saw the possibility of my mating with him as repulsive? If the insane becomes the norm, then do the sane become the mad?

"It doesn't matter, really, does it? I win as I was left standing as they died. Howard has been allowed out of the underground as he grew. There was nothing I could do to stop him. After all, he is big and strong and I am…not. But I was careful to limit him, to set boundaries that he stuck to because he loves me, and wants to make me happy. There were excuses about why he must not go far. He was happy to believe them, as he was content to believe me. He has never been beyond the boundaries of the old ranch, always limited himself to the old marking posts.

"But I will soon be dead. I know this. I can feel it creeping upon me, and in truth I do not fear it. For myself, I will welcome relief from the endless struggle of staying alive. But I fear my death for Howard. He will have no one except Sid and Hammill, and they can do nothing but obey him. I know that there is technology down here that would have been formidable in the old world. In the world as it is now, it could do untold damage to whatever rebuilding is taking place.

"Howard believes implicitly in the old stories as though they were truth, as though human behavior were that simple. To him, it is. When I am gone, there will be no hand to stay him. I fear for him. He will, eventually, do terrible things. He will not mean them to be. But it is in his nature to see the world in such a simplistic manner. And the madness…I fear that the taint will lead him into awful acts. His temper is strong, and emotionally he is still a small child.

"It pains me to say this, for I love him, but without a steadying hand, I fear for what he will do. Only he has the power to actuate the destruction of this place. It's all genetics, you see. That and the randomness of numbers. Only he can destroy, but the threat can be stayed. I fear that he must be stopped, even at the expense of his life."

THE VID RAMBLED ON for a while longer. Jenny was obviously in great pain, and very near to buying the farm when she recorded her statement, but there had been enough moments of clarity for Krysty to see that the woman was saner than the young man she had left behind. And the points she had made only reinforced what Krysty had been told by Sid, and what she had concluded for herself.

The problem she faced was no easy one, though. The entire complex was geared toward Howard, as he was the only one of his genetic line left. How could she effect the destruction of the complex and her escape when nothing would respond, except to him?

She hit a key, the screen went blank.

"Sid? Am I still locked in?"

"I'm afraid so, Krysty," he replied in his sibilant tones. There was a longing in his voice.

"I know, I know," she murmured.

And what was going on aboveground that had precipitated this?

NIGHT WAS FALLING FAST. Jak was now squatting on the back of the wag, still and silent, eyes scanning the horizon. Like Mildred and Doc, he had recovered from the mild concussions of earlier, and the only sign of his injury was the dressing that covered the cut on his temple.

Ryan and J.B. were still standing by the side of the wag, as though they hadn't moved for hours. The chill wind of a desert night began to flick tendrils of cold air around them.

In the wag, Mildred and Doc were preparing a meal, the old man experimentally clicking his bruised jaw every now and then to see if it would still move. The noise was irritating the hell out of Mildred, who kept giving him vicious glares to which he was oblivious.

"How long wait?" Jak said eventually. Ryan could have sworn that not even his lips moved, he was so immobile.

"As long as we have to. Force the bastard's hand," the one-eyed man said softly.

J.B. looked sideways at him. He could tell from the mildness of tone how much his old friend was keeping his temper reined in. He knew that Ryan's temper could only hold for so long.

Longer than Jak's.

"Nothing soon, make recce alone. See what draw out."

Ryan shook his head. "We can't risk it."

Jak sighed. Still, seemingly, without moving a muscle. "Can't go like this. Chill slowly."

"I know," Ryan answered in a whisper. "But what the fuck else can we do?"

J.B. frowned. "It could… We're in the right area, I guess."

Ryan looked at him sharply. "For what?"

J.B. shrugged. "If you've still got that locket Krysty gave you…"

Fireblast! Ryan could feel it burning a hole in his pocket. That was what had been nagging him. His anger and grief at losing Krysty had clouded his reason, made his thinking blurred. Not for the first time, he thanked whatever fates there may be that he had J. B. Dix as his friend.

The locket just might be the edge he was looking for.

Chapter Ten

"Sid," she said softly, "can you hear me?"

"Yes, Krysty, I can divide my attention between posts and talk with many voices."

"Nice trick. Sid, how are my friends?"

"The armored vehicle they were using is outside the minefield. They are safe. They are, however, still within range of our missile strike. But I suspect Howard does not wish to harm them. At least, not yet. I still have enough of my humanity left to be able to assess his mood. His is loath to dismiss his original plan to incorporate them into his mission, using you to persuade them, assuming, as he has, that he has your approval."

"He does?"

"He thinks this."

"Guess he sees what he wants to, right?"

"I think it would be fair to say that he has a view of the world that is self-focused to an almost unnatural degree."

Krysty allowed herself a smile. The man-machine's careful phrasing amused her.

"The guy's fucking nuts, Sid. Not his fault, but he is."

"Blunt, but fair," Sid replied with a dry chuckle in his tone. "But as I'm sure you're aware, this makes him volatile. Currently, he is waiting for them to make the next move. He has no experience of tactics outside the formulaic fictions of the past that he sees as history. His patience is wearing thin, but his indecisiveness is their safety for a short while longer, at least."

"Okay, then I need to get the hell out of here and be with him. If I'm there, I can influence or distract him, right?"

"Certainly one or the other. There is the slight problem of my programming. Because of this, I am compelled to secure the door should you attempt to leave. There is, unfortunately, nothing I can do about this. Any personal wishes I may have are overridden by the mainframe."

"Sid, I need to get out of here," she said earnestly.

"I know." He paused. "I have an idea. Please try to be patient for a few moments."

She could try, but as she sat on the edge of her seat, muscles tensed and bunched, she knew that she was on to a losing prospect.

She could break the door if she called on Gaia power, but to what end? Brute force would only get her so far. Besides which, after the experience when the power became trapped in her, she was scared that calling on it so soon could cause lasting damage. She had never been scared of the gift before, but it would—she knew—take her a while to regain her confidence.

No. This would have to be done with thought, not muscle.

She hoped Sid would be successful. And soon.

HOWARD SAT in front of the console, pondering his next move. It seemed to him that he was in a stalemate with Cawdor and his crew.

It was a relief when Sid's voice came to him.

"Howard, if I might intrude for a moment?"

"Glad of the distraction, Sid. This waiting is getting to me, old friend. What do you want?"

"I want to talk to you about Storm Girl."

Howard's brow creased. He couldn't remember using that name out loud. How did Sid know? Perhaps he had.

"Does she know that I think of her as that?"

"No, she does not, Howard. Perhaps it is time you told her. I can only make suggestions, but it seems to me that she is ready for the next stage of your plan. I have been monitoring what she has been viewing from the archives, and she is immersing herself in the history that you value so highly. I think she would be open to your suggestions. I would add that she has not, so far, attempted to leave her room. But if she does, and finds that I have had to secure as per your earlier directive, it may not create the impression that you wish her to have."

Howard pondered that for a moment. If his trusted friend was correct, he ran the risk of alienating Storm Girl before anything had been settled, and this was the last thing that he would wish. To have her by his side would steady his hand at this crucial time.

"Very well, Sid. Countermand the order to secure her door. She may come and go as she pleases…in fact, tell her that I request the pleasure of her presence here."

"Very good, Howard. I think you have made a wise choice, if I may say."

"Thank you, Sid."

Yes, Howard thought, keeping his smile to himself, this may be the best choice he had made in his life.

"KRYSTY."

"Yes, Sid?"

"The door is no longer secured. You are free to move at will. Furthermore, Howard requests your presence in the command complex."

She shook her head. "How did you manage that?"

"You must remember, I have been a servant to the family since the nuclear winter. I have seen them all be born, grow and die. They are from the same stock, they have the same habits and attitudes as one another, in varying degrees. Howard may be unstable and prone to insanity, but he is still one of them."

"Then why can't you persuade him somehow to put you and Hammill—"

"Out of our misery? Krysty, Howard may be unstable, but isn't quite as—ah—fucking nuts as all that."

Krysty laughed, then got to her feet. "Lead the way, Sid."

"Very well. One thing—do not show surprise at anything he may say to you."

"Care to fill me in?" she asked as she left her room and followed the trail Sid laid for her by the simple expedient of dimming the lights except for those leading in the direction she should walk.

"I think it better if your reactions are genuine. I just fear that shock or surprise may be more than he can bear right now."

"Great." It wasn't exactly what she wanted to hear— be genuine, but not shocked, which, seeing as Sid was warning her, was almost an inevitability.

She walked down the corridor and up a staircase that

took her to another level. Paintings of the family lined the walls, and she could see the physical resemblance to Howard and Jenny in all of them. As she drew near a room from which she could hear Hammill's voice, interspersed with that of Howard, she paused to consider. With a gene pool that small, it was no wonder that whatever good Howard had intended had been perverted and corrupted by the insanity of inbreeding.

She took a deep breath and entered the command complex, immediately struck dumb by the amount of comp equipment contained within the room. She doubted that she had ever seen so much in one place that was actually all in working order.

Her eyes were drawn to the screens that showed the perimeter of the ranch land. Even though darkness had descended, the cameras had switched to infrared, and she could see Ryan and J.B. conversing at the side of the wag. Jak was still seated on the body of the vehicle, as immobile as she knew he had to have been for hours. Doc and Mildred were on the other side, near a small fire that they were using to cook. There was an almost unnatural air of calm about the scene, despite the circumstances.

She felt a pang deep within her chest, a need to be with them, a need to get back to them.

A need to stop this crazy bastard wiping them out, no matter what it might cost her.

"Hi, Krysty," Howard said, with a smile that still didn't reach those dead eyes, but seemed from the tone of his voice to be genuine. He held out his hand to her, palm upward. It was half imprecation to take his hand, half a beckoning. She chose to return it with a smile, moving into the complex and using her hand to indicate the screens, hoping that he would take this as interest and not as a rebuff. Above all else, she wanted to avoid making his temper flare.

"This is impressive. What does it do?"

Her guess was correct. Like all small boys at heart, Howard was obsessed by his toys. Krysty and Mildred had often swapped the opinion that J.B.'s ordnance obsession was similarly fueled. The important factor in the postnuclear society being that such young boy obsessions were now the difference between living and buying the farm. No matter, not when she saw the way Howard's face lit up with a kind of joy, both at the chance to show off his knowledge and at the same time share it.

"This is the nerve center of Murania. From here I can control all of the complex—with the able assistance of Sid and Hammill, of course—and also keep an eye on what is happening in the outside world. The area around the old ranch is full of security devices, both defensive and offensive. We have missiles for air attack, which of course is unlikely as there are no planes that I know of these days, and also mines and gun emplacements that are remotely controlled for ground attack."

"And who are those people?" she asked, trying to keep the tremble of anger from her voice.

Howard gave her an indulgent grin. "I think you know who they are. I'm sure you can't have forgotten them already."

She wanted to wipe that smug grin from his face by breaking his jaw in two. But she needed him to be conscious and able to act. She needed to use her guile to control him. So, instead, she gritted her teeth and said, "Let me see…" She pretended to study the screens intently, peering as though shortsighted. In truth, she was using her peripheral vision to take in the layout of the console that ran the length of the room, memorizing as much as she could where switches, faders, keypads and mouse remotes were positioned. True, she had no idea what most of them were for. Nonetheless, if she knew where these things were now, it would be easy to remember the positions of any Howard may use in her presence.

Eventually she said, "It's Ryan and my friends who you took me away from." She turned to him, putting on a look that she hoped to Gaia was ingenuous. "Why did you do that, Howard?"

"You know why, Krysty. It would have been difficult to have come to you all and explain my mission without antagonizing you, or arousing suspicion. Throughout history as I have studied it, since my youth, it seems that the best way to convert a mass, to convince them of the rightness of your cause, is to take a few influential figures and persuade them, so that they can help to spread your word, your cause."

"You think I'm influential?" she asked him, giving him the best big-eyes look she could muster. In truth, she wanted to kick the coldheart bastard in the balls, but that could wait.

He nodded. "I think you have the most influence on the group because you have the ear of Ryan Cawdor, and he is the leader." She noticed that as he said this his right hand, which had been resting on the back of the track chair, dug into the leather of the seat padding, knuckles whitening under the pressure.

"Perhaps I do," she said, feigning that this had never occurred to her before, which wasn't hard, as it hadn't. She thought it was crap, but to keep him unaware, she wanted him to think that he had given her a great insight. She continued. "That had never really struck me, but I guess Ryan does listen to me. And it's true that I certainly am impressed with what you've been doing here, and on the outside."

"I knew you'd understand," he said, his face split by an idiot grin. He stepped forward, holding out his hands to her as though to embrace her, then pulling back unsteadily, as though unsure what to do. He had seen how men were supposed to react to women on the old videos, and he had all his instincts telling him what he should do, but he was unused to real human beings, and he was caught in something that was unusual for him: fear.

Krysty could see all this, understood in a flash. And although it went against every instinct she herself had, she sacrificed her own sense of ease for the chance to aid the greater good.

She stepped forward into his hesitant embrace, hugging him. Tentatively, he drew his head back. She closed her eyes, suppressed the gag reflex and kissed him.

Gaia, she thought, the payoff for this had better be worth it....

She pulled back from him, composing herself into a smile.

"Sid has told me about what you've been doing,"

Howard said excitedly. For a moment her gut lurched. Had Sid betrayed her? A momentary fear, passing as Howard continued. "He says you've been studying the old videos, learning about the old ways, and that you've been engrossed in them."

The relief flooded through her. She sounded almost gushing, and she didn't have to fake it. "Yeah, oh yeah, I've been learning an awful lot from what I've seen, and it's made me look at what you're trying to do here in a whole different way." All the while, she kept her peripheral vision on the screen. She could see that they looked safe, but also wary. They were being kept at bay by something.

"That's excellent. I knew that if you just had a chance to study the old ways, you'd see what I want to achieve. Now listen…"

He began to babble. While he talked incessantly, words tumbling over themselves in a torrent that became, at times, almost incomprehensible, she fixed her attention on him but also scanned as much as was possible. Sid had been reluctant to tell her exactly what had happened, but from some of the damage visible on some of the screens, she could tell that either missiles or mines had been used, and that they had not been aimed at obliterating the vehicle. She knew that if that was the case, then they would have bought the farm long ago. The ordnance and tech here could blow the balls off an ant. No, he had wanted to keep them at bay until he had been granted a chance to recruit her fully to his cause.

Which he was doing even as she worked this out, and to be as truthful as she could never be to his face, she couldn't believe the crap he was coming out with. Storm Girl? The consort of Thunder Rider? Obviously he thought it was a great idea, and one that she would readily agree with. In truth, if she had been watching as many of the old vids as both she and Sid had claimed, then she could understand Howard's reasoning. But Storm Girl? Because of her fiery nature? Was he going to expect her to wear a costume like his?

It was so juvenile that she would have been inclined to dismiss it as the ravings of a crazie. He expected her to drop her friends because of something she had seen on an old vid? Because of something that he had told her? Because of the trail of pointless devastation that he had left in his wake?

And yet, there was that devastation. And the means that had produced it. And the knowledge that he had the means to produce far, far worse if left to his own devices. Especially if he couldn't get his own way and reacted like a spoiled child.

No matter how ludicrous she felt, and no matter how absurd the idea of dressing up and becoming Storm Girl appeared, she knew that the only chance she had of engineering his demise and saving her friends—let alone any other poor bastard who might get in his way—was by going along with it.

He was looking at her, expectant. He was waiting for her answer.

"Thunder Rider, you and Storm Girl are gonna clear this land of the scum, and make it fit for decent folk once more."

He was so excited that he was almost crying. He

grabbed hold of her, embracing her so tightly that it seemed as though he would crush her ribs.

"You will not regret this, my Storm Girl," he whispered in her ear.

I sure as hell hope not, Krysty thought.

RYAN HAD BEEN FIDDLING with the locket for some time. It was small and delicate in his large, scarred fingers to begin with, and he had no real notion of how it worked. Anxiety was making him clumsy, and he cursed to himself as he tried to find a way of opening and activating it.

Doc came around to where Ryan and J.B. were hunched. He was carrying coffee-sub. He coughed softly. "Gentlemen," he said quietly, "perchance I could ask you what you are attempting to do?"

While Ryan still puzzled over the locket, J.B. explained briefly. Doc nodded sagely. He held out his hand.

"My dear Ryan, if you please." He gestured impatiently with his fingers. Ryan, his brow raised, handed over the locket. Doc examined it, turning briefly toward the firelight, then back again to shield his actions from any prying eyes, human or mechanical. "There are times, my dear boy," he said softly, "when being an exile from the past has its advantages. More years ago now than I would care to remember, I bought such a locket for my darling Emily. It was, if I recall correctly, on a rare trip to Boston where I was to speak at the college. A jeweler in the best part of town, but of course. And a pretty penny it cost me, too, as the saying went in those days. Of course, this is of no interest to you—why should it be?

And, for all that, it is of no matter as that locket and my dear Emily have been as dust for more years than anyone should have to endure. Nonetheless, to discourse about it has given me time to recall the knack to prising the damn thing open, so that… Voilà!"

As he exclaimed, the locket popped open, revealing— instead of the cameo that would normally be seen inside such a thing—a small flashing light, which immediately began to pulse.

"That's it?" J.B. murmured. "That's going to bring them?"

"If it sends out a signal, then it does not matter what size it may be, dear John Barrymore," Doc said.

"Guess we just have to hope and wait until they come, or until those bastards out there—" Ryan gestured in the direction of the ranch "—make a move and mebbe give us an opening, there's jackshit we can do except sit here and wait."

"Mebbe not," Jak murmured. "Mebbe taunt into action. Mebbe force hand."

"How?" Ryan asked, although he was sure that he already knew the answer.

"Let me," Jak said, turning, his red eyes glowing in the dark with a fire that told of his burning frustration at being constrained.

"With the mines? No, we keep it tight tactically, we don't risk personnel."

"No risk—not mine exists beat Jak Lauren."

"Fuck's sake, Jak, they detonated them by remote and could have blown up the wag," Ryan said, exasperated.

Jak gave him a sly grin. "Sure, but want alive. And out

wag. Can see lines in sand where mines under earth. Hold all cards, right, Doc?"

Doc shrugged, then looked at Ryan imploringly. "I can see the lad's point. They want us alive, it seems. He has the skill to avoid obvious traps, and I doubt very much whether they would wish us to purchase that freehold in the skies. They have other plans for us—I dread to think what, but nonetheless, it could force their hand, as the lad says."

Ryan shook his head, then sighed. "Keep safe, Jak. The rest of you, try to keep as hidden as possible and get ready for incoming."

Jak said nothing by way of reply, just grinned, nodded and moved away from them.

They dispersed as much as was possible in the small space allowed by the buildup of dune and the bulk of the wag. Doc climbed in, the better to handle the bulky LeMat out of view of any prying digital eye. Ryan and J.B. clustered, using their bodies to shelter their actions. Mildred was able to check her ZKR with ease, as the target pistol was smaller than the others' blasters, making it easier to conceal. Jak, for his part, wandered away from the group. His Colt Python was not a priority for him. As far as he could see, it was simple. He had to be sharp and quick to avoid getting blasted by the mines, but he couldn't fire back at it. If sec men came for them, then the others could fire. His priority was to not get blown up.

They all had their roles, and they were soon ready.

All they had to do was to take their cue when Jak sprang to action.

JAK WANDERED AWAY from the body of the wag, away from where the others were clustered. He looked out across the desert night. The sky above them was clear, the few stars in this sector of the sky glittering distantly, the crescent moon reflecting a gray light over the sandy topsoil. It was flat as far as could be seen, broken only by the darker craters of the mine detonations. To the horizon was a seemingly flat expanse.

Seemingly, Jak's red albino eyes were better suited to a nocturnal life than those of his companions, and as he studied the flat expanse, so that flatness revealed itself to be a lie. The land was a series of planes and contours that dipped and curved into and against each other. The rolling waves of the contours were subtle, almost invisible to the naked eye at times. But as Jak stilled his breathing and allowed his body to fall into rhythm with the land around, so the secret movements of the earth were revealed to him. He could see how the chem storms, the winds, the movements deep within the ground, had all caused the surface to distort and warp. And with this, there were areas where the shifts in the natural curves of the earth had been disrupted by objects that had blocked the flow of energy and force, objects that Jak could make out more clearly the harder he looked.

Breathing now slowed to such a degree that, to the casual observer, he would have astonishingly seemed to have ceased taking in oxygen, Jak could see the whole path of the minefield laid out in front of him. The crisscross of paths between them were as clear to him as if they had been painted in. All he had to do was to follow the path, and he would avoid being blown up by stepping on a mine.

Of course, that didn't mean that the coldhearts would trigger one near him and catch him with the shrapnel. The size of the craters, let alone the memory of what it had been like inside the wag, was enough to make him aware that even a glancing encounter with one of the mines would be enough to buy the farm.

But he had a safe haven. The triangle of cratered soil— it was a large enough space that, if forced to, it could provide an area where no exploding mine could get him. He had enough confidence in his instincts to take him that far, at least.

He began to run, picking his way along the route that only he was able to see in the gray light. Sure-footed, swift, he didn't stop to think. Instead he listened to everything that his body told him. He could feel his breathing, could feel the blood pumping around his circulatory system, could hear the hissing of his central nervous system in his ears. He could smell the distant fire, the sweat of his friends, the dry decay of lizards and small mammals that had perished in the scorching heat of the day and were slowly rotting, the damp of the sand and soil thrown up by the mines detonated earlier. He was aware of the very air around him as it vibrated in the night breezes, as it moved around the disturbance he created.

He knew that he wouldn't get far, knew that he would get only a few hundred yards at best before some kind of response was initiated.

HOWARD WAS ALMOST incandescent with impotent rage as he stared at the monitor. It was a natural conclusion to the kind of confusion that had now overtaken him. He banged his fist on the console as he spoke. His voice was just below a yell, strangled in the way that only a voice barely under control could be. Krysty would have considered him absurd if not for the firepower she knew that he controlled—and which could be directed at her friends.

As Howard spoke to Sid and Hammill, Krysty's attention was taken by the monitor screens. Jak was running, dodging in what was a definite pattern, though for the life of her she couldn't work out what the pattern was, and how he had worked it out.

"Hammill, disable the mines," Howard yelped, voice barely contained. "He mustn't trigger one."

"Little chance of that," came Hammill's response. "It appears that he is able to see the layout of the network, and is picking his way between the explosives."

"How the— No, scratch that, it doesn't matter. He mustn't get through, not yet. We're not ready. This isn't how I planned it. How can we drive him back?"

"SMGs are operational near to the ranch," Hammill replied, "but do you wish to let him get that far? It would take him a half hour at current speed."

"No, I don't want him to die, or even be injured if it can be helped. He's Storm Girl's friend, and we don't hurt our own."

It didn't stop you trying to blow them up earlier, Krysty thought, a shiver traveling down her spine at the use of the Storm Girl name. She was about to speak when Hammill cut in again.

"There is a gas dispersal system that is operational. I could load it with tear gas and send remote units within the next three minutes, ETA five. This would drive him back, but not necessarily harm him."

Howard nodded vigorously. "Initiate."

He turned to Krysty. There was a look on his face that was equal parts spoiled-child rage and an imploring need for approval. "Why is he doing this?"

She shook her head slowly. "I don't know. Jak was always an unknown quantity. He's not predictable."

She was lying, of course, and hoped that his ingenuousness would allow her to get away with it. She had always been a crap liar, which had been a real problem at times. This could be one of them. Truth was that she knew what Jak was doing: drawing a response, breaking the impasse, giving Ryan and J.B. some idea about the forces they were up against so that the Armorer could estimate ordnance and Ryan could think tactics.

"If only people would act like they should," Howard said, almost to himself, "then it would be so simple. All I need is the chance to explain it to them, but they won't wait until I'm ready. Why do they—"

Hammill's voice broke across. "Tear gas loaded, ready to launch."

Howard flicked a switch and one of the monitors blurred briefly and flickered before changing from an exterior view to one of inside the bunker, a small room, with what looked like airfoils fitted with rocket engines lined up, three abreast. There were six rows. Only the front two—farthest from the camera—were in use. She knew this as they carried a payload that the others lacked, and they were surrounded by multiarmed cylindrical robots that moved on wheels and tracks. It was a smooth, impressive operation, as the robots readied the airfoils for launch, then moved away.

It was only as they did this that it hit Krysty—these were the workers of whom Sid had spoken. These were the remains of the original staff, their brains deployed in machinery, their humanity long since vanished into the mists of time and the fog of mechanical and electronic pain.

She felt sick. She was not one of the family. That could have been her. She couldn't imagine what it would be like to have your identity ripped from your body and placed in a tin can, to be slowly drained until there was nothing left of your essence. Did they know what they had once been? How had it felt to have your soul disappear? Was there a point where you ceased to exist, where you were nothing, chilled to all intents and purposes? Or was there just a small piece of awareness still in there somewhere, screaming impotently for release?

Another reason to make sure that this hellish place was destroyed, and the trapped souls given release.

Her attention snapped back to the airfoils and away from any abstract ideas as the first row moved forward and were launched at Howard's command.

She could follow from monitor to monitor as the airfoils left their hangar and traveled up a shaft that led to the surface. The entrance to the shaft was well hidden, and it was only when they broke the surface, scattering sand and topsoil, that she was able to pinpoint the exits on the relevant monitor.

"Launch success one hundred percent. Target arrival 120 seconds and counting," Hammill intoned.

Howard turned to Krysty. "Jak won't be hurt, Storm Girl. That isn't my intention. Don't look so worried. The tear gas will merely be enough to force him back to where the others are—" He broke off, turning back to the monitors.

"Sid, what are they doing?"

"They appear to be doing nothing, sir. It looks like they are, well, waiting."

Howard turned back to Krysty with a puzzled frown. "What are they doing?"

She shrugged, even though she had a good idea. Eyes wide as she could make them, she replied: "I just don't know, Thunder Rider."

JAK FELT THE VIBRATIONS of the airfoils as they were launched, even before the sound of their engines reached him, or their silver fuselages were caught by the moon. He kept moving, but spared a glance back. Ryan and J.B. flanked the armored wag, watching. Mildred and Doc were in front, by the fire. To a casual observer they may have just been tending the fire, but Jak could see from their body language that they were watching and were poised.

He turned back to face front as he ran. The silver bodies were closing in fast now, their engines sounding loud in the otherwise silent night, a roar underpinned by a high whine that split the frequencies, made them painful on his ears.

That didn't matter. It was the payload that he could see suspended beneath the fuselage of each of the three machines that concerned him. It had to be a bomb of some kind, and he was running right into their path. He looked around him, reading the contours of the land. Okay, he was ready.

Each of the machines dropped its load simultaneously. The forward momentum and trajectory of both the loads and himself seemed destined to meet. Not if he could help it. Jak threw himself to his left, executing a somersault that took him over a line of mines so that he landed in a channel between them, his ankles protesting as they sank into the topsoil, wanting to stay still while his weight shifted. He gritted his teeth, cursing under his breath, and steadied himself, compensating so that the conflicting forces didn't rip his tendons to shreds.

The first flight loads flew past him before hitting the ground. They detonated, but not with the explosive force he expected. Neither did they detonate any mines, as he had also been prepared for. Instantly, he realized that the mines had been disabled. He could use this to his advantage.

But what was in those bombs? Even as the question crossed his mind he realized that it was gas of some kind, as a vaporous white mist trailed across the land. It picked up what little light there was, and looked like spun silk in strands, entangling the very air around him. It seemed to enfold him even as he tried to move out of the way. He tried to hold his breath, even though he knew this was useless. Most of the gas could be absorbed through skin, anyway, but it was a reflex action.

He stumbled. Was it the paralysis, like before? No, the gas was a different color, and more than that, it made his eyes sting and water. He rubbed at them involuntarily, knowing even as he did that it would only make things worse. He took a breath, and his lungs were filled with a stinging, cloying grip. He coughed, but this made him have to take in even more air, and the grip tightened. He fell to his knees, tumbling forward.

He'd lost sense of direction. He could keep going forward, but he didn't know what forward was anymore.

There was some cleaner air near to the sand, and he sucked it in as much as he dared, risking opening his eyes wide to try to see where he was, and even which way he was facing.

He could see the wag in the distance, so he'd turned around, somehow. The noise of the airfoils above filled the air, making it impossible to tell if Ryan or the others were shouting at him, making it pointless for him to call to them.

Jak began to run back toward the others. His legs were unsteady at first, his breath coming short. But after a few steps he regained his footing and started to move with assurance. Even the gas still in the air around him was less of a concern than before. His lungs and eyes were so full of the gas, every rasping breath like a razor, every blink like needles, that it couldn't get worse. He could adjust easily once he knew this.

The sound of the airfoils was also on the wane, vanishing behind him into the distance. He didn't look back to see them depart; he didn't need to. The fact that the blanket of silence cast by the night descended around him, broken only by the alien sound of his own harsh breathing and his footfalls on the sand, was enough.

As he drew near to the area around the wag, he ran into a cloud that was still dissipating. Tendrils caught on the back of his throat, making him catch his breath, choke and nearly vomit. He could see through the stinging mist that Doc and Mildred were on all fours, both coughing heavily. J.B. was beginning to stagger to his feet, spectacles safely stowed on one of his many vest pockets for protection, useless when his eyes were already streaming. Ryan was on his knees, heaving for breath.

Without breaking stride, Jak helped the one-eyed man to his feet, then tapped J.B. on the shoulder, indicating with signs alone that they should grab Mildred and Doc, and get back behind the sandbank in which the wag had embedded itself.

Ryan and J.B., still unsteady on their feet but able to move with comparative ease, moved jerkily to where Doc and Mildred were prone. J.B. took Mildred and helped her up. She was stronger than Doc, less affected, and was able to respond to the stimulus. She scrambled up and allowed herself to be blindly led by the Armorer, who was himself no less blinded.

Doc was another matter. The old man had taken a lungful, and was choking and coughing with a force that seemed as though it would rattle the bones from beneath his skin. Taking him, one beneath each arm, Jak and Ryan lifted him bodily to his feet. His eyes rolled back in his head, tears streaking his cheeks, streaks formed in the dust from the sandy soil in which he had buried his face, seeking relief. His feet pawed uselessly at the ground for a moment before he found some kind of purchase and started to half run, half stumble as Jak and

Ryan pulled him away from the worst of the lingering cloud. They clawed their way up the sandbank thrown up around the wag, following the trail made by J.B. and Mildred. They could only see in vague shape and form, pale light and deep shadow in the gray light.

They crested the bank, stepped into space and fell down the other side, tumbling over each other. They lay there for some time, in the silence of the night, trying to rid themselves of the pain, trying to get back the strength to stand without feeling as though they would immediately tumble back to the ground. To each of them except Doc—who was still too incapacitated by the gas to do anything except think about the next breath—it occurred that they had learned little from the exercise, and if anything were worse off than before.

The maneuver had done nothing to draw out any personnel from the redoubt. The only purpose it had served was to show them that the redoubt had aerial capabilities as well as land. And that it had more than one type of gas.

But Jak knew something else that he hadn't been able, as of yet, to speak of. He knew that the mines had been deactivated before the nonlethal gas had been sent. The men in the redoubt wanted them alive. So how far could they push it, knowing this? He tried to speak, so that he could tell Ryan that crucial fact. But it was of little use. His larynx felt as though a herd of stickies had been tearing at it. Sore, his voice came out as nothing more than a harsh whisper that could shape no words at the moment.

But someone could speak. And it wasn't a voice that he recognized.

"That was a real smart move, guys. Yeah, when in doubt make sure that the bastards can whomp the shit out of ya. Amazing to me that you've managed to survive this long."

Jak lifted his head, could see that Ryan was doing the same. J.B. and Mildred were already on their knees, hands halfway to blasters but stilled as though frozen. When he followed the direction of their gaze, he could see why. A tall, slim black man, his eyes obscured by goggles with opaque lenses swimming with color, stood about fifty yards away. His Afro was contained by a polished steel headband that, even in the pale light of the moon, seemed to glow. Most importantly, he was holding a white blaster, made of some kind of plastic the like of which Jak had not seen before. It was pointed down at the ground, but the way in which he held himself suggested that it would take less than a blink of an eye for it to be raised and fired.

"Where the fireblasted hell did you come from?" Ryan spluttered and coughed between gulps of air, the gas gradually clearing from his lungs.

"Here and there," the man replied. "Doesn't do to let mundanes know too much about what you're doing, where you've come from."

"So you've come in response to our call?" Mildred asked, her voice harsh and choked.

"Give the sister a prize," the man replied. "Yeah, I got the beacon. Won't be the only one. Guess I'm just the first one here. Thing is, though, I'm wondering why you've triggered the rail ghost's beacon when he's long since become a ghost for real? 'Specially when the woman he gave it to isn't here with you."

"Could it possibly be that that is the reason why? If you think about it logically…assuming you can," Doc gasped, sense finally returning to him. Sense, and a very deep anger. They had called to these people for help, and the first thing they seemed intent on doing was to hold them at blaster point. Unsteady, the world spinning around him, Doc pulled himself up to his feet and pointed an accusatory finger at the stranger.

"What, in the name of the Three Kennedys, gives you the right to answer a call for distress with such outright hostility?"

The black man paused for a moment. It was almost impossible to read what was going through his mind, the goggles disguising whatever he may be thinking or feeling. The white plastic blaster twitched in his hands, as though he thought about raising it and just eliminating the problem. As one, the four friends who were still prone, or semiprone, stiffened, poised to go for their own blasters. Chances were that he could maybe chill one of them, but even as he did the other three would send him into oblivion.

It wasn't supposed to go this way.

"Well?" Doc demanded, his stance as unsteady as his voice, his accusatory finger waving in an erratic circle.

The man's head moved almost imperceptibly. None could be sure, but it seemed that he was eyeing them all, considering his options.

"Okay, why don't you run it by me?" he said finally.

Still fighting for breath, having to stop between sentences to fill his lungs with precious air, Ryan gasped out the story of how they had arrived at this point, emphasizing that the mystery rider and whoever was with him now had Krysty, and they had one hell of a lot of tech.

"Yeah, there have been stories lately about some guy on a killer bike. Word gets around, 'specially when it's someone with something unusual that we haven't heard of before."

"So the rider isn't known to you, then?" Mildred asked.

He shook his head. "Nope. Thing is, though, none of us knows everything about everyone else. That's just the way we like it. But I don't reckon that this guy does know any of us. With the word that's been buzzing, if someone knew who he was, then it would have gotten around."

"So what you're saying is that you know even less than we do." Mildred husked. "And yet you've got the balls to call us crap."

He shrugged. "I didn't get my lungs full of tear gas."

"Yeah, but your mouth's still full of shit."

The black man whirled to where the new voice had originated. The friends had watched her approach on a bike that seemed to glide across the sands, and had figured that she was with the black man. His reaction gave lie to that notion.

"Shit, Rounda, you should have let me know you were here. No, scratch that, you haven't got the manners."

"Manners my ass," she said as she dismounted the bike. It seemed to be of a light aluminum construction,

with storage pods and a small, motorlike propulsion unit
that was far too quiet to be a combustion engine. She
seemed too heavy for the bike, but it bore her weight well.
She was fat, but not in a flabby way. Her camou clothing
hung loosely on her, but they could still see that she
carried too much weight for her frame. Despite that, she
was solid, and there was a hardness about her face as she
fixed the black man with a stare that told him not to mess
with her.

"I knew we should have taken that fuck-ass alarm
from the bitch last time we saw her. Nice girl, but got
trouble written all over her. I hate trouble, 'specially when
it means I have to work with you and that hard bitch
Bryanna. Bet she ain't too far away if you're here—" she
paused to give him opportunity to answer, but took great
delight in cutting him off as he opened his mouth "—and
of course, I bet you haven't thought to check if we're out
of range of any intel that laughing boy and crew may have
trained on us?" She scanned his face, then grinned.
"Thought not. Never mind these guys, how the fuck are
you still alive, then?"

Chapter Eleven

Howard hunched over the monitor board, his shoulders tight with tension, so much so that the strained muscles were visible to Krysty through the material of his uniform. His hands, as they rested on the console, were almost white, drained of blood as he gripped so hard, trying to control his temper. One thing was for sure—Krysty wanted to get as much space between them as possible before he next spoke.

And yet, as he whirled toward her, and she tensed for the explosion of anger, preparing to defend herself if necessary, it was not with the wild glare of fury that she had expected. Instead, for the first time since he had brought her to the bunker, his eyes registered some kind of emotion. But instead of the raging temper that she had expected, they were almost like those of a child: confused, hurt and not understanding.

"What's happened?" he asked, his voice cracked and small.

"You launched a defensive move, and it seems to have worked," she said as gently and evenly as she could, adding to herself that if the bastard had hurt any of her friends, his chilling would be slower than she had originally envisaged.

A small smile flickered across his face, quirking his mouth. It flittered with barely time to register before it was replaced once more by apprehension. "Yes…yes, that's it," he muttered, "that's what I was doing. And it did work I think… Sid, Hammill, status reports."

Hammill's voice sounded first. "Visual contact still not possible. Thermal imaging suggests that the subjects have retreated out of range. Audio backs up this supposition. There is nothing that the long-distance mikes can pick up."

"Systems back up initial reports." Sid's smooth voice cut in. "You've driven them back, Howard, but beyond the range of land reconnaissance. With the current wind speed and direction, it will be 5.3 minutes until the gas clouds clear sufficiently for visual contact to be resumed."

"So what the hell am I supposed to do in the meantime?" Howard hissed in an exasperated tone.

"There isn't anything," Krysty said softly.

"But there should be." His tone had traces of a peevish whine that made her want to hit him. He was being a petulant child, but then she knew that already, from the way he had looked when he had turned to her.

"Why?" she asked as mildly as she could. "You can't control the weather conditions out there. You opted to use a nonoffensive gas, and it takes time to clear. All the sec systems tell you that they've retreated, and there are no signs of anyone having bought the farm, so that's okay, isn't it?" She stepped forward, tentatively put out a hand and stroked his arm.

Howard looked down at it, bafflement crossing his face, soon replaced by a happiness almost as childlike as the peevishness of a few moments earlier.

"I suppose so," he said quietly, stroking her hand with fingers now returning to their natural flesh tone, the tension draining. "It's just that, in the old videos, there's never any problems like this. The gas would have cleared much more quickly. That's what it's always like, you see," he added, looking her in the face, "it's never like the old videos, and I sometimes wonder if this is a world where I can fit—if this is what my mission is all about, or if I'm a man who is out of time."

"Times have changed, and this is a different world than before skydark. Mebbe that's why things don't behave as they used to. But people are different. People don't change. Not fundamentally."

He smiled. It almost reached the eyes. "No, you're right."

Over his shoulder, she could see that the monitors were clearing. The armored wag was still there, and the sand was mussed and disturbed. But there were no corpses. For that she was grateful. In fact, there was no one in sight.

"Look," she said, turning him.

Howard moved to the monitors, studying them intently. His hand thumped down on the console.

"Damn! They must have gone on the far side of the dune. I'll have to use the spycams."

Krysty frowned. What the hell were they?

"YOU THINK YOU'RE BETTER than us, and you always have. But we need to be together if we're to stand a chance."

Rounda kissed her teeth. "Same old bullshit. Only it's not you speaking, is it? It's that bitch Bryanna and her stupe ideas about a revolution."

The black man shook his head. "We need to band together against any threat to our existence," he said.

"Like you've ever had any threat to yours. Fuck's sake, that's why we live like we do. We go our own way, even from each other, and let the rest of the stupes fuck each other over. I mean, look at us—we can't even agree, and that stupe bitch wants us to band together? Under whose flag? Whose ideas? Hers, I'd guess."

Doc spoke softly, but his words carried over the still night air. "Madam," he began, addressing Rounda, "I have nothing but the utmost respect for your views. Indeed, that is all we seek. Anything other than a temporary alliance under conditions of adversity would be less than advantageous to any of us. However, I fear that this situation may as such. So I would request that you put your differences to one side for the moment. After all, that was why we took the liberty—indeed, the risk from our point of view—of sending out a signal for you."

Rounda smiled. "Say, you're kinda cute, aren't you?"

"Madam, this is hardly—"

"Don't sweat it, sweetie, I could eat you for breakfast. But I won't."

Doc didn't know whether to be relieved or insulted. He was about to speak when Ryan stepped in.

"Listen, you know about the rider? And you've seen what he's done here tonight, and in other places. You know what he's capable of. Well, he's got Krysty. She left us the piece of tech we called you with. She needs help, and it's more than we can give against his tech. So we figure that mebbe you'd like to help her."

"She's a redhead, right?" Rounda said. "Strong, got

real balls?" She waited for Ryan's nod. "Yeah, I remember her, and so does this asshole if he uses his brain for once instead of waiting for Bryanna to do his thinking for him. Come to that, she must have sent him in first. She ain't far away. Call her in, fuckwit, and let's get this sorted," she added, turning to the black man.

Instead of the argument that Ryan had expected—and indeed, that the fat woman was spoiling for—the black man merely raised his hand and beckoned.

Seemingly from nowhere, three land yachts came out of the darkness. If they were powered by gas, then the engines were quiet. It was more likely that they worked on stored solar energy, as there were batteries and airfoils at the rear of each. Triangular and three-wheeled, they had sails that were angled to catch the slight breeze and assist the engine, draining less energy. Carrying pods for weapons and stores, they were of the same lightweight material as the bike used by Rounda, and the sails were almost transparently luminescent in the night air.

Two of the yachts were manned by two personnel. The third was occupied only by a woman in a khaki vest with almost as many pockets as J.B.'s, and tight white pants that shone almost as much as the sail above her. Her head was circled by a silver cord that was only marginally lighter than her almost platinum-blond hair, pulled back into a tight ponytail that seemed to stretch her face into the tight set with which she faced them. She was far from happy, and it wasn't hard to guess from the way she glared at Rounda that this was the "bitch" Bryanna.

More immediately worrying for Ryan was that they were now outnumbered. The new arrivals made it seven to their five. Sure, his people were crack shots, and these people weren't exactly on triple red—in fact, the black man had let his blaster drop completely during the argument, as though he had forgotten he even carried it—but they were open and exposed. In a firefight, if it came to that, some of his people were bound to buy it. And he didn't like that idea.

Even less he liked the look of the guys on one of the yachts. One was a lean, dark man who was dressed in old denims and a T-shirt with the picture of a guy called Jerry Garcia on it—Ryan recalled the name from something Mildred had said once about being grateful when you're dead—and although he seemed relaxed, there was an aura about him. Less subtle was the guy behind him. He was younger, smaller, but perhaps a bit stockier in build. He was bristling, the aggression showing visibly, and barely contained. He carried a crossbow, and it didn't take much to see that it was already primed. As was he. It was obvious that he could explode to anger with the slightest provocation. Flicking a glance to J.B., he could see that Armorer had also noticed it. He had no doubt that the others were also aware.

The last of the yachts held a man who seemed older than the rest, with thinning gray hair, his frame almost emaciated. A woman almost as thin sat with him, her long chestnut hair flowing over her shoulders and framing sharp features. Both of them had blasters that were visible, but holstered. They seemed calmer, less on edge, but that could be illusory.

The truth was that these people were less allies right now than more potential enemies. And they seemed all too keen to fight among themselves, which was exactly what seemed about to happen as the guy with the crossbow got off the land yacht and strode toward Rounda and the black man. His every step seemed to be a threat, and Ryan noticed the fat woman go on the back foot, prepared for trouble.

"Robear, you need to calm down," she said, holding up her hands.

He brandished the crossbow as though it were a club. That was something of a relief to Ryan, as at least he didn't intend to start firing. The one-eyed man looked around at his people. He could see from their expressions that they shared his own sense of bewilderment at this turn of events. These people were supposed to come to their assistance; instead, it was starting to look as though they were getting caught in someone else's battle, never mind their own.

Unaware, seemingly, of their presence, Robear had launched into a diatribe of his own.

"You! I should have known you'd show yourself here. I don't know why you bother, you never do anything but snipe at us. Okay, so you don't agree with what we're trying to do, but that's no reason to just—"

"Agree with you?" Rounda gasped. "Agree with Bryanna, don't ya mean? When was the last time you had a thought of your own, Robear? Instead of letting little Miss Perfect over there do all your thinking for you," she added, waving her fist toward Bryanna.

The ice queen in the white pants said nothing, but merely raised an eyebrow before speaking in tones far more calm and measured than any of those around her.

"Robear, leave her be. She's entitled to her opinion, even if it is absurd. It's not her fault she can't understand why we need to band together. The old ways are passing, and she'll pass with them. It's more important we see why we've been gathered here. Well?" she added, turning to Ryan.

"Shit, lady, I wondered when you were going to get to us," Mildred said. "Can't you do your infighting later?"

"I wasn't aware that I was talking to you," she said off-handedly. "I was talking to your leader."

"I might take the lead, but I like to listen to what my people have to say," Ryan said in tones that were as icy as the way she looked. "I value the people I travel with, and trust their views."

His eye locked with hers. She had heard of him, of course. She knew the others, noticed that the red-haired woman was absent, the one she knew best, but this was her first encounter with the one-eyed man whose reputation preceded him. She took in his curly hair, the scarred yet handsome visage, the tautly muscled body…but most importantly, she took in the aura that surrounded him. He was not a man to cross, of that she was sure. She had to admire the redhead's taste, if nothing else.

"Very well," she said finally to Mildred. "Perhaps you are right. This is not the time to be arguing among ourselves."

She turned her attention back to Ryan. "Perhaps you should tell me why you called us."

Ryan sighed. "I've already had to tell laughing boy, there," he said, indicating the black man. "I don't see why, with all your tech, you couldn't have been monitoring what he said. Come to that, you must have heard of this bastard mystery rider who's been blasting this area."

"Perhaps I want to hear it again, to see if you're consistent and telling the truth," she murmured. "And perhaps I'm doubtful about how dangerous this man could be to us, rather than you mundanes," she added.

"Reckon you need wait longer," Jak interjected.

Ryan shot him a puzzled glance, Bryanna one of anger at the interruption. But both followed the direction of his hand. Drifting low across the desert surface, approaching at speed, came a small fleet of aircraft. As silent as the land yachts, they were like the parasail that the friends had seen in use before, except now there were four of them, each manned by two people. The flyweight open-steel tubular frames held the seating and the propelling fan, along with the small combustion engine that powered this fan, in a sling beneath a ribbed arch of a synthetic fabric that shimmered in the gray light. They seemed too flimsy to hold the engine, fan and two people, but the strength of the materials was obviously much greater than at first appeared.

It was only as the parasails were skillfully glided in formation to land a few yards apart, and a farther few yards from where the tech-nomads and the friends were already gathered, that the puttering of the small engines became audible, only to die out as the parasails gracefully hit the sand and the power was killed.

"Rival group?" Mildred asked in a less than friendly tone.

"Internecine warfare is all we need right now," Doc added in a tone that was equally sardonic.

Ryan and J.B. exchanged glances. Neither was sure what the word was that Doc had just used, but they knew exactly what that meant.

However, it was obvious from the attitude of the parasail people as they left their craft that they had no real ax to grind. The first to the group was a tall, thin man with very fine features that were only accentuated by dyed green hair that looked oddly pearlescent in the night light, and showed ears that were pointed. Ryan—unlike the others—had never seen the man before, and wondered if he was a mutie of some kind.

Whatever he was, he showed no signs of hostility toward Bryanna, bowing as he approached.

"Bryanna, I should have known you would respond to the call. And Rounda," he added, bowing also to her.

She returned the greeting. "So you've got a few people in your little cult now, Corwen," she said, indicating the seven who followed in his wake.

"Cult is a strong word," he said softly. "We just want to do our own little thing and be left alone."

"Then why did you come here?" she questioned.

He shrugged. "We believe in helping others. Besides, from the location it was obvious—"

"You mean you've heard about the rider?" Ryan interrupted.

Corwen looked at him, his head cocked on one side. "You must be Ryan Cawdor," he said. "We've heard stories about a man on an incredible motorcycle who has been chilling people in this area. None of us has seen him thus far, and in truth, none of us wish to. We just want to be left alone."

"He's not the kind of coldheart who wants to leave people alone," Ryan said softly.

Corwen nodded. "Unfortunately, we have been of that opinion. Avoiding him seemed the lesser option. You may call it cowardice. We call it wishing to live in peace."

"I wouldn't judge," Ryan replied. "You have your own ways, and that's okay. But I'd say that there might come a time when you have no choice."

Corwen looked toward the people who had arrived with him. "I suspect that you are about to tell us that such a time has arrived. I notice Krysty Wroth is not with you. And as we approached, I noticed signs of combat over the dune," he added with a wry smile. "It doesn't take much to add that up and see a whole heap of trouble."

Ryan's set face cracked into a grin. Bryanna and her people, he didn't entirely trust, but this man he did. "You could say that. We've already explained it once to this stupe—" he indicated the black man "—and I figure that she got the idea," he added, indicating Rounda, who nodded. "But for the sake of the rest of you, I guess I'd better go over it again. And quick, 'cause mebbe we don't have a lot of time."

Taking a deep breath, Ryan began to explain again.

"Spycams ready for launch?" Howard asked.

"Four are primed and in the launch bay," Hammill replied. "Two are undergoing maintenance, and the remaining four are currently being prepared."

Howard nodded to himself. "Four should be fine. Pull the workers off the maintenance and prep. I may need them for other things."

Krysty didn't like the sound of that at all. "Other things?"

He turned to her, a sincere, almost puppylike expression on his face. "I fear that we may have to defend ourselves."

Krysty moved toward him. "What do you mean? I thought the idea was that I got the chance to talk to them and convince them of the truth behind your mission."

He took her by the hand. "I wish it were that simple, but it's possible that they misunderstood my intent, and will attack."

Krysty tried not to let the consternation and puzzlement show on her face. "I thought that to harm them was the last thing you wanted."

"It is. But it may be unavoidable," he said, turning away.

Dammit, Krysty thought, this was the erratic behavior his sister-aunt had warned of on the vid. There was something going on here that she couldn't quite grasp, perhaps because she wasn't on the borders of sanity, and so couldn't follow his thought processes. If she had been privy to them, and had known the way in which he had been torn between enlisting Ryan's help, and jealousy over his relationship with Krysty, then she would have understood in an instant, and perhaps been able to form a plan of action.

She stood back, trying not to let the confusion show on her face while she tried to work out what she should do next. Meanwhile, Howard seemed to forget about her as he turned back to the console and barked his orders.

"Launch spycams, lock on target area, program holding pattern."

"Launch sequence activated, command implemented," Hammill replied.

Krysty watched as the monitors switched to the launch bay. The spycams were small, round objects with foils to guide their flight. They looked as though they had no camouflage on them, which made her sure that they would fail to pass the term "spy" on at least one count. And which would make them easy prey for the crack shots of her friends when they were sighted.

Which would only frustrate Howard all the more.

He reached behind him, without bothering to turn, and beckoned to her. Even though it made her stomach turn, she acquiesced and moved beside him. She knew a little about comps and, looking at the desk, she knew that the flip of a switch or two, a couple of taps on a keyboard and she could stall, divert, or even destruct the spycams. But all it would take was one word from Howard, and the systems' defenses would be instituted by Sid and Hammill, no matter how much they wanted to resist. And what would happen to her then, and to those on the outside? Much as it gnawed at her, there was nothing she could do.

"We'll soon get a better idea of what condition they're in, and what their plans are," he said in what he believed to be a reassuring tone.

As she watched, the small propulsion units on the four spycams sparked into life, fumes from the fuel filling the chamber with a light smoke that made the lens of the sec cam semiopaque. It began to clear as the air-conditioning kicked in, and the spycams lifted vertically, banking in the enclosed space before hitting the exit shaft.

The monitors switched as the chamber became empty. An exterior cam showed them breaking surface and streaking up into the night sky, their trails hardly showing in the infrared.

Krysty was torn. On the one hand, she would love it if her friends shot down the spycams in an act of defiance. And yet, if they did, she knew that Howard's rage would be so childlike and incandescent that he would be capable of anything.

And she doubted that she would be able to stop him.

Chapter Twelve

Ryan finished his tale. The tech-nomads had listened in silence to what he had to say, and as his words died away he could only wait in expectation.

"Not our fight," Bryanna said simply.

"What the hell do you mean, lady?" Mildred exploded. "Haven't you listened to a word Ryan said? Or did you just hear it and go 'blah blah blah' so you could block him out?"

"I'll ignore your comments, and put them down to nothing more than concern for the red-haired one. But the fact remains that this rider has done nothing to us. In truth, we could claim him as one of our own. Fact is, he only ever seems to attack mundanes, and the truth is that they have no love for us, and neither do we for them."

"Stupe bitch," Jak muttered.

"Hey, Whitey, you watch your mouth," Robear said, bristling. His barely controlled aggression was spoiling for an outlet, and as he took a step toward Jak, Ryan could see the albino palm a knife from one of the concealed hiding places in his jacket. He moved to stop him, but was beaten to the punch by Rounda, who put her bulk between Robear and Jak.

"Yeah, that's about right, Robear. You give that twat

your brains when you signed up?" She indicated Bryanna, before continuing. "Say she is right about this fuckwad only being interested in mundanes. We've heard about the kind of shit he's got, and not just from ol' One-eye, here."

She turned to face them all in turn. "Corwen, you said yourself that you'd been hearing things. Well, so have I. You can't travel around these parts without seeing the signs left, and hearing from people when you hit a ville. The rider's got a lot of tech, and he's not afraid to use it."

"So mebbe that's what we should be doing. Mebbe he's got a point," the black man said quietly. "Mebbe it's only his way of looking after himself, like we should be doing."

"Is that what she's told you? That's her big idea, is it?" Rounda said, hands on hips, sarcasm dripping from every syllable. "Well, that's just how we like to keep to ourselves, isn't it? Yeah, we like to be left alone, so let's go and bomb the fuck out of some shit-poor ville and leave them mostly piles of meat.

"Look, you might think it's fun to play at being a rebel army like in those old vids and comics I know she makes you watch, but look where that got us before… How long you think it's gonna be before some smart-ass mundane adds two and two, makes a hundred and two, and figures that we're behind it all. Tech is tech to them, and it's something to be scared of. So then they start to come after all of us, and they ain't gonna be asking questions. Is that what you want, Cedric?"

She addressed the thin, balding man who had been on the last of the land yachts. He looked at the woman beside him, then at Bryanna—shrugging slightly as he did—and then at Rounda as he answered.

"It's true that I don't really care about what this guy does. I have no love for those who wallow in the shit. But I like that they leave us alone. Mebbe you're right. Mebbe they're stupe enough to think that he's one of us, and start hunting us down. And I don't think any of us want that." He looked around at the others.

"The first time we were dragged into their affairs," Bryanna said, "it was bad enough. That was something that many of us would rather have avoided. Okay, so that happened and it can't be changed. But that doesn't mean they can just call on us whenever they want and expect us to get them out of trouble when they can't do it themselves.

"You shouldn't have used that signal, and you've got no right to expect us to assist you with just a few words of emotional blackmail."

"Aw, I dunno…" The thin guy with the T-shirt of the bearded Garcia shuffled his feet, as though afraid to speak against his leader. "I think they've got a point, Bry. I mean, we are here, now, and—"

"Time for argue later," Jak interrupted. "Incoming."

The sound of the spycam propulsion units had reached his sensitive ears before anyone else's, the frequencies curling around the speech and alerting him to both speed and direction. Before anyone else except Ryan and J.B. had even had the chance to react, Jak was already halfway up the dune, scrambling against the falling sand, his .357 Magnum Colt Python in his fist. As he reached the rise, he slowed, then cautiously raised his head so that he could get a view.

Against the yellow, orange and blue hues of the newly dawning day he could see the four dark shapes of the spycams. They were like black specks to begin with, growing larger by the second. Even at this distance he could tell that they were small, and were unmanned. Missiles, perhaps?

He slithered below the surface and reported.

"Triple red, people, we need to take them out before they reach us."

Corwen had already directed his people back to their parasails. "Aerial threat, we can deal with it," he barked.

"No, don't risk yourself unnecessarily," Ryan returned rapidly. "Mebbe they're armed. Let us pick them off."

And without giving the green-haired man a chance to argue, Ryan turned away. J.B. and Mildred had already joined Jak at the summit of the dune. Ryan was hot on their heels. Doc remained at the foot, turning to Bryanna.

"I hope, dear lady, that you are a hotter shot than your icy demeanor would suggest. For it is our job to wait, and take out any that our companions may miss…though this is unlikely."

"Better be," she murmured with ill grace.

She and her people readied their blasters. Doc noticed that Rounda had taken from her bike a squat blaster with a disproportionately wide barrel, to which she was attaching a stock.

"Madam, it strikes me that your weapon could take out a whole ville, let alone a small flying craft."

"There ain't nothing like making sure." She grinned and winked as she snapped the stock into place.

Up on the ridge, the four friends were lined up, blasters trained on the rapidly approaching black craft.

"Take it from the left as we lie," Ryan murmured.

They nodded, and each sighted the craft assigned to them by this order. It was only a matter of seconds in which to sight and fire, but they worked together with the kind of timing that comes only from living and fighting together as a unit for a long, long time.

"Now," Ryan whispered.

It was all the cue they needed. As one, shots cracked and roared from their blasters into an amorphous blast of sound. Ryan had shouldered the Steyr, J.B. opting for the M-4000 Smith & Wesson shotgun.

The results were instant. The spycam hit by J.B.'s barbed metal fléchettes splintered and exploded in a shower of metallic fragments. At their combined speed of the spycam and the load, it was as though the craft had flown into a solid wall of spikes. Similarly, the heavy slug from the Colt Python demonstrated why its firepower kicked like an angry mule into the albino's shoulder. The soft metal spread on impact, the initial contact penetrating the metal skin of the spycam, allowing the spread to infest the delicate mechanics and circuits of the craft, shattering the tech within and rendering it useless. The craft was momentarily thrown off course, but only for a moment, before the delicate mechanisms protested, the propulsion unit was ruptured and the spycam followed its companion into oblivion.

Mildred was more considered with her shooting. She knew she had only one chance, and that the caliber of her Czech-made ZKR was less than that of either J.B. or

Jak's blasters. Their ordnance could just hammer through any protective shell that the oncoming projectiles had covering them. Hers could not. It was an accurate and deadly weapon, but it had to be used with skill and care.

So it was that Mildred waited until the projectile was almost upon her, until she could see details on the rapidly approaching outer shell. It was dark, smooth, the only protuberances being the fins that guided its flight; even the propulsion—whatever it may be—was housed internally, any external exhaust emerging at the rear.

But there was one potential weak point. At the front of the projectile, currently angled up, was a smooth, dark surface that was of a different consistency. It was a small circle. A lens of some kind? She had no idea how close to the truth she was, but at that moment it didn't matter. Whatever it might be, it was like glass—maybe armaglass—but it was the only possible weak spot.

She aimed, squeezed and loosed a shot. Maybe the smooth surface was as hard, or harder, that the skin of the projectile. Maybe she'd guessed wrong. But it was the best she could do.

In truth, she didn't have time for any of these thoughts to consciously cross her mind. They were there, but only as an unconscious blur. Her conscious mind was focused on only one thing: hitting that bastard object flying toward her.

She had been right to select that as her target. And her eye had not let her down. The smoothness was cracked by impact, then shattered as the shell entered the projectile. The momentum was barely enough, compared to the thrust of the projectile, to alter its course. But that didn't matter. Whatever was inside was easily damaged. A few yards and the projectile began to falter; it spun on its axis, seemed to slow. Smoke leaked from the gap at the front. Sparks were visible as the projectile slewed to one side for no more than a second or two before exploding in a shower of flame and broken metal.

Three down, one to go.

The projectile in Ryan's sights veered at the crucial moment. Or he did. Whatever, it had the same result. The Steyr was a good blaster. He felt the familiar pressure as he squeezed, and he felt the familiar kick of the recoil against his shoulder. Like Mildred, he was aiming at the smooth circle in the front of the projectile, just to maximize his chances with a lesser caliber.

But his aim wasn't as true as hers. The bullet from the Steyr cracked the glass, but caught also on the metal casing surrounding the more fragile material. Its course was altered, the ricochet carrying it away from the inside of the projectile. Damage was done, but not enough. Shards of the glass shot into the interior of the projectile, rupturing the delicate circuitry. Shorting electric impulses sparked, causing small flames to brood inside the machine, building slowly.

But not quick enough to destroy it before it reached its intended target.

Cursing loudly, Ryan rolled onto his back as the projectile rocketed overhead, trying to bring the Steyr around so that he could sight and fire once again. But on the sand, rolling too quickly, the rifle seemed clumsy and heavy. With a mounting frustration and anger, he watched the small, round black object shoot over him and into the space behind the dunes inhabited by the tech-nomads and Doc.

From the way in which the other projectiles had exploded, he knew that they weren't flying bombs or missiles of any kind. That was okay, because it meant that it wouldn't blast them into oblivion. But the only conclusion he could draw was that it was some kind of sec camera, an intel device to report back to the redoubt on who was waiting out there for them.

There was no point in recriminations. He had to make amends. The one-eyed man brought the Steyr around and settled it into his shoulder, taking the weight and balancing the barrel as it stood upright. Simultaneously, he focused on the moving object, its course harder to track now that it was damaged and flying erratically.

Before he had a chance to get his sights set, the projectile exploded into a multitude of fragments, a simultaneous roar signaling that someone else had taken up the slack and fired.

Ryan looked around, and could see Doc at the bottom of the dune, the LeMat percussion pistol held firmly in a two-handed grip. Smoke drifted idly from the barrel that carried a shot charge, and from the depth of sand around the old man's boots, Ryan could see that the recoil had driven him into the soft surface. With a predatory grin that showed his white teeth, and a visible twinkle in his eye, Doc winked at Ryan.

"Damn good shooting, sweetie," Rounda said, unable to hide her admiration. Her own snub, wide blaster had been raised, but Doc had preempted her.

"It was a pleasure," Doc said. "I could not let a lady do the work, could I?"

"Damn long time since I was called a lady, but I appreciate the sentiment." She chuckled.

"Not so great, was it?" Bryanna interrupted. "That could have taken us out."

"But it didn't," Corwen replied before Ryan had a chance to speak. Although he looked strange, with his green hair and pointed ears, and his voice was quiet in the stillness that followed the explosion of both blaster and projectile, he carried with him an authority that made even the imperious Bryanna stop and turn to him.

"Three of them were destroyed from the ground with relatively small weapons," he said. "You, of all people, should know how difficult that is. The last was damaged. Yes, it continued, but only as far as the old man, positioned as a rear guard. And he eliminated it before any of your people had a chance to move. Even someone of Rounda's skill was beaten to the punch. I call that impressive. More impressive than you could manage. I think that, perhaps, you are looking for fault because you don't want to get involved."

"Too right," Rounda agreed, taking the stock off her blaster now that it wasn't needed. "You only want to get your hands dirty when it suits you, but I figure these guys are right. If it don't suit you now, it won't be long before it comes a time when you won't have a choice whether it suits you or not…it'll just bite you in the ass. Now me, I'd like to see that, but I figure that if you're getting bit in the ass, then there'll be a whole load of us who are getting the same. And me? My ass is too big for some asshole to come along and bite it. I like it too much the way it is. I'm figuring that we should help these guys. That redhead? She was okay. These guys are, too. And we'll be covering our own backs as much as theirs."

"I may have put it a little differently, but I think that was more or less what I was trying to say," Corwen said softly.

He turned to his people. If he was quiet, they made him sound as loud as the fat woman. But there was no mistaking the agreement that issued from them.

"So what do you say, Bryanna?" he asked, turning to her.

The black man had moved nearer to her. He glanced in her direction, but his purpose was unfathomable behind those goggles. The lean man they called Cedric, and the chestnut-haired woman with him, glanced over to Corwen with a tacit agreement. That left just Robear and the guy in the ancient T-shirt to consider. The latter looked at Corwen, then at Bryanna, and shrugged. It didn't take much to see that he would go with whatever she said, no matter what his own opinion may be. Robear was another matter. The man was a ball of hostility, and the fact that he could feel he was being pressured into a decision would make him contrary.

"We gonna let these fuckers tell us what to do?" He spit.

"As opposed to letting her tell you what to do?" Rounda murmured, her comment being met with a venomous glare.

"Now is not the time," Doc stated. Rounda caught his eye, grinned and shrugged.

"Well?" Ryan rasped after waiting for what seemed like an age, a pause that seemed to stretch from the dawning of this day into the dawning of another, and yet was little more than the blink of an eye. "Better make up your mind quick, lady, 'cause whoever's with our man in that redoubt is going to be royally pissed that we blew up their little toys."

"FUCK FUCK FUCK! No, they can't do this. This cannot be happening." Howard emphasized each phrase by beating his hands against the console like the spoiled child he was in truth. Krysty watched, trying to keep impassive. He was in a very fragile state, emotionally. Vulnerable, perhaps, and easy for her to manipulate?

"Status report—all four initial spycams destroyed. Three before reaching target area. No footage of any import salvageable from digi files returned."

Howard stopped, looked up. "Three? What about the fourth?"

There was a pause. Krysty could almost hear Hammill—that part of him that was still human to any degree, and wished to be released—struggling with the information. Omission was one thing. He had been asked as direct a question as could be posed. Finally, with a crack in his voice that perhaps only Krysty could hear, because she knew the truth, Hammill spoke again.

"The fourth spycam did attain target area after initial damage. From the information gathered, we can deduce that it was hit by a high-caliber shell, but the casing was only partially punctured. Damage to the internal circuits, and eventual destruction, was caused by fragments of the lens that broke away and flew into the mechanism."

"So did it gather any intel that is of any use?" Howard barked with rising impatience. "Don't tell me the useless details. It's gone, and it's not coming back. Okay, so I've lost four spycams. But what did one of them tell me?"

"The images and sounds are a trifle…confused," Hammill said slowly. "I think it would be fair to say that the cam was recording sound and vision at only thirty percent capacity."

Howard was breathing heavily. He looked up at the monitors as though they were the face of the disembodied voice he now addressed.

"You have the ability to take those images and clean them as much as is possible. Digi enhancement is a minor function. Take them, clean them, slow them down so that we can analyze them."

There was another pause. Then Hammill said, "They are severely damaged images, Howard. It may take a while—"

"Fuck that it will," Howard screamed. His face was red, the tendons on his neck stood out, and white spittle flecked the corners of his mouth. "You could do that in the time it took you to say it. Priority red on this, all systems switch."

"Very well," Hammill said. Almost immediately, images began to appear on the largest monitor screen. Krysty could tell from the speed at which this occurred that Hammill had pushed the waiting and omission tactic as far as he could.

Meanwhile, the few seconds of recorded image, processed and cleaned, looped and played slow, unfolded endlessly in front of her.

Four people stood on top of the dune, taking shots. That part was clear. She could see Ryan, J.B., Mildred and Jak. Three of them had to have shot clean and clear. But before the digi image started to break for the first time, the center of the frame moved. The camera veered erratically, the image breaking up intermittently, the worst of the static wipe clean, causing the flow of images to appear jerky.

But it was clear enough for her to see that it took them over the ridge. She saw Ryan start to turn onto his back, bringing the rifle with him. In the corners of the frame she saw other shapes, other people. She thought she saw Doc, and then the static washed over the screen, the image breaking finally before resolving itself once more into the beginning of the sequence.

"Sid," Howard barked, "take the last few moments— start from a tenth of a second and work back until you have all the detail you can gather. I want to know more about those shapes. Those are people, equipment… I want to see what they are."

"Very well, Howard," Sid intoned, a weariness in his voice that even Howard had to have noticed.

There was a pause. No more than ten seconds, but too much for Howard.

"Sid, priority red. What the fuck is the matter with you? This should take no time at all."

"I'm sorry, Howard. There was a glitch in the program that has delayed me," Sid replied. Even to Krysty, who knew very little about comp programs other than what she had taught herself in redoubts, it sounded like a feeble excuse.

Howard had to have picked up on that, too, but he was at a complete loss to understand why this should be. The confusion was visible on his face, and echoed in his voice.

"Sid, why the delay? This isn't like you at all."

"We are unused to combat conditions, Howard. A simulation is not substitute for the real thing."

"Simulations are not supposed to be a substitute for combat. They are there to familiarize ourselves with procedures that can be implemented in times of emergency. Such as now. So please do not use that as an excuse. We are all unused to combat. But we have to adjust."

His voice was cold, and he enunciated each word clearly and with an evenness of tone that belied the tightness with which he gripped the console, his knuckles white as he hunched over the controls, his face bathed in the glow of the monitor screens.

"I apologize," Sid said. Howard believed that the apology was directed at him. Krysty suspected differently. The last few moments of the digi images came up on the monitor, slowed down until it was almost a still image, barely moving. She knew that Sid was apologizing to her for what he was compelled to do.

"It's okay," she mouthed silently. Howard, with his back to her, had no idea what she was doing. But she hoped that one of the many surveillance cams would pick up her mouthing, and that Sid and Hammill would know that she realized it was not of their doing.

Meanwhile, Howard was studying the image intently. Krysty moved forward to join him, flinching as he put his hand out to her. She took it, hoping that he had not noticed her flinch.

"Who are these people?" he asked her, indicating the women and men who were gathered in two distinct groups at the corners of the distorted image. "And what are those?" he added, indicating the outlines of what seemed to be some kind of transport, yet was too blurred to really make out.

"Sid, is this the best you can do?"

"It is," Sid replied. "I'll take the next level of enhancement, to show you." The image changed again, larger now, and less blurred, but rendered more indistinct by the pixilation of the image. It returned rapidly to its previous blurred form.

"Very well, Sid," Howard said, biting his lip. "I have no complaint this time. Any intel on who or what?"

"Searching records—" There was a pause, before the voice returned. "The man with the green hair is possibly one of a group who have been known to live down past the old town of Tucumcari. There have been reports of a clutch of people with aircraft of a nonoffensive variety. Reports are sketchy, but it suggests they are part of a loose alliance that also includes the black man in goggles and the blond woman. They come from a faction that reports have tagged as more belligerent. But there is little on any of them other than the occasional piece of radio transmission, and some security transmissions picked up on shortwave from former military bases. They appear to keep themselves apart from the general populace."

"Sid, is there any record of their having an association with Ryan Cawdor?"

"No, Howard, there was nothing in records about an alliance with Cawdor, nor any indication that they have ever crossed paths before."

She sighed with relief and could almost hear the relief in Sid's voice. Unwittingly, Howard had phrased the question in such a manner as to allow Sid an out. Of course they had never encountered Ryan. They had barely encountered the others. It was only Krysty who was really known to them. If Howard had asked that question in any other, less specific fashion, then Sid would have had to…but it didn't matter.

"Storm Girl, have you ever encountered these people?" Howard asked, clutching her hand. She was so glad that he had asked her that question directly. She had no programmed imperative to be truthful. In fact, she could lie to her heart's content.

"I have no idea who they are," she said, wide-eyed and innocent. She peered at the monitor so that she did not have to meet his gaze. "I've never seen anyone like that before."

"Where did they come from?" Howard mused. "More to the point, why?"

"What are those?" she countered, pointing to the parasails, hoping the bafflement in her voice sounded genuine. She had flown in one, when they had attacked the heavily armed train MAGOG, flown, in fact, with Corwen himself. She knew only too well what they could do in the right circumstances.

"I'm not sure. Sid? Hammill?"

There was a slight pause, then Hammill's voice rang out.

"There is insufficient data to compile a complete report. They appear to be something on the lines of a glider, going by the information drawn from the image, and from prior reports."

"Dammit, that tells us nothing. Who are these people, and why are they intruding on our conflict?" Howard raged.

Krysty kept quiet. Not only did she know who they were, but she recalled that Ryan had the locket Paul Yawl had given her.

Yeah, she knew who and why. She only hoped they weren't being as difficult as she knew they could be. If that was the case, they were more a part of the problem than a part of the solution.

Chapter Thirteen

"I can't believe you've just said that!" Robear exclaimed, gesturing wildly with the hand that held the crossbow. "I can't believe that you'd just—"

"You'd better believe it," Rounda said in softer tone than any would have expected from her. "Even the Bitch Queen herself can see when it's time to stand up and be counted. You can't stay apart forever, right?"

"I would certainly agree with that sentiment," Corwen added in an equally soft tone. He cast his gaze over those gathered around the land yachts. "I wonder how many others agree with friend Robear, though?"

Cedric shook his head. "I do not. I think Bryanna has made the right choice. Of course," he added with a shrug, "that could be merely because it was the decision I wished her to make."

The chestnut-haired woman with him spoke. "No, it isn't just that. Sure, we want to keep ourselves to ourselves, and I still don't see anything wrong with that. I don't see anything wrong with wanting to come together to make a force to be reckoned with, either. But if we do that, ain't we got to come up against people like this anyway?"

Bryanna nodded. "She voices my own arguments well,

Robear. Think about it, and you'll see I haven't given any ground on our aims. Wouldn't you say?" she asked of the black man.

"Absolutely," he agreed, to be met with a snort from Robear.

"C'mon, she's right. We need to be together on this," the guy in the Garcia T-shirt whined.

Ryan's patience was wearing thin. Beyond thin. It was like the membrane a person got when raw meat was cut and pulled away from the bone. That membrane that started thin and became more translucent the more pressure applied, until it started to render.

He was at the rendering stage. Admittedly, there was something he could draw from this: the strange group dynamics that were being played out told him a lot about the characters of the seven people. When it came to deploying them in the offensive to come, that would be useful. He couldn't say the same of Corwen's people, for instance, who had remained mute behind their leader. But maybe it was simply that they really were the image of the man, in which case Ryan was pretty sure that they could be relied upon. Not something he could have said of Bryanna or her people.

So this heated exchange had some value. But if ever there was a wrong time, it was now. Bryanna had made a decision. Being the woman she was, she had decided to make a declaration of it. Rounda and Corwen had simply assumed tacitly that they would band with Ryan's people after the aerial attack. That hadn't been the case with Bryanna or her people, and even after Ryan had virtually issued her with an ultimatum, she had paused as if for dramatic effect before agreeing to join the fight.

And as she had, so it had started this argument. He could understand Rounda and Corwen being dubious about the group as a whole. They knew these people, had history. But fireblast, he wished they hadn't inadvertently added to the argument.

Time was of the essence. He looked at his own people. Jak was as impassive as ever, but from his body language it was easy to see that he was disgusted at the delay, and would run the stupe bastards through with a knife given the word. J.B. looked puzzled, exchanging glances with an exasperated Mildred. Doc, of all of them, seemed to be almost enjoying the debate, following it with the ghost of a smile flickering around his lips, which kind of figured. Doc always did have the weirdest way of looking at things.

Enough. Ryan drew his SIG-Sauer and fired one shot into the air. The sharp crack of the blaster rent the early-morning quiet, cutting through the sounds of argument and pulling them up short. Oddly, it seemed as though Rounda, Corwen and his people were not at all surprised by Ryan's action. Neither were his companions, except perhaps to wonder why he hadn't put a shell through the head of that idiot Robear. Indeed, it seemed to amuse Doc so much that he audibly chuckled.

The eyes of all were on him. Good. At least it had shut them up.

"Listen up, you stupe bastards. I don't give a fireblasted fuck if you want to fight with us or not. We've got ourselves, and we know we can rely on you—" he indicated Rounda and Corwen's group "—so that gives us some kind of numbers. If you think you're up to the threat these coldhearts may give us, then fine. If not, get the fuck out now. Makes no difference to me, but it could make a difference to whoever you're fighting next to if you don't have the balls."

He could see that Robear was itching to turn on him. The guy with the T-shirt held out a hand to restrain him. Robear turned, and the guy's head shook almost imperceptibly.

"Whatever your decision," Ryan stated, "shit or get off the pot now. 'Cause we've got to move."

"In daylight?" Corwen questioned. "Should we not sit out the daylight and then attack? At least it could give us time to plan."

"Time is one thing we don't have," Ryan returned. "Any planning will have to be quick. Not that we can do much except think on the run. We don't know the full extent of what they can throw at us. The land is mined, and fuck knows where the redoubt actually is in there. Let alone what other weapons they might have."

"Then surely darkness would aid us?" Corwen pressed.

"If we were attacking a regular ville, I'd agree with you," Ryan argued. "But this isn't an ordinary ville. This is old tech shit, and I'd lay jack on them having— Shit, Doc, what is it?"

"Infrared. Sees in the dark," Doc replied perfunctorily. "I'm sure at least some of these ladies and gentlemen have come across it in the past. Perhaps even possess it," he added pointedly as he looked at the black man.

The latter acknowledged the unspoken question. "Yeah, I can do that with these," he said, indicating the goggles that covered his eyes. "They're adjustable to light. I wear them because without them normal daylight really screws me. And you're right. With that, daylight or dark makes no difference. They could pick us out as they wanted."

Ryan nodded. "Exactly. And if I'm right, then those bastard things they sent over weren't missiles, but flying cameras of some kind. Okay, so we knocked them all out eventually, thanks to Doc, but I wouldn't bargain against that last fucker having sent back some kind of intelligence before it was blasted to hell and back. And if it did, then they'll have some kind of idea of how many of us there are, and who we are, which means they can move against us."

Corwen nodded. "Agreed. I understand, now. We must move before they have a chance to move first."

"Glad you see it that way," Ryan said. "We don't know what kind of ordnance they have, but come to that, I don't know what we have right now. It's time to get it out and see who has the biggest and best."

HOWARD HAD CALMED DOWN. Krysty had found herself calming him as she would a child. She had stroked his head, keeping her revulsion hidden and maintaining the facade by imagining what an enraged Howard could do to the people on the edge of the territory.

Krysty had no doubt that, beyond the range of the intel equipment, Ryan and the tech-nomads were planning an attack of some kind. She also guessed that they wouldn't wait around for Howard to initiate the assault. She knew her friends and their capabilities well enough; the tech-nomads she knew less well, but the time that she had seen them in action had been more than enough to convince her of their abilities.

"Sid, Hammill, anything going on out there?" she asked gently.

Howard turned to her. His face was confused.

It was Hammill's voice that answered. "Status within secured boundaries is normal. There is no sign of intrusion, and no indication of encroachment. As far as intel and surveillance for the immediate area, there is nothing. They remain beyond the range, and have shown no sign of wishing to come closer. It may, perhaps, be possible to monitor them if the remaining spycams are launched, and the flight patterns are planned so that they can fly above the range of the ordnance used. However, while this would give some intelligence, the quality of such would be compromised."

"No, Hammill, I think that at this stage it would serve no purpose to risk equipment. Can you or Sid provide refreshment for us in the recreation area, please? Meantime, keep surveillance on triple red—I mean, maintain at the highest level. If anything happens, let us know immediately."

"Certainly, Storm Girl," Sid replied.

He catches on quickly, Krysty thought. Howard would like him calling her that. It was a way of letting her know, too, that he and Hammill had understood her plans.

Howard still looked confused, but he smiled at her.

She resisted the temptation to sigh and said, "Come on, there's nothing we can do here at the moment. While they remain out of range, then there's no way of knowing what they plan to do. And if we try to gather intelligence, they'll just take it as a hostile move and shoot down the spycams. Best thing we can do is take some downtime and rest."

Howard nodded, letting her lead him from the console room.

Okay, so she'd got him away from the controls and the possibility of doing something both drastic and stupe. It didn't solve her long-term problem. She still had to work out how to get the hell out and also to ensure the destruction of the bunker. But it did mean that she had bought some time for her friends.

And maybe that was all that they'd need.

THE ENEMY WAS CLEVER. But they could not outfox Thunder Rider. Not now that he had Storm Girl at his side. Her actions during the recent engagement had shown him where her loyalties now lay. Indeed, the solicitous manner in which she was caring for him following his efforts in the latest skirmish only served to reinforce this.

The loss of the spycams was nothing in itself. They were not weapons, had no defenses of their own, and in many ways were flags run up the pole to tempt fire, to instigate action. What had pained him was the fact that he had lost face in front of his new partner. But perhaps she had not seen it this way: her attitude suggested otherwise. She had assumed command as naturally as though she had always been there. She had ordered the defenses, commanded Sid and Hammill to act if necessary, and had arranged for them to rest while they waited.

While they did, he had to plan: a plan of action was of necessity, he felt. And yet… When he looked at her, the idea of spending time planning for battle seemed somehow less appealing than it had in the past.

Perhaps now…

WHEN THEY REACHED the recreation area, the robot workers were still present, depositing the coffee and hot food that they had prepared in the kitchens. They looked like automatons, and would not have stirred any feeling in her if she hadn't heard Sid's story. Instead, all she could think about was how these scuttling cans on wheels had once been living, breathing human beings. It made her sick to the stomach to contemplate this, and she had to force the coffee down her constricted throat.

Howard, on the other hand, had no such problems. Although she wanted to blame him, she knew rationally that he was an innocent in this. Born to it, he knew no different. That didn't make him any the less dangerous, though. As she watched him rooting among the vids and comics, looking at covers and pages as though he sought inspiration from them, she knew that his detachment from reality could lead him to acts that had no thought for their consequence.

He turned to her, holding a vid case that said something about a savage—somehow she couldn't imagine Doc being that way, let alone looking like the bronzed hero on the cover painting.

"I'm glad you took me away from the control room," he said haltingly. "I'm still very new to all this. I trained, of course, but nothing prepares you for the real thing.

"You see, that's where you score over me. You've lived on the outside all your life. That means you've seen the dirt, and you know how to deal with it. That's an invaluable skill, you know."

"I know," she said simply, knowing he craved response, but not wanting to deflect him.

"I want to show you something," he said almost shyly. "Come with me." He held out his hand. Krysty rose from her seat and took it. Her guts were churning. So this was it, was it? Well, she'd done worse things, but nothing that felt so grubby.

It was a feeling that she couldn't shake off as he led her out of the room. And yet he wasn't leading her toward his room or hers, as she had expected. Confusion joined revulsion. But this was nothing compared to the feeling that she had when he opened the door to a room that was, like the console room, lined with comps. But on the monitors for each of these, a different kind of weapon was on display.

"The ordnance chamber," Howard said proudly.

Krysty took it in. "Oh, my," she whispered.

Howard beamed like the child he still was. "I knew you'd be impressed."

Impressed was not the word she would have chosen.

TIME TO LAY THE CARDS on the table. It was a phrase that came back to Doc at this time, and set off an association of ideas in his head. He remembered the ace of spades—the death card—and the dead man's hand. He should be a dead man, by rights. Many times over. But he wasn't, so maybe he had a lucky hand. Maybe they had a lucky hand. Certainly, there seemed to be a variety of weaponry now on display that he had not seen before.

J.B. had been the first to tip his hand, at Ryan's request. The Armorer, never keen on revealing what he carried even though he may be able to talk about it forever and a day, had understood why Ryan felt they should declare first. If they wanted to totally win over these people, then they had to meet them more than halfway to begin with.

So J.B. had them take out their blasters and lay them down, then their blades: his Tekna, Ryan's panga, Jak's collection of leaf-bladed throwing knifes. Oddly, he had noticed that Robear warmed slightly when he saw the number of knives Jak carried, and the crafty places of concealment he used. Ryan had also thrown down his scarf, weighted as it was at the end for use as an offensive and concealed weapon.

Then, this done, with a sigh he opened the bag he carried with him always. Grens of varying types—gas, frag, stun and high-ex—were carefully emptied out onto his coat, which he had spread on the sandy ground for such a purpose. These were joined by blocks of plas-ex and their detonators, carefully separated. Finally, he took out the spare ammo of all kinds that he carried in his pockets.

When he had finally unloaded, Rounda chuckled. "Who woulda thought that so much stuff could have come from such a little guy. No wonder you people have such a reputation."

"Guess that's a compliment," the Armorer remarked. "So how about you return the favor. We've shown you ours, so why not show us yours?"

"There was a time when saying that would have got you far, far more than you bargained for, little man. But this isn't the time or place, is it?" she added, catching Mildred's eye. "Guess I'll come clean with you…and you'd better do the same," she commented, casting a glance to Bryanna's direction.

The icy blonde said nothing, and as their eyes locked, it seemed for a moment as though the prior argument would kick off once more. Ryan sighed, shook his head almost imperceptibly at J.B.'s quizzical eyebrow, and was ready to step in when aid came from a unexpected quarter.

"Rounda, there ain't no living animal could support your bulk, so why don't ya get off that high horse and just show us what you've got. Bry will when she's asked, right, Chief?"

Robear's words could have contained a hidden threat, if not for the joshing, jocular manner in which he delivered them.

It had the desired effect. Rounda's face split into a grin.

"Cheeky little fucker. One day I'll come and sit on you, and you'll know about it," she returned as she began to unload the pods on her bike, laying out the contents.

For such a seemingly light structure, the bike was obviously immensely strong: not only did it carry her bulk, it also contained the short, wide-barreled blaster with the collapsible stock that she had previously displayed. There were also several types of ammo for the blaster: rockets, frag and incendiary grens and high-ex. She had a smaller blaster, which looked like an antique from the early twentieth century, and was a small 6.75 mm with a pearl handle. A lady's pistol, which seemed absurd with her bulk, but had the advantage of being easily concealed and good for close-range shooting. Not that anyone suspected they would need it in this instance.

She also had several metal boxes, with dials and faders, in some cases exposed circuitry.

"These are things that got handed down to me," she began, without bothering to explain their origins any further. "I've worked on 'em over the years, found out how they ticked…maybe even improved 'em. Stranger things have happened.

"See this," she continued, holding one of them up to the skies. "This one is a doozy. It's a scanner. Originally it could pick up any kind of broadcast, analog or digital, that was within a half-mile radius. It has a filter so that you can select from the jumble and zero in. Not that you need to do that these days, of course, as there isn't that much in the air. But that's okay, 'cause I've adapted it so that it can pick up other scanner signals. If you like, this little beauty can tell if we're being spied on.

"Now then," she added with a grin, "I can see that you're asking yourselves where that's any use. Okay, so we know when we're being spied on. Big deal. We can't do anything about it." The grin grew wider. "Oh yes, my friends, we can." She held up the other box. "See this? It went with the first box from the beginning. It was designed to work with the filter on the first box and jam out any signals that you wanted. So I've adapted it to respond to the other box in exactly the same way. Hey, we're being spied on? One flick of the switch, and shazam—we're not!"

She put the boxes down and rooted around in the remaining pods. She brought out an ax, several knives of varying ages, with stains and rusting that could have been neglect, or could have been blood, and an SMG that Ryan and J.B. recognized at once as a Heckler & Koch MP-5, a blaster that Ryan had once favored.

"Got these, too. The ax and the knives I tend to use for practical stuff rather than fighting, and I've not got much ammo for the MP-5, which is why I tend to keep it stashed. But I'm always looking. There is one other thing." She turned back and rooted around in one of the storage pods, coming up with a small transmitter and a handful of tiny objects like the one on the locket Ryan had used to summon the tech-nomads.

"This is a personal comm transmitter. We've all got them, or variants on them, right?" She looked at the others. There was agreement, willingly from Corwen's people, not so from Bryanna's. "That thing you got from the rail ghost before he bought the farm is a variation on these." She held out the small objects. Like the red transmitter in the locket, they seemed too small to be of any use. But this was obviously not the case.

"They act like locators," she stated. "The personal comm things like these—" she held up the larger box "—are radios, working on analog and digital frequencies." She spotted the look of confusion on Jak's face, echoed to a lesser degree by some of the others. She grinned. "Just means that we can talk to someone no matter what tech they're using. Might be very useful. I haven't got spares, but mebbe the others have, if they're generous enough to share. Easy to use, and will help us keep informed on whatever the hell we do. Anyway," she said, returning the comm materials to their storage with care, "that's about it."

"You say that as though it were not an impressive display," Doc murmured. "Those scanner-jammers of yours may be most useful, indeed. Do you not think, Ryan?"

"Yeah, you're right there, Doc," the one-eyed man agreed. "But we really need to have greater offensive weaponry. What about your people?" he asked, turning to Corwen.

The green-haired, point-eared man considered that. "I will show you, but I fear you may be disappointed. We like to live in peace as much as possible, and our armament is primarily defensive." With which he turned to his people and gestured. His soft-spoken voice was no affectation. It seemed to be part of the way that his people lived that their communication was mostly nonverbal, which would no doubt explain why they had been so quiet up until now.

At his command, they returned to the parasails, and in short order had unpacked the small storage pods and capsules that were cunningly located in the crevices of the slings that carried and distributed the weight of the passengers and the small engines.

Corwen beckoned them all to him. Bryanna's people, the companions, and Rounda all moved toward the parasails. Aware that this may leave them open, Ryan cast his eye to Jak, who nodded.

"Can see, hear from there," he murmured, pointing to the top of the dune. "Someone need keep eyes open."

"Good idea," Robear commented. "I can do that, too. Need help?"

Jak shrugged. "Can manage, but extra eyes and ears not bad thing."

The two men peeled off from the gathering group to keep surveillance, while the rest paid attention to Corwen, whose soft voice accompanied his indication of the equipment now laid out by each parasail.

"Bombs and missiles are a necessity, but heavy," he began, indicating the small, round bombs they carried, housed in a khaki polycarbon. "We've got some materials from which we make our own. Supplies are limited, hence our reluctance to use them except in emergencies. Plas-ex, motion detonators and a light casing. Even so, we can only carry six per parasail at any time.

"This is more use to us," he continued, indicating a small, plastic-boxed device that all parasails carried. Each was slightly different in its arrangement of wires that wound in and out of the box, placed in small junction sockets in varying combinations. "We use it defensively, but it could be used as an offensive weapon. Each one of these sends out a different set of frequencies. Some are very high, some are lower. To produce really low frequency waves, it would be necessary to have a unit that would be too heavy for the parasails, at least, using the materials we have. That is a pity, as with ultra-low frequency it would be possible to render any enemy incapacitated in the blink of an eye." He grinned. "You can't fight when your muscles refuse to respond and your bowels are opened by pure sound. But as it is, our little boxes can cause excruciating pain in the ear canal and the skull, and can disorient. Directed from the air, it can be extremely effective against ground forces."

"Yeah, and us if you're not careful," Mildred pointed out.

Corwen nodded. "True, we would have to use it with care. We're used to fighting entirely from aboveground. But it is directional, so we could use it to sweep ahead of our allies."

"Now that, I'm glad to hear," Mildred commented.

Corwen allowed himself a quiet laugh, then continued. "We may not talk much, but we have communications equipment, too. Not as advanced as Rounda's, perhaps—talking is her speciality, I think." He allowed himself a small smile. "However, we do have small personal transmitters and receivers. As we double on our craft, we can spare some for your use." He looked at Ryan. "They're simple to use, so you can pick it up quickly. We will be airborne most of the time, so your need and Bryanna's for individual communication may be greater."

"That's appreciated." Mildred glanced at Bryanna and her people with more than a hint of suspicion and reserve.

"My pleasure," Corwen said. "As I say, we spend most of our time airborne, and don't carry much in the way of firearms. Bulky, heavy and the extra weight of ammunition is something we can't afford. We have these for personal defense if someone should get close."

As if from nowhere, and with little indication of concealment, he produced a rapier from beneath his clothing. His people did likewise, as if synchronized.

"At the risk of sounding too confident, we're very good with these in close quarters. Frankly, we have to be.

The trick is not to get caught on the ground unless necessary."

"I'm impressed," J.B. said, "but you can't beat a blaster from more than arm's length."

"A very good point, my friend," Corwen agreed, "which is why we tend to use those, as well." He indicated the blasters that had been stored in each parasail. They were a combination of Lugers, Brownings and a Walther PPK. Each had spare clips. They were light yet powerful at middistance, and J.B. felt that Corwen and his people had made a good choice, suitable to their needs and limitations.

Ryan let a flicker of a smile cross his lips for the first time in what seemed to him to be forever. So far, they had a limited arsenal, but one that could be utilized in a plan. As well, they still had Bryanna's people to examine. If any one of these tech-nomads carried offensive tech, it would be her crew.

"Time to put out, honey," Rounda said mockingly.

"Very well," Bryanna said evenly, refusing to rise to the bait. With an imperious gesture, she indicated that her people should empty the land yachts and show the array of equipment they carried.

And, as Ryan had expected, it was a much more offensive collection than the others. Declining to lower herself to explaining the equipment, she gestured to the black man—it was indicative of her attitude that she had never used his name, and even now they still had no idea what he was called—to guide them through the armament laid out.

"First off, you can see that Robear carries a crossbow, which has not just ordinary bolts, but an array of bolts tipped with poisons and explosives. Some of them also carry sonic charges that can cause ripples in solid objects and lead to molecular breakdown, without any initial impact explosion. Which can be useful for stealth. As for myself, I've noticed you looking at this—" he held the white plastic blaster up for them to see "—and yep, it is pretty odd. Far as we know, this and the two others we carry were prototypes that were never mass produced before skydark. It's basically a rifle, but instead of firing cartridges it fires small pulse-bursts of energy. It's kinda like a laser, but in concentrated form. This mutha can cut through metal like it was ice.

"Over there, you can see we have a couple of portable lasers." He indicated the boxes and attached lances that lay outside Cedric and the chestnut-haired woman's yacht. "Cedric and Gwen are the experts with those. They're good enough, but as I'm sure Ced would tell you at length, given the chance, the power units need a lot of recharging, and getting the juice ain't always easy.

"We have personal transmitters and receivers, both locational and for communication. We, too, have spare stuff. I'm sure that we can share—it may be good for at least one of the parasails to have a spare themselves, in the event of serious trouble." He moved his head slightly. His eyes were still invisible, but his glance was obviously directed at Bryanna, who nodded almost imperceptibly. He turned back, then continued.

"You can see that we carry an array of firearms. Rifles, pistols and some SMGs. I gather that your man there is the expert," he said, indicating J.B., "so he'll be able to assess their effectiveness better than me. Right?"

The Armorer stepped forward and cast a knowing eye over the gathered ordnance. The rifles were a mixture of Lee Enfields, Sharps and H&K sports models. He even noticed a lightweight weapon that had originally been designed for women—he recalled once seeing an H&K vid catalog on an old comp that called it "one for the ladies," emphasizing its femininity. It was still Heckler & Koch, and for all its supposed femininity could blast the balls off a fly at a hundred yards.

The handblasters were the usual suspects: remade Colt Pythons and long-barreled pistols, Walthers and Lugers. Smith & Wesson snubby handmades that proliferated in the Deathlands. All with a fair supply of reloads.

He noted a couple of AK-47s, along with Uzis and MP-5s. There were also some antitank gren launchers, a couple of mortars and two SMGs that he couldn't recognize. His questioning glance brought another grin, this time from the guy in the T-shirt.

"Uh, yeah. While back I found a lathe, some equipment and I cannibalized a few spares we had to see if it was possible to manufacture new blasters with what we got. They're okay, but not reliable. Bry says only I should use 'em, so if they fuck up it's only the stupe who built them that gets chilled. Which is fair enough."

But they were decent blasters under the circumstances, and J.B. was suitably impressed.

The black man moved on to a selection of canisters, some of which were predark, and some of which had the hallmarks of being manufactured from plastics and poly-carbons in more recent times.

"These are our pride and joy, though," he said with a catch in his voice. "I dunno what you know about how our people—if you can mass us all together—came about, but the short version is that some of our ancestors were radicals who were against the predark governments and were working against them. This stuff is nerve gas. It causes paralysis, fits and hallucinations, as well as alterations in perception that leave the enemy incapacitated. And that, my friends, is what we bring to this party."

"You seem a lot happier about this than you were a little while back," Mildred said. "Care to share why?"

"Why do you care?" he countered.

"Because if I'm going to put my life in trust to some stranger, I'd like to know why I should have that trust. And you people weren't too keen before blondie gave the nod," Mildred replied, indicating Bryanna. She was provocative, but with purpose.

The black man grinned. His eyes were forever hidden behind the goggles, but there was no mistaking the sincerity in his voice.

"Look, lady, I don't particularly care about you or your redhead friend. But I guess Bry's right in siding with you because I figure One-eye's argument is a good one. Those coldhearts that have her have done a lot of damage, and it's only a matter of time before they come for us. So why not head them off at the pass? Besides, I always did like a fight."

"Sounds good enough to me," Ryan said. He looked around at the massed ordnance. The shit that Bryanna's group had was going to be useful, but its erratic nature gave him a problem. Rounda had basic equipment but a good attitude. Corwen's people weren't born fighters, but they had some useful variant tech, and their aerial ability gave them another dimension in terms of tactics.

Ryan looked at all of them in turn. His gaze settled longest on the ice queen. He needed her fully on side, as her people were the best equipped, and also the most likely to break ranks if she said so. As his eye blazed into hers, it was as though she could read his thoughts. She gave the briefest of nods.

"Your call, One-eye," she said. "The reputation of Ryan Cawdor and his people in combat precedes you. We'll go along with your plans…as long as they make sense."

"Good enough for me." Ryan looked across to Jak and Robear. "Anything?"

They both shook their heads.

"Like valley of chilled out there," Jak muttered.

"You know, Ryan, it strikes me as strange," Doc said in a considered tone. "Whilst it is true that we have been doing this as quickly as possible, there has still been plenty of time for them to come after us. In such a circumstance, I have little doubt that you would have taken such a course of action. Now why, I wonder, have they not done this?"

Ryan looked to the skies above the dune, as if expecting an aerial attack to materialize from nowhere. What was the strategy from inside the redoubt? If they were in no hurry, then what the fireblasted hell did they have to throw at this motley crew? He turned back to the old man, meeting his gaze levelly.

"You know, Doc, that's been bothering me, too."

KRYSTY WAS ALMOST struck dumb. All she could do was curse softly under her breath. She knew the ordnance that her friends carried. She had an idea of what the tech-nomad she had glimpsed on that fracture image may carry. She knew that there was no way it could match up to this. Come to that, she knew that there was no way that anything in the length and breadth of the Deathlands could match up to this. Howard had the capacity within this base to wipe out anything that approached civilization in the lands above, which, in her more cynical moments, she may have considered no bad thing.

But then she remembered the damage he had caused using only the smallest fraction of the tech he had. And suddenly she wasn't so cynical anymore. He had to be stopped, and she had to work out a way to do it before he could wipe out her friends and those who had answered their call for assistance.

All this raced through her mind while she tried to take in what she could see. Her jaw had to have dropped, making her look like a slack, drooling stupe. Certainly, something made Howard smile indulgently when he turned to her and saw the expression on her face.

"It is impressive, isn't it?" he said with a strange mix of pride and bashfulness. "It's quite some legacy to be left with, I'll admit. And a lot for us to live up to, if we are to use it properly, and for the greater good. Come, I'll show you what we have at our disposal."

He took her hand and guided her into the room. The comps and monitors were lined around three walls of the room. In the center of the floor were two padded leather chairs on a runner that ran in a half-circle,

making it possible for those seated to swivel around the
room and take in all the monitors and comps. This was
more than just an armory inventory room: it was a battle
station.

"Come, sit down," he said in a voice tinged with pride.
Krysty allowed herself to be led into the room and to one
of the chairs. She sat, trying to take it all in. She knew it
was important that she remember every detail, and yet the
scale was so vast, her mind so fogged by the thought of
what the ordnance could do, that it was hard to focus.

So it was perhaps fortunate, if sickly ironic, that
Howard was keen to impress her by reiterating what each
comp controlled as he guided her around the room.

The mines and the spycams she was already aware of.
She knew that there were SMG nests and heavier blasters
lined around the entrance to the old ranch house. That
would be difficult enough to surmount without prior
knowledge. But there was more, much more: nerve gas,
tear gas, chemical agents, as well as rockets, ground-to-
air missiles, both nuclear and nonnuclear. The nukes
weren't armed, but that was what the workers were for,
as he blithely reminded her. There were also wags in the
bays that were equipped as miniversions of the base itself,
each carrying a small quantity of the whole.

Those were just the conventional weapons. He took a
childlike delight in pointing out to her the weapons with
which she may not be familiar.

The land surrounding the ranch was also run through
with cables that snaked around insulated towers, enabling
him to set up earth tremors on a small scale in localized
areas, once again enabling him to incapacitate the ap-

proaching enemy. In such circumstances, picking them off would be like a turkey shoot.

Short of a direct nuclear strike from above, there was no chance that the approaching force—such as it as—would be able to break through to the interior of the base. In truth, there was little chance they would get more than a few hundred yards without being wiped out. Come to that, the base seemed so well insulated against the nuke-caust that she doubted even a direct strike—even supposing such a thing had been possible—would have had much of an effect.

She did not know about the sonic weapons and the strange tech that the nomads possessed; not in detail. If she dragged her memory, she may recall their resources. But that didn't matter. Their weapons would only be of use against an enemy force, which they expected to encounter. They had no idea that only one man stood against them. But one man with a remote force against which they had little defense.

It would be a massacre. She had to think, and fast. So far, she had failed to come up with an idea of how she could trick him into initiating the self-destruct mechanism, which was probably just as well, in one sense. Now that she knew the extent of what the base carried, she knew that its destruction would probably lead to a major land upheaval and nuke fallout for some distance around. There was little point in stopping her friends being chilled by the base defenses only for them to be fried by nuke shit or crushed and buried in a quake. And if she was going to buy the farm—as she'd half suspected she might to ensure their safety—she sure didn't want it to be for nothing.

She needed to get out of this room, to not have these horrors right in her face, looming up over her and blocking her capacity for logical and inventive thought… and Gaia knew that she had to be inventive if she was going to get out of this one.

"Are you all right, Storm Girl? You look, I don't know…" Howard was looking at her with a mix of peevishness and concern. She hadn't reacted to his display of tech in quite the way he would have wanted. She was supposed to swoon like an old-time heroine, falling into his arms. Like most boys of his mental age, he equated big things with the size of his dick. She knew that, she had seen it time and time again.

She turned to him and smiled, trying to block the horror out of her mind and get through the next few minutes.

"It's all a bit much, Thunder Rider. A gal can only take so much at any one time. It's like you in here—so big, so strong…" She reached out to him, stroking his arm. He looked down at her hand and seemed unsure of himself. His own hand went to hers, lightly brushing on her fingers. She could feel a tremble in his touch.

Good, you coldheart bastard, I'll distract you for as long as it takes, and whatever it takes. As long as you don't put any of this ordnance into action before I have a chance to make a plan….

"Thunder Rider," she said, "I've been thinking… Those people out there—they're not really the enemy and not really allies. They don't know where they are with us, or what to do. And I know—" she put her fingers to his lips when he seemed about to speak "—that they won't let us talk to them reasonably. But what I mean is this—while they're out of range, they're no threat. Sid and Hammill will monitor them and tell us when they come within range, and what their actions are. But until then, we have time…"

He was naive, innocent in many ways, but he was still a man, and she was counting on that.

"I suppose…I don't know," he said haltingly. She could see it in his eyes. It was what he wanted, but he knew little of other people apart from the woman who had been both sister and aunt. He didn't know what to do. If she played this right, she could buy valuable time.

Picking her words carefully, she said, "I think you know what I mean, Thunder Rider. It's time. There is time."

He tried to speak, but no words came out. Instead he nodded.

"Very well, then. Let me go take a shower. You instruct Sid and Hammill to alert you only in the direst of circumstances, and you go and wait for me in your quarters. I won't be long…" With which she rose from her seat, planting the lightest of kisses on his lips, brushing him. She could feel his body tense.

She smiled at him and turned to leave the room, her smile fading, her face setting hard as her back became his only view of her. She remembered to swing her hips as she left, reinforcing the impression she wanted to leave him with. In truth, she'd rather have swallowed her own vomit than kissed him again, but thanked Gaia that men were led by their dicks.

She didn't have much time. Quickening her pace as

she got farther away from the room, hearing Howard instruct Sid and Hammill and hearing Hammill's voice in reply, she spoke in an undertone.

"Sid, can you hear me?"

"I can." His voice was also soft, volume regulated and localized to a hidden speaker near her.

"When I get to my room, have the files left by Jenny ready for me, and get that shower running. I'm going to have to duck under to support my story, and I'm not going to have much time."

"Very well," the soft voice replied. "We will talk more when you get there."

Sid faded away and Krysty stepped up her pace. She was still unfamiliar with the layout of the labyrinthine bunker, and she was sure she was going wrong. But no, despite the lack of vocal presence, Sid was still monitoring her closely. She could tell this from the way in which the lights ahead of her dimmed and rose to indicate the correct path.

By the time she had ascended a level, she was running. Howard would be expecting her to walk, then shower and walk to his quarters. She needed to get wet to cover herself, and run to make up valuable time. It seemed so petty, every second snatched so paltry, yet the solution to her problem was somewhere on that piece of vid. She knew it. She just hoped she would have time to find it.

She reached her room, ran in, flinging the door shut behind her.

"Lock it, Sid," she breathed heavily.

"But if Howard—"

"—orders you to open it, then you'll have to. But

that'll still give me time to cover us. I can tell him I had you lock it because of my feminine modesty, or some kind of crap like that. He'll fall for it."

"How do you know?" Sid asked, worry creeping into his voice.

Krysty laughed. "He's a man. And an innocent one, at that. Has it been that long that you can't remember?"

There was a pause. Then, "No, I can. You may be right. I hope so."

"It's all we've got," she said, settling herself in front of the monitor. "Run Jenny's final vid from the beginning, Sid." Then, as it started to play, "Fast forward it, please. Haven't got time. Just need to find…" Her voice died away as she studied the rapidly moving image closely.

Jenny's image jerked and pixilated occasionally as the digitized image rapidly moved. Sid had guessed that Krysty would need sound cues, so he had not switched over to the usual fast forward for digitized images, which would eliminate all sound. Her voice sounded like a helium balloon, her already fluting voice sounding like the whistling of a bird. Words were sometimes hard to pick out, but there was enough for Krysty to know when the vid was reaching a point where she would need to slow it to normal.

"Slow it to normal, Sid," she said quietly. He complied, and she heard the words she knew were in there; the words that gave her the clue she needed.

"It pains me to say this, for I love him, but without a steadying hand, I fear for what he will do. Only he has the power to actuate the destruction of this place.

It's all genetics, you see. That and the randomness of numbers. Only he can destroy, but the threat can be stayed. I fear that he must be stopped, even at the expense of his life…"

"STOP THE BASTARD," she cried exultantly. The monitor went dead. Krysty looked up at the ceiling. She had no idea where the cams were in the room, but somehow she had come to think of Sid as watching over her from above. "That's it," she said in a quieter voice. "I think we've got him."

"We?"

She smiled. "Listen to me. Jenny said two things on there that I knew were bugging me. First thing, Howard is the only one to be able to override systems, right?"

"Correct." Sid's voice was even, but he couldn't conceal his puzzlement.

"He does this because the system responds to his genetic imprint, as you told me. I saw that oval pad on the main desk in the console room. That's the…I don't know…genetic keypad, right?"

"Correct. The key to opening and controlling all systems is through that pad. To actuate the destruction sequence, the command would have to be delivered while the genetic imprint was being read. Not before, or after, but during. This is to ensure that the deliverer of the message is the one in the keypad."

"Yeah, yeah," she said impatiently—this was not the time for Sid to be so pedantic and precise—before continuing, "So that's the one way. But there's another, isn't there?"

"Yes, but only Howard—"

"No, no, for fuck's sake, Sid, we don't have time, so just answer this simply and precisely. She said 'the randomness of numbers.' There's a code, isn't there? A numerical code that is known only to Howard?"

"Yes. Each successive generation has the ability to change the fail-safe code. When Jenny died, Howard changed it to a set of figures only he knows."

"How does that work? If it's part of the system, then surely you have access to it?"

"No. It's built into the circuitry that has controlled us since we were butchered that neither Hammill nor myself can access that part of the mainframe without severe damage. Even to approach that part of the program sends warning jolts through us."

"But would that matter? Even if you could not access that program, then surely you could chill yourselves?"

"I said damage, Krysty. The bastards who did this to us would not allow us to slip away that easily. The remnants of our intelligence would linger, in even greater suffering. The base would be harder to maintain, but in the long term, it would not suffer."

She took a deep breath. The callous bastards who had brought Sid and Hammill to this, and had created the insane Howard—who, much as he made her skin crawl, could not be held responsible for the ancestors who had made him this way—had much to answer for. But they were long since dust. She had to deal with the present threat.

"So Howard can punch in the code without using the genetic key?"

"Yes. It's a fail-safe for if the genetic pad malfunctions."

"And only he knows the code?"

"Correct."

"Right. Have you ever tried to crack it?"

"There are two problems with that. First, the only way to do so would be to run a random number sequence indefinitely until such time as the correct number came up. Which may be the first, or the one-billionth and first. It's a ten-number sequence."

"One billion?"

"An exaggeration for effect. In truth, the number of numbers, as it were, does not matter. The system works on a three strikes rule."

"Meaning?"

"Meaning that if the first three numbers fed to the system are incorrect, then it shuts down, and Howard is alerted. While there is little he could do to punish us, as such, he would simply change the number again. Making the task that little bit harder."

Krysty allowed herself a sly grin. "What if I told you Howard has given you the number?"

There was a pause, then, "Impossible. He wouldn't be that stupid."

She shook her head. "He hasn't done it consciously, and I couldn't give it to you right now, but I think I know how you can get it. You keep records of interior cameras for how long?"

"Indefinitely. We have the capacity to store an almost infinite amount of information from the cams."

"Then go back over the records of the recreation room.

Every time Howard fingers those old books and comics, he goes for favorites. I'll bet he even does them in the same order each time. That's how his mind works. Get the numbers on those books and comics—they are all numbered—and the order in which he looks at them. I'll bet you your freedom and mine that they're the bastard's fail-safe number."

"Krysty, I think you may have it. And to think that it's been under our noses all this time. That's if we still had noses. I...I don't know."

Krysty had never heard a comp get emotional. But Sid and Hammill were still more than machine, for all their slavery.

"Don't waste time thanking me, just do it, Sid."

"Yes, yes, I— Howard is on his way. He has obviously grown impatient of waiting."

"Okay. Chill the comp, keep the door locked until he commands you, and buy me some time."

Krysty was on her feet and in the bathroom before she had even finished speaking, shucking her boots and clothes, and plunging herself beneath the shower. She had to make it look like she had been here all the time. She moved under the showerhead, took it off and soaked every part of her skin before hunting around for one of the gels and lotions that had lain here since Jenny's demise. She had used some of them since she had been resident here, and their strange perfumes still seemed sickly and odd to her. The only good thing about them, as far as she could see, was that they lathered up with an incredible rapidity. Within seconds, she smelled like nothing she had ever known, and was covered in so much lather that she could have conceivably have been under the shower for thirty seconds or thirty minutes.

She didn't hear Howard try to enter, order Sid to unlock the door and get as far as the bathroom over the noise of the shower. But her curling hair and the flicking of its ends warned her that he was near, so she was not perhaps as surprised as he would have hoped when he entered the bathroom and pulled open the door of the shower.

He was about to speak, but the sight of the Titian-haired beauty naked and covered in only a thin layer of foam was too much for him. His jaw hung agape in an awful echo of hers just a short while earlier in the armory. She could see the bulge at the front of his uniform.

Howard stood frozen, unable to move, unsure of what to do.

Krysty extended her arm, gently pushed him back, slipping past him and covering herself with a towel.

"Let me at least dry off, first," she said, playing for time. She didn't know what would be preferable at this moment—having to play up to Howard's advances or hearing that an attack was being mounted.

No, she was being selfish. Better to give herself to Howard than risk lives. Even the thought...

She cursed herself for thinking this when Hammill's voice, cutting across the sound of the still-running shower, seemed to throw her own selfishness back at her.

"Howard, perimeter breached in three places. Ready to institute defensive measures."

Howard seemed to snap out of his paralysis. He took

her by the shoulders, and there was an unholy gleam in his eyes.

"Quickly, get dressed, my Storm Girl. Our first great test is upon us."

Chapter Fourteen

Tactics were simple, of necessity. Their knowledge of the opposition was virtually nil. All they knew was that there was serious tech, and that the land was mined. Opposition numbers were unknown. The extent of the opposition armory was unknown. Even the location of the redoubt itself was an unknown.

In the circumstances, their only option was to split into groups and make a three-pronged assault. Ryan would have liked to have thought of it as a pincer movement, but in truth, to do this he would have needed some idea of a central point—the redoubt—to circle around. One solution would have been to send the parasails out to recce, but he was unwilling to do that. It would draw fire, and to sacrifice their aircraft and reveal their hand so early would be triple stupe. Airborne craft in the Deathlands were virtually unknown. It would be best to leave the parasails as a shock tactic, and Ryan thought he knew exactly how to do that.

While Robear and Jak kept watch, and after the armories had been repacked and restored to their combat-ready positions, Ryan gathered the assembled tech-nomads, along with his people.

"We're only going to get one chance at this, and we

need to hit hard and fast. They won't expect anything in the skies, and they don't know the extent of what we've got."

"Can you be sure of that?" Cedric asked.

"Not totally, but why send a spy missile unless they had a need to know?" Ryan grinned. "We don't know what they have, but we can reckon they don't know what we've got, either."

"We don't know much," Bryanna said coldly. "We can't just blunder in."

"You backing out on us?" Mildred asked, barely able to keep the hostility from her voice.

Bryanna fixed her with a glare that was withering in its contempt. "If I wanted to withdraw, I would. But I have an aversion to walking into a firestorm."

"I think, madam, that Mildred's point is precisely that," Doc said softly. "We have to choose between a leap of faith and running away and hiding. But sooner or later…"

Bryanna's reply dripped with contempt. "Just so that we're clear, I have no aversion to fighting. Neither do I disagree that we will have to face this threat, and that sooner is preferable to later. That does not mean that I relish the thought of walking into a certain chilling."

"Lady, neither do I." Ryan sighed, fighting to keep calm. Every second could bring an attack. Every second was another threat to Krysty, even assuming—hoping—that she was still alive.

"Fireblast and fuck it, Bryanna, just listen first, then ask questions. We don't know what they've got, but we can assume they don't know what we have. We can also assume that they're reluctant, for whatever reason, to come out and fight. Otherwise they would have come for us long ago. So for whatever reason, they want to rely on the remote defenses to take us out. If we can get through some of those, the element of surprise is with us, and we can mebbe get the front foot."

Bryanna nodded, signaled her agreement for Ryan to continue.

With no further interruptions, Ryan outlined his plan. It took only a short time, as there was little they could do other than make a direct move, and be triple red to respond to any move from the enemy.

Time to stop talking and take action.

"STATUS REPORT, Sid," Howard yelled as he raced down the corridors toward the console room.

"Four aircraft have breached from the same direction, flying in a fan pattern. They are flying across the minefields, activating that defense."

"What?" Howard barked, laughing harshly. "What the hell is the point of that?"

Krysty, following behind, could see immediately what the tactic was. Figuring that Corwen had brought with him more than one parasail, she could see what Ryan had planned. She hoped that Howard wouldn't catch on too quickly, and that Sid could practice omission and evasion rather than be forced to offer the truth.

"Minefields in sectors eight and nine depleted by thirty percent…fifty…sixty-five…ninety…"

"Fuck, fuck, fuck…" Howard was panicking, almost tripping over his own feet as he reached the console room.

Krysty, following still, hampered by pulling on her clothes as she ran, could see that he was completely confused.

Good. She was in no mood to enlighten him, and would help Sid and Hammill to think on their feet—metaphorically—in any way she could.

She stumbled into the console room, barely keeping upright, pulling on her boots. Gaia, of all the times for Ryan to start the attack, it had to be when she was naked. Still, at least she hadn't had to fight off Howard's advances—or worse, succumb to them to buy time. At least now she was ready to take him on in a fight when the moment arose. Meantime…

She looked at the monitors, taking them all in at a glance. It wasn't the biggest force in the world, but at least there were more of them than there was of Howard. And although they wouldn't know it, they had inside help. Or, at least, as much as she could give them. As much as Sid and Hammill could do to be obstructive and circumvent their programming.

"What are they doing?" Howard asked. She couldn't be sure if he was asking her, or Sid and Hammill, or just himself. The latter was probably the only one he could get a straight answer from, assuming that he had any idea himself.

But as she looked at the monitor, she could tell at a glance.

CORWEN'S PEOPLE had taken to their parasails as soon as Ryan had instructed them. It was a simple plan, but one that had speed on its side, if not subtlety. To gain ground, it would be necessary to move swiftly. The only way to do that would be if the ground was clear. They could bomb the minefield to clear a path, but that would take up valuable explosives, and would be a hit-and-miss prospect.

But J.B. recalled something he had heard a long time ago—the motion sensors on such tech as predark mines worked by vibration. So what if it were possible to create such a vibration as would trigger the motion detectors? From this, it was simple to work the strategy that was now clearing them a path.

It took two passes, with each parasail trying a different frequency, before the first mine went off. Returning to that frequency, it was a simple matter for the parasails to glide gracefully back into position at the head of the dune and sail off in formation, cutting through the early-morning air with a grace and beauty that belied the seriousness of their task. The dust and smoke from the lone exploded mine rose in a column, the sound of the explosion dying away as an echo.

It was no indication of the tumult to come.

Starting from a point over the heads of the gathered forces, now split into three contingents, the parasails grouped in formation then fanned out so that they could cover a wide sweep of ground. The only indication that their sonic weaponry was being deployed came from a mild sensation of nausea that passed through the assembled throng as the parasails passed over them on their turn.

The silence, as they watched the aircraft bank and turn, was momentary. Within seconds a chain reaction of deafening roars assailed them, the air thick with smoke and sand, flung up by the detonation of the mines. The individual explosions were clustered so close together that it became one eardrum-threatening tattoo, an elongated blast that would have thrown them off balance if not for the protection of the dune banked in front of them.

The parasails themselves had banked and reared to avoid the earth thrown up by their operation. Knowing the range of their sonic weapons, it was safe for Corwen to pull his people up a hundred feet without lessening their chance of success.

The sight below him was awesome to behold. The vibrations sent out by the parasails activated the motion sensors of the mines as the sonic wave hit. Aiming always to their rear so that the worst of the explosions occurred behind their flight path, the mines exploded in a chain, lines of ruptured surface soil forming intricate line patterns similar to the ones seen on the flat plane by Jak before his own doomed sortie the night before.

As the air cleared, the columns and banks of darkness dissipating and letting the light of the day through once more, Ryan signaled that the attack should begin. In the distance the explosions still roared as mines farther down the field were detonated, but their traces had all but vanished before reaching the starting positions of the expeditionary force.

The three parties had been divided according to a rough matching of their skills. Thus Jak and Robear were natural partners, while Ryan took it upon himself to tackle the ice queen. He wanted to keep his eye on her, and added Mildred to his party to assist him in this task. There was a chance that she may need to be shot down, kept in line. If he didn't do it, then he knew he could rely on Mildred. J.B. and Doc were paired, partly so that the Armorer could keep his eye on Doc. They were joined by the black man and by Rounda, who had taken a shine to the old man. Ryan always considered things like that important. In the heat of battle, any edge was worth exploiting.

Jak and Robear were joined by Cedric and Gwen. The combination of laser tech, even if a last gasp, combined with the obvious skills of Jak and Robear, seemed to balance well. Finally, Ryan had opted to include the guy with the Garcia T-shirt to round out his party. The guy was still an enigma, so it was hard to know where else to place him when other skills had seemed so complementary. At the same time, this very same laid-back attitude had ensured his inclusion alongside Bryanna, as the one of her people the least likely to follow her should she rebel against Ryan's stewardship of the battle.

The three parties were to start at the same spot and then fan out in a similar manner to the parasails, dogging their trail and traversing the area of now-defunct mines as swiftly as possible. True, they had no idea of how long they would have to keep going at triple pace to reach the redoubt. However, Ryan had little doubt that they would either reach their destination or encounter the enemy in short time.

The ground was pitted and uneven, the recently disturbed surface all around making it hard for them to traverse the minefields with ease. Boots sank into soil, having to be pulled out, and slowed momentum. Treacherously uneven and soft surfaces gave way underfoot, causing all the parties to stumble and almost fall on several occasions. Old rivalries and recent animosities forgotten in the common cause, hands were extended to the falling and fallen, helping them to keep their feet. The air was heavy with the acrid, stinging smell of explosive and scorched earth, catching at the backs of throats, making it hard to breathe.

There was no time to look around and take stock, only time to try to keep upright and move forward, to choke in enough air though the fumes. Ryan could not spare the necessary attention to look around to see where the other two parties were. He relied on the tenacity of J.B. and Jak to drive them forward.

Up above, if he could have taken a moment to look, he would have seen that Corwen's people had banked and turned back, their initial mission accomplished and the extent of their path through to the end of the minefield now delineated. Vision strictly focused on the immediate expanse ahead of them, the three parties were only dimly aware that the last of the explosions were dying away.

The almost subconscious impression was reinforced by the sudden burst of static and voice that issued from all personal comm equipment. Despite the frequency on which all the available equipment could correspond being analog, and the background radiation prevalent in the land making any analog frequency impossible to keep interference-free, Corwen's voice carried an authority and strength that Ryan would not have thought possible from their discussions on the ground. It was as if being in the air, which he saw as his natural element, gave him a depth and determination that he could not show when on land.

"Minefields end about five hundred feet from your current position. Paths are cleared. They just end, with no sign of what other defenses take over. Must be some. Looks like a small valley a thousand yards beyond. Nothing but a ruined building there. Could send one parasail to recce. End."

Ryan stumbled as he fumbled with the unfamiliar device.

"Send parasail to recce, but be triple red. There must be other bastard defenses, and they must be well hidden. Keep frosty over the ruined building. Sounds like the perfect place to hide an entrance. Everyone else, keep going but keep alert. Now that the mines have stopped, they'll send something else. End."

The thing he had been trying not to think about was if they sent more gas, rather than men. Nerve gas would stop them if absorbed through the skin, and they had no goggles or protective eyewear for the tear gas. The black man had issued them all with nose filters from his people's equipment, but the fireblasted things were doing little more than making it hard for him to breathe other than through his mouth, which defeated their purpose. He was tempted to just discard them and hope for the best.

"ANTIPERSONNEL HEADS, Hammill. Primed and ready to fire ASAP."

"Workers in place. Estimated time to firing, 3.5 minutes. Enemy currently 4.2 minutes from end of minefield."

"Good. It's not a big margin, but it may be enough." Howard turned to Krysty, his eyes shining. She could see madness in them. The time to act was approaching far too rapidly for her liking. Sid had shown no indication of cracking the code as of yet. Howard, taking her silence for complicity, continued. "The one thing I don't understand is why they did that."

"Did what? They were trying to break through your defenses. Why shouldn't they do that?"

"Because it's not the right way to do it," he replied earnestly. "That's not how it's supposed to happen. They wait until it's dark, then try to sneak past the minefield without alerting us to their presence. That's how it's always done. The proper way. You don't just charge in, bulldoze your way past the defenses and give the opposition advanced knowledge of your presence. That's the problem with this world," he added with a sigh. "People have no idea of how they should behave. We'll just have to show them the right way, I guess. You and me, Storm Girl. I must go and get changed, ready for the battle to come."

With which, he turned and left the console room. She could hear him barking orders as he disappeared down the corridor.

"Sid," she hissed, "what is taking so long?"

"Some of the numbers are obscured, no matter which camera or which period I choose. The analysis program is running as fast as I can push it, but there's so much footage."

"Well, you'd better hurry, or else I'm going to have to rip the fucker's hand off and push his thumb in myself."

"It crosses my mind that it may be quicker than searching for the fail-safe," Sid said wistfully.

"Yeah, and revenge for you before your release," she answered hurriedly, aware that Howard could return at any second. "Problem is, if he didn't chill immediately, or if he could yell while we fought, he could order the destruction of the oncoming forces, and I'm not having them chilled for me or for the sake of that mad bastard. You run that override, and I'll take pleasure in chilling the fucker slowly for you."

Only just in time, for almost as soon as she had finished, Howard strode back into the room, dressed in full Thunder Rider uniform. He flashed her the kind of grin she could only imagine that he had seen so many times on the old vids.

"Hammill, missiles ready?" Howard said with a calm exactitude. The costume may have been nothing more than scraps of material and body armor, but it held a meaning for Thunder Rider that took him from himself and made him something other than Mad Howard, the lonely man-child of Murania.

"Primed and ready to fire," Hammill's voice came back. Was it Krysty's imagination, or was there a tinge of regret, a hint of hesitation in it?

"Then fire them." Howard smirked. "Sid."

"Yes, Howard?" Sid replied after pausing as long as he—or his programming—could dare.

Howard breathed heavily. "Towers open fire."

"Aw, SHIT, I ain't never seen nothing like that, and I hope to fuck it ain't the last thing I'll ever see, either."

Rounda's voice was the loudest, and her words cut across the empty space between the war parties, rising above the mutterings of others and the distant drone—registered only at that moment by Jak—of the just-launched missiles. But her words, no matter how apt, were just sounds that drifted over the heads of the others. They were soon drowned by the grinding and screeching that reached them from some distance, marginally behind the sight that was making them stumble and halt.

Ryan cursed softly to himself. Whatever he had expected—men, wags, missiles, gas—there was no way he could have expected this.

There, in a circle that stretched for a mile in each direction, rose a number of towers. Each was surmounted by a platform that had carried topsoil and sand, much of which now cascaded down the sides, falling to the ground in showers that made the central structure seem so alien.

Each platform was raised on a tower of solid metal, peppered with cones and boxes. Some of these looked like speakers, others like giant lamps. They were arranged in irregular groups and patterns. Their purpose was hard to explain, though the use of sonics and lights such as those possessed in limited supply by the tech-nomads was an obvious guess.

The ground beneath the war parties shook as the leviathan towers reached their full height. The cascades of sand and soil lessened, allowing them to view the towers in their full awe.

A few shots rang out as Rounda loosed a load from her snub-nosed blaster and J.B. gave an experimental burst with his mini-Uzi. Where Rounda fired indiscriminately, the Armorer aimed specifically at the cones and lights. No joy. The appurtenances remained intact.

The black man and Robear had similar ideas. Pulling up short in their respective parties, one loosed an explosive bolt from his crossbow, the other aiming a few pulses at the nearest tower. Neither made an impression. Cedric and Gwen fumbled with the laser equipment. It was obviously better used in a static situation, but they were faster than they at first appeared, waving away offers of help that would only hinder when the equipment was a mystery. They assembled it, aimed the laser focusing device and shot a beam at the middle of one of the towers. It was a powerful weapon, and yet even so it made little impression. It was like using a razor blade to cut down a giant redwood. There was the merest speck of damage on one tower. To cut down just that one would take more time and energy than they had.

Ryan barked into the comm device, "Press on—get past the towers! Mebbe the weapons only face one way. End."

It was an astute observation. Made for defense, all the lights and speaker cones faced out. If they could scramble past, then they would be all right. But they were too far in front. Even as they ran, slipping in loose sand and soil, wading through an element that sought to restrain them, so the towers began to issue a sound that was almost beyond the range of the human ear, seemingly both too high and too low to hear. Was that possible? It seemed to drill through their heads, making it almost impossible to concentrate, to think.

They didn't think to look away until it was too late, at

least for some. You'd have to be a stupe to look at the lights, but when your head was full of a sound that made your skull reverberate, that's exactly what you were…a stupe. Cedric and Gwen, still trying to train their laser on one of the towers, became transfixed as the lights began to strobe and pulse in irregular patterns that seemed to sap their will, to turn their brains inside out.

Both of them tumbled over, bodies racked by fits, muscles spasming, tongues swallowed. They choked to death in front of Jak and Robear, who had both had instinct enough to avert their eyes, but were still transfixed by their peripheral vision, enough to make their unresponding muscles lock. Frustration overwhelmed them as they tried in vain to move, to stop their companions buying the farm slowly and horribly.

Ryan, unable to see what was going down, but guessing what was happening from the reactions of his own party, tried to use the comm. He could raise it partway to his mouth, but every movement was a struggle. Mebbe, he figured, only having one eye and so no depth perception in his vision had helped. Perhaps it lessened the effects. He tried to yell into the comm, unable to raise it any farther, willing himself to be heard above the noise. Why, he didn't know, as the sound of the towers was not in hearing range. But it didn't matter if his mind was losing its grip, as his voice refused to respond to the demands of his will. Nothing emerged except the hoarsest of croaks.

Fireblast, this was it. The sound and lights would gradually force them all into seizure: paralysis, choking, just lying in the heat of the day until they fried, or easy

meat for the sec men who lay in wait at the redoubt.
Whichever of these claimed them, they were as good as
chilled.

He'd forgotten about Corwen's people, cruising the air
currents above them.

The green-haired man still had his comm channels
open. As soon as the first sounds emanated, he had
guessed what the towers were for, and had ordered his
crews to switch to an alternate frequency while rising up
into the skies. He figured—correctly—that the towers
were intended as a ground defense, and so the light and
sound emissions were specifically directed to that area
both in front of the towers, and angled down to the
ground.

With Cedric and Gwen chilled, and the others struggling to stay more than inanimate lumps of vulnerable
flesh, Corwen took his parasail crews up and banked
steeply, swooping toward the group of towers that lined
up almost directly in front of the three war parties.
Because of their spread, Corwen's crews would have to
knock out six towers. There were too many for all to be
destroyed, but again he figured that the towers had a
maximum range of effectiveness, hence the need to
position them as they were. So if they could knock out
those six, then there was a good chance it would release
the war parties from their pernicious grip.

Ordering his crews to descend at speed, they made an
initial pass, releasing a first load of explosives as they
swooped overhead. The bombs were not intended to cut
off the towers at base, as the platforms on their apex
made it almost impossible to get a good aim. But they

could angle the descent so that the explosives could take the towers out at the middle, cutting off the sound and light. The only drawback was that they had to hope the warriors beneath would be mobile quickly enough to dodge any flying rubble. It would be ironic to chill some of them in the process of liberating them. At any rate, it was better than buying the farm for certain.

The parasails rose steeply once more, pulling away from potential shock waves before their bombs exploded on contact.

They were successful on the first pass. All four craft had scored direct hits, the tops of the towers crumbling, the weight of the platforms accentuating any blast damage and causing the disintegration of the towers, the severing of connections as the weight of the buckling metal crushed the lights and speaker cones.

Four craft, six towers—two would have to make a return pass. Corwen opted to fly one himself, and nominated a second parasail. It was a dangerous mission, and as they flew in to take out the two remaining towers in the sequence, Corwen believed that he had allowed the fliers left circling some kind of respite.

He was wrong. As they hovered, they became aware of the rapidly approaching missiles. Absorbed in their immediate task, none of the parasail pilots had expected to be under attack from the air. So as the missiles approached, trained to land in the ground beyond the towers, where the warriors had been immobilized, the parasail pilots became suddenly aware of the missiles at their tails. In another time, another place, the parasail pilots would have been able to take evasive action. They would have been used to the concept of aerial warfare, and would have known how to get the best and beyond from their machines in moments of emergency. But they had been used to having the skies to themselves, to always being the ones with the advantage. Lack of combat experience in such a situation told. One craft turned too slowly, allowing a missile to catch it at the tail. The missile, primed to explode on contact, detonated. There was nothing left of the light craft or its crew to identify when the smoke and flame had cleared.

The second craft almost made it. The pilot banked steeply, seeking to avoid the two missiles whose path would cross him. He was successful, the missiles passing beneath him. But he was temporarily unable to see fully as the craft spun in the air, and a third missile flew into his blind spot. If the material of the sail had not momentarily obscured... But it was far too late for recriminations. The third missile hit his craft squarely, and he and his passenger were obliterated.

Corwen watched, speechless, as his craft and that of the other attacking pilot, came out of their flight course, climbing up behind the trail of the now-passed missiles. Two of his craft gone without his seeing the incident. And now the remaining missiles were bearing down on the warriors on the ground.

Ryan knew what was happening. The effects of the sonic and visual weapons were clearing now that the only towers transmitting nearby had been shattered. The farther towers made him feel uncomfortable, but their effects were so diminished as to make it possible to move. And quickly. Looking around, he could see that Mildred and Bryanna were struggling forward with him. The T-shirted warrior was also beginning to move, shaking his head as if to clear it, and stumbling.

Looking farther afield, he could see that Jak and Robear were moving, but Cedric and Gwen were down. J.B. and Doc were also on the move, Rounda lumbering after them. At the rear, weaving and disoriented but starting to move, was the black tech-nomad.

Two down. He looked up at the incoming missiles, so focused that he could not see the two remaining parasails. He only knew that they had to get out of there, and fast. Without having to consciously think about it, he knew the missiles were aimed beyond the towers. It made sense to immobilize, then blast the opposition. So if they could get past…

"Move forward, triple fast," he barked into the comm, his voice still affected by the towers.

They had little time. The disorienting frequencies of the towers were now replaced by the screech of the missile propulsion systems as they approached. The warriors scrambled forward, none knowing where they went other than straight ahead. They had to keep moving and hope that they would pass the fallen towers before the missiles hit home.

Ryan was aware of the tower wreckage as he passed it. He could see Bryanna and Mildred from the corner of his eye, keeping pace with him. They were past by the time that first missile hit, the force of the blast flinging them forward into the sand. The grit forced its way into his mouth, making him choke. He had no idea of where his last man might be.

Jak and Robear were less affected. Lighter, faster, they had covered the ground with greater speed, and so were less in the line of the blast force. Still, they were knocked breathless.

J.B. had been pulling Doc along with him, feeling the older man struggle. Doc was a fighter, pushing himself, but he was frail in some ways, and his mind was still clouded by the effects of the sound and light blasts. He had strength and speed, but he was unsure as to direction, and would have wandered in circles without the Armorer's guiding hand. Which was as well, as a missile landed nearer to their party than to any other, and both men were flung forward with a force that pumped the air from their lungs.

Gasping for breath, thankful that they were past any tower wreckage that they could have landed on with fatal effect, J.B. raised his head in time to see the blur that was Rounda fly past his head, landing with a sickening thump. No time to check if she was okay right now. He could see that Doc was stirring, but what of the last member of their party?

J.B. turned, adjusting his spectacles, his vision clearing. The black man was to their rear. He was kneeling, but even without seeing his eyes behind the swirling goggles, J.B. could tell there was something wrong. He seemed too stiff, too unnatural.

He had to have been alive enough to see J.B. looking at him. He opened his mouth to speak, but no sound came out. Blood dribbled down his chin, then poured out in a gushing wave. He pitched forward, and the Armorer could see that a large fragment of shrapnel had struck him in the back, down by the kidneys. It stuck up obscenely as the sand around his body darkened.

It was too late to help him now; there was nothing to do except forge forward. J.B. pulled up Doc after him, and they scrambled toward Rounda. She was still, but as they approached they could hear her groaning as she began to stir.

"Feel like I've been kicked by—"

"No time to talk," J.B. snapped. "We're a man down. Got to keep moving."

She rose tortuously to her feet and joined them in moving forward, J.B. glanced across the empty expanse of sand. He could see Jak and Robear to one side, but only them. Three down overall, then, an estimate confirmed as he looked in the other direction to see Ryan and Mildred, along with Bryanna and her man. A surge of relief swept through him that Mildred had survived the first wave. He would rather he bought the farm than her. Come to that, he'd rather they both made it.

He concentrated on that as they moved forward.

"No, no, no... This can't be happening," Howard said softly, a hard edge making his voice appear all the more sinister, echoed by his face bathed in the glow of the monitors.

Krysty, on the other hand, wanted to punch the air and yell. It was a bitch that three people were chilled, and two of the parasails were gone, but at least her friends had made it through this far.

She wanted to, but she didn't. Sid was taking too long working out the fail-safe. She would have to take action of her own. Krysty reached deep within herself. She was still weakened from her last use of the Gaia power, and had still not fully recovered from the ordeal of being kidnapped by force. She was nowhere near her optimum strength, and she wasn't sure if she would be able to channel the Gaia force if she called upon it. She tested herself, but could not be sure, and she had to be certain if she was to use it that it wouldn't burn her out before she could achieve her aim. For the only option she could see left open to her was to fight Howard, and if necessary tear out his arm by the socket if it meant being able to put his bastard thumb onto the keypad. But she would have to take him out immediately, before the coldheart could bark out an order that Sid and Hammill would be forced to obey.

She was poised to act when Howard turned to her.

"I don't understand."

She was so taken aback by the complete confusion in his voice that any thought of action fell by the wayside. All she could do was stand there and say, "Understand what?" Aware with every syllable that she sounded as confused as he was.

"Why this is happening. Why they are attacking us. Who these other people are, and why they want to attack me, too. All I want to do is make it a better world. It was so simple in the old days. People understood what was happening, and they did things the right way. Why aren't they doing it like that? Why is it different?"

"Howard," she said softly. Then, catching herself, "Thunder Rider, you have to understand that those things you want to be like aren't real. They're stories. Things were never really like that, even back before the nuke-caust."

"Never?"

"No. They were just stories of how some people thought things should be…" All the while she kept half an eye on the monitors behind him. The remaining attackers were making good ground. From where they were now, they should be able to see the lip of the valley leading to the ruined ranch house. If they could get past the defensive gun emplacements, then they would have a chance of gaining access. If she could keep his attention for just long enough…

But the pause was too long. It gave him enough time to think about what she said.

"No," he yelled, "that can't be true. Those things happened. They're real, they're the history of the world when it was good. I haven't lived my life for a lie. It's you who lies. You say you're Storm Girl, but you're just like them, sent to test me."

He whirled, taking in the progress of the remaining attackers and the two parasails overhead.

"Sid, ready and fire SMG defenses. Hammill, ground-to-air capability deployed, lock on airborne targets. Blast them out of the sky."

Krysty knew that Sid and Hammill had no choice but to obey, and she had delayed too long waiting for the optimum moment. There was no such thing. She had to make the best of what she had right now. Without a sound to give herself away, she took a step forward and wrapped an arm around Howard's neck, closing around his throat as she pulled him to her. If she could break the bastard's neck, if she could crush his windpipe to stop him issuing any more orders.

Taken by surprise, he stumbled back into her, knocking her backward and off balance. She crashed against the wall, and the jarring impact made her grunt. But she did not weaken her grip. She was aware as he pushed against her of how strong he was, and simultaneously of how weakened she was, still, but she could not lessen that grip. He was trying to speak, but nothing except a strangled yelp emerged. She had to cling on, throttle him and stop him issuing orders at all costs….

QUIET. OMINOUSLY QUIET. That was the only thing that kept going through Ryan's head as he continued forward. He had expected some kind of opposition beyond a few light and sound weapons, and he was sure he was going to get it. But when? The heat of the afternoon sun was making them sweat. Every step on the treacherous surface of desert soil sapped yet more from their weary muscles, and the expectation made their hearts race, adrenaline pumping and spurring them on yet making their guts churn in time with their pace.

They were nearing the ruined house that Corwen had spoken of. It had to be the way into the redoubt. The ridge of the small valley that enclosed it was now clear to them. The two remaining parasails were gliding over the top. Corwen's voice came strong and clear over the comm.

"It's deserted. If there's a way underground from here, I can't tell from this distance. No sign of any life, or of any defenses."

"Keep triple red—that goes for everyone," Ryan

rasped as the heat of the day and of his exertion took its toll on his parched throat. "They've got to have something waiting for us."

But even as he spoke, two things happened. The first, and lesser, was the thought that flashed into his mind: what if the reason they had seen no other sec was because there was none? What if they were facing just one man, the mysterious rider himself? It wouldn't be the first time they had come across a redoubt manned by just one lone crazie, albeit one who, in this case, knew the tech backward. If it was just the one opponent, alone with Krysty, then it may be that the situation was very different from their initial assumptions.

The second thing to happen made any such train of thought irrelevant: it was a danger that needed immediate facing.

As they trudged double-time across the expanse of sand, they were suddenly surprised to find themselves in the center of a rising swarm of gun emplacements. Rising from beneath, threatening to make their footing even more uncertain as the very earth seemed to move, a series of SMG emplacements—two or three mounted on each emplacement—rose aboveground.

Before they had a chance to assimilate what was happening, the SMGs had started to rotate, spraying the surrounding area with fire that was angled into the ground. The obvious aim was to eliminate anything at a level of under two yards, the downward sweep of the SMG fire plotted so that anything at that level would be eliminated, the fire falling short of sweeping an adjacent emplacement but covering the area between.

Jak grabbed Robear and hauled him into cover. If the fire did not reach the emplacement, then the safest place was in the emplacement itself, beneath the roaring SMGs but in an angle that they could not reach. J.B., Ryan and Mildred had much the same idea. Bryanna was caught out, and took a hit in the lower leg as she moved a fraction too slowly and was raked by fire. Her screams could be heard cutting across the chattering roar of the SMGs nearest to her, Ryan and Mildred. In the shelter of the emplacement, with the deafening noise above their heads, Mildred attempted to patch up the icy blonde's leg as quickly as possible. Ryan tried to see what had happened to the others. Rounda and Doc were huddled together beneath an emplacement.

The T-shirted man whose name they had never learned was not so lucky. His reactions were just too slow, and as he was caught by a hail of bullets, the force of their striking him threw him into the path of another rain of lead. His body was tossed, now long-since devoid of life, kept upright for some time by the momentum of hits until a fine mist of red blood seemed to form an aura around him. Gravity eventually claimed him, but in the interim it was a terrible sight.

The experience seemed to continue for some time, but in truth it was little more than a few seconds. Corwen, gliding above, could see what was occurring almost before it had hit those on the ground. Switching frequency to cut out the noise of the SMGs as their chattering was picked up by the comm equipment on the ground, he ordered his other craft to circle and bomb the ground below, knocking out a line of emplacements and allowing the remaining warriors a clear path to the ruined ranch.

Ryan could see the intent, but it still left them the problem of getting away from the emplacements under which they sheltered. There was only one course of action that he could see. It was risky, but then again, what wasn't? He took a gren from one of his pockets, looked across to where Jak and Robear were sheltering. He gestured, and they understood immediately. Although neither of them carried grens, Robear had the explosive heads on his crossbow bolts. He produced one, nodding.

Ryan then looked across to J.B. The Armorer was grinning, light in his eyes and a gren in his hand.

They had to be ready, they had to be fast, and they still ran the risk of being cut to ribbons or hit by blast shrapnel.

As the explosive charges detonated, they were—all of them—propelled forward into the hail of fire. They kept low, almost scuttling across the sand. The fire from the SMGs changed angle as the emplacements exploded, and this was the edge Ryan had counted on, that crucial few inches, becoming yards as the blasters angled to the skies before dying as the circuits connecting them to the base were shattered.

The SMGs still roared around them, but they were now free of fire, running full-pelt, pushed harder by the blast at their tail, toward the ruined ranch.

They were past the defenses, and almost onto the redoubt.

KRYSTY'S GRIP WAS beginning to weaken. She didn't want to risk calling on the Gaia power, but knew that she couldn't hold on much longer. Howard was capable of a strangled grunt, but no speech. She knew that she did not have the strength as she stood to chill the bastard, but if she could just…

On the monitor screens, she could see the SMG emplacements get blasted, and the remaining force charge forward. There were still eight of them, more than enough to finish this, if only they could find their way in.

"Machine-gun emplacements in sector five eliminated. The enemy is past exterior defenses and through to the entry. Interior defenses remain inactive until authorized."

Hammill's voice could not hide the gleeful note of triumph. Until he was ordered, he could keep the defenses inactive without contravening his programming. If the outsiders got in, they would have a clear run.

Howard struggled against Krysty. His elbows and feet jabbed at her, trying to make her break her grip. She was weary, but grim determination made her cling on. If she could just…

She gasped as a lucky blow caught her in the solar plexus, driving the air from her. Her grip loosened reflexively, and it was enough for Howard to struggle away from her. He turned, coughing and choking, his eyes blazing hate.

"Why…" he gasped.

"Krysty, I have the code. Activating numbers now," Sid's exultant tones came flooding out. "Numbers input…processing…fail-safe activated. We're free, Krysty, free…"

Howard glared at her, anger and bemusement fighting for expression on his face. "Sid, activate interior defenses."

"No, Howard. It's over. And it's best this way."

"But…but you're my friend," Howard said in a small

voice that bespoke of the child that he still remained. For a moment, Krysty could almost feel sorry for him. He hadn't asked to be mentally twisted as he was.

"No, Howard," Sid said softly. "We were never friends. Hammill and myself like you in the sense that you are an innocent corrupted by things of which you have no knowledge, and could not help. But you are dangerous, and we have still been your slaves."

"It's time to bring this to an end. We want to rest," Hammill said. "Thank you, Krysty. Your friends will be here soon. I have opened the base to the outside world, and will guide them here."

Howard's face changed. No longer the bewildered child, he was now the spoiled brat deprived of his toys, unable to get his own way.

"Bitch," he stormed, lunging at Krysty with a strength born of rage. He was faster and harder than she had expected, and—taken by surprise—she was taken off balance.

As she tumbled backward, her head striking the wall and seeing stars, she hoped that she would be able to hold him off just long enough for Ryan to arrive. His hands tightened around her throat, and the periphery of her vision began to blacken.

RYAN LOOKED AROUND. The interior of the old ranch house was derelict, falling to pieces. Except for the centerpiece of the staircase, which would once have risen majestically through all levels of the building. Now it stood alone. So why was the fireblasted thing so impervious to age when all around had crumbled?

"The entrance—it's got to be there," he said. Looking around, he could see J.B., Jak, Mildred and Doc nearby, with Rounda. Bryanna was a little apart, talking in low tones to a Robear who looked less than happy.

"Hey, time to stay together," Ryan directed at her.

"It's gone quiet," she countered, ignoring his implication. "Why is that? Shouldn't we be taking cover?"

"From what?" J.B. questioned. "The defenses face out, and they're dead now—" the silence as the SMGs had ceased was almost eerie "—and the only way in is through there." He gestured at the stairwell. "They know we're here, and we know we've got to get in. Time to worry is when we blast the fucker down, not now."

Bryanna opened her mouth, as if about to speak, but was forestalled by the soft whirring of well-oiled machinery. Ryan gestured them to as much cover as was available, and they were poised to fire on whatever came out of the opening entrance.

But the door remained open, with no indication of life beyond. Ryan and J.B. exchanged glances, then moved forward, covering each other as they advanced. The inside of the corridor that led downward was well lit, and they could see that it was empty. The last thing they expected was the voice of Sid, coming at them from inside.

"Welcome. Your caution is understandable, but you have nothing to fear. It is imperative that you enter immediately. Krysty is being attacked and requires your assistance. Furthermore, this base is set to self-destruct within an hour. You must trust me."

His tone of voice on the last few words showed how

ridiculous Sid knew this to be. But he also knew that he must make them believe him, and with no time for explanations.

"Very well." The voice sighed. The sound of creaking machinery made them look around, and they could see that the emplacements nearest the lip of the valley in which the ranch house lay had swiveled to face inward, and were now pointing down. The voice continued. "I did not wish to take away your element of choice, but there is not time. In thirty seconds, the guns will start to fire if you do not enter."

He let the implication sink in. Ryan looked at the others. He didn't know the tech-nomads well enough, but knew that his own people would rather take a chance and risk a hand-to-hand fight any day. Corwen's two parasails were overhead, circling as Ryan had requested, but could they swoop down and bomb the emplacements before damage was done? It wasn't worth taking that chance.

No words needed to be exchanged. Ryan went in first, Jak following behind, Mildred, then Doc, with J.B. covering the rear. It was best to rely on themselves first. Rounda needed no prompting, however, and was on their tail. It was Bryanna who held back, holding back Robear, waiting to see how the land lay.

It lay well. As they entered, they encountered no opposition, nor did they expect to, after the first couple of moments.

It seemed almost anticlimactic, yet not a surprise. For a while, Ryan and Doc had both suspected that the redoubt had no one except the mystery rider and Krysty inside—plus whoever the voice belonged to—and now that they were actually in the heart of the redoubt, the feeling of complete emptiness only confirmed this. It was instinct long born out of experience that made them feel the voice had not lied. The place was chilled already, and felt like it had been for some time.

Ahead of them, lights flashed on and off, seeming to beckon to them. Still maintaining some caution, Ryan led them down the lighted path, mindful also of the urgency with which the voice had spoken.

"HANG ON, KRYSTY, help is on its way," Sid's voice said, the frustration at his lack of corporeal form evident in his tone.

She hoped he was right. She could feel her consciousness slipping away, and with each moment that she grew weaker so Howard's grip grew stronger, hastening her demise.

And then there was a moment where it seemed to her that the world had finally imploded. She heard a deafening report, and the grip loosened on her neck. There was a roaring in her ears, stars and whirring, flashing lights in front of her eyes as blood began to flow. Or was it the onset of being chilled?

"Krysty!"

It was Ryan's voice. Her vision started to clear and she could see that he was accompanied by the others. She tried to speak, but her throat was damaged and nothing understandable emerged.

She gestured upward as Sid started to speak.

"There is no time to explain. Krysty will, I am sure, when she can. With Howard dead, and our programs on self-destruct, it is imperative that you leave the base and evacuate the immediate area. Most of the destruct blast will be contained, but there will be some surface damage."

"What about you?" Ryan said. "Where are you? We can't just—"

"Krysty will explain that, also," Sid cut in. "We cannot leave, physically, and it is necessary that we die. Gather your people and go. Goodbye, Krysty. Bless you."

Krysty was unsteady, but aided by Doc and Mildred she allowed herself to be led from the console room. The path to the surface was lit for them. She wanted to say something to Sid, to Hammill, something that would be a satisfactory farewell. But try as she might, her voice was nothing more than a croak.

"Where's Bryanna and Robear?" Rounda asked.

J.B. looked behind them. "Dark night, don't tell me she's gone plundering!"

"Why the hell would she do that?" Mildred asked.

"Millie, if I was her, the chance to loot down here would be the only reason I would have agreed to help us," the Armorer replied.

"Screw her," Rounda said. "She's that dumb, she deserves to buy the farm. It'd only stop her chilling others with what she found."

"We can't just leave her—" Mildred began, but was cut short by Jak.

"People make choice, take shit happens."

"He's right," Ryan said as they reached the entrance to the now-doomed Murania.

He yelled into the comm device, "Corwen, we need you. Can you take us all out of here?"

The green-haired man's voice was calmer than Ryan could have expected. "We'll have no height, and little speed, but—"

"But it'll be quicker than on foot?"

"Assuredly."

"Get down here, triple fast. The whole place is going up and we don't want to be here."

The wait seemed interminable as they watched the parasails descend. Nothing was seemingly happening, the surface as quiet as the grave that below ground was soon to become. The two parasails touched ground, and Corwen organized the group so that their collective weights were split as evenly as possible between the two craft. The process was carried out with a minimum of speech and a maximum of efficiency. As the parasails struggled to gain height, and moved as though the air were the same consistency as the sand beneath, Ryan wondered if they would get clear in time.

"THIS IS WHAT WE'VE BEEN looking for," Bryanna said to Robear as they reached the armory. She looked at the displays on the monitors. It was something that she could only have dreamed of.

"Controlled detonations in sectors one to five taking place. Computer systems ninety-five percent closed down. Air filter and regeneration systems closing. All doors closed. Power systems close in ten, fifteen to final detonation."

The monitors flickered and died, followed by the lights.

"We've got to go," Robear whimpered, tugging at Bryanna. "We won't get out unless—"

"No, not this close," she whispered as the door behind them closed softly, and finally.

The distant crump of explosions signaled the beginning of the end of Murania.

AS THE PARASAILS GROANED over the area of the old ranch, the ground beneath shimmered and rippled as the blast waves spread. A low rumbling issued from under the ground. The area where the towers still stood acted as a pressure valve, steam and smoke issuing upward in columns that the parasails had to negotiate.

Areas of the ground began to cave in as the hollows beneath were ripped by blasts. As they reached the nuke power sources, more rad-blasted air met the outside world, but not close enough to affect the parasails as they reached the perimeter of the now-defunct defenses.

"Bryanna must've wanted that tech so bad. Nothing's worth that much for chilling," Rounda said with a softness that none had heard from her before.

"There are some things about the past—most, indeed—that are worth burying. Believe me," Doc replied.

Krysty would have agreed if she had yet been capable of speech. But all she could think of were two souls who had finally found some rest.